ROLL OF A LIFETIME

ALSO BY MELANIE GREENE

Roll of the Dice Series

Rocket Man *(Serena & Dillon)*

Ready to Roll *(Janice & Miguel)*

Eye of the Tiger *(Natalie & Evan)*

Let the Good Times Roll *(Chloe & Gabriel)*

Roll of a Lifetime *(Rachel & Theo)*

Roll Play *(Kim & Tómas)*

Stand-alone Contemporary Romances

Retreat to Love *(Ashlyn & Caleb)*

Feather in Her Cap *(Jeannie & Brendan)*

ROLL OF A LIFETIME

A Roll of the Dice Novel

MELANIE GREENE

GreeneLeaves

*Many of my very favorite people turned 50 as I wrote this novel.
Mark, Jennifer, and (always) Robert, this is in celebration of you!*

CHAPTER ONE

RACHEL PACED the convenience store aisles, paying little attention to the packaged foods, the stacked cases of beer, the three donuts left in the bakery case. All she noticed was time ticking away at the rate of two strides per second. Four seconds per aisle, turn, four seconds more. With each step, something on the sole of her left shoe clung, lightly, to the linoleum. It didn't alter her pace.

She would stick to her pace until her ex pulled into the parking lot with their daughter.

He was late. Still no text. Still no call.

Three minutes, fine. He'd been three minutes late with handoff before. Five. Eight. Thirteen.

Eighteen.

She checked the map app. No signs of slow traffic anywhere near. No accidents or high water, despite the rain darkening the sky. She gripped her phone as she paced, hedging against thunder drowning out the sound of a call.

If he was driving, navigating slick roads and maybe Hannah getting cranky as dinnertime approached, she didn't want him answering a call. Fumbling for his phone instead of keeping his hands on the wheel.

Chip aisle. She scanned for snack options. Wouldn't be the first time he'd failed to account for normal toddler pickiness and returned her hungry.

Candy.

Automotive accessories.

Energy drinks.

She pulled up next to the sunglasses display, where she had a partial view of the parking lot between signs for the Texas Lotto and a flyer for the local high school's year-end musical. The phone rang four times before someone at the host stand picked up. "Thanks for calling Elixir, how can I help?"

"Is Sergei there?" He wasn't supposed to work during his custody weekends, especially when his mom was out of town. Didn't stop him from dragging her daughter to the brewpub.

She got a cheerful "Hold on," and curled the phone to her clavicle to avoid listening to the recorded upbeat spiel about new summer beers and Thursday Trivia Nights. It took deliberate effort to avoid memorizing it. She turned towards the magazines. But all the glossy covers under fluorescent lights made her queasy. She could practically smell the competing perfume samples in the women's mags, and as for the men's stuff. No. She didn't need to be yelled at by a bunch of cars and boobs.

The voice returned. "Sorry! Can't locate him for the moment. Can I leave a message?"

She managed politeness as she declined. Not this guy's fault his boss's voice snaked through her mind. *Pestering my employees now, Rachel? Try a little self-control for once, can't you? Stop acting like every half-formed thought that makes it into your head constitutes a national emergency.*

She flinched, and then glanced at the man behind the counter to smile an apology for making a spectacle. He shrugged back at her. Setting an oat bar and juice bottle on the counter, she searched for more time-consuming distractions. Even if he'd just left work, they'd arrive within ten minutes. She would do herself a favor and not spend them counting the seconds.

Back to the sunglasses rack and the partial view. Not that seeing the parking lot magicked Sergei's car into it. At least the rain had slowed to a mist. Rachel sighed and uncrossed her arms, the better to rotate the display of eyewear. She alternated trying the white-framed Jackie O style and the smoky aviators as if choosing was the weightiest decision she'd faced in the thousand or so days of her daughter's life. Maybe the glittery purple pair with star-shaped lenses? Hannah would adore them, but she couldn't picture cycling to the daycare wearing them. They'd probably bash the underside of her helmet.

Just past the slim strip of mirror, she caught sight of the dark, sporty SUV that still twisted her stomach five months after he steered its shiny rims off the lot. Sergei was still paying back child support from his between-jobs periods, but his silhouette at the wheel was as nonchalant and above it all as always.

She was at the vehicle before the door chimes had quieted. He was bent into the back to retrieve their daughter. Fine. No matter how it galled her, getting loud directly to his smug face still gave her the shakes afterwards. So she ranted at his narrow ass. "We have a schedule. *She* has a schedule. Did you ignore it the whole time you had her, or only this afternoon? How is she supposed to —who the hell are you?"

THEO CUT off his one-sided conversation with the toddler and, hitching the overnight bag higher on his shoulder, turned to locate the owner of the royally pissed voice.

"Mama," said Hannah, lunging at the woman so eagerly she for once loosed her grip on her blue elephant. Theo gathered her to him, trapping the stuffed animal between them, and earned a whap from the plastic brachiosaurus in her other hand as thanks.

Wincing, he asked, "Rachel Groff?" He held off on passing back the girl, just in case. It wasn't that he doubted it—her daughter's reaction was enough to go by, even without Sergei's inadequate sketch of a description. Blonde. Shortish. Dressed in 'mom clothes,' whatever Sergei meant by that. He'd given Theo a blank look when he asked for a picture, as if the idea of having a shot of Rachel in his phone was absurd. Theo had a few of his ex, and not because he was hung up on Annalisa. She texted him pics of their son, and sometimes she was in them. If he'd sent Andres off with some random guy in search of her, he'd at least be able to show the random guy what Annalisa looked like.

Not that he was random. Which he needed to explain to Rachel before she blew another fuse. "I'm Theo."

"Good for you. Is that supposed to explain why you have Hannah? And yes, I'm Rachel. Give me my daughter."

She didn't wait for his compliance, but reached over and helped herself to the child. He held up the bag. "Want me to stick this in your car for you?"

"Where is Sergei? And who are you? Why do you have my child? Did you even belt her in right?" She was peering into the back seat as if the configuration of car seat straps would prove his negligence.

"Of course I did. Look, I have a little boy; I know how to work car seats. And Sergei's the one who put her in the seat. And I checked it before we left."

She was still exuding non-verbal displeasure.

"Sergei works for me," he said again. Or maybe for the first time. The woman had him off-kilter. "I'm Theo. Theo Melis? Did Sergei not tell you I'd be bringing her to you?"

She made it clear the question didn't need answering. Not that he hadn't gleaned the truth. Seemed Sergei's hand wave when he'd checked about this plan was dismissal, not acknowledgment. All so the man didn't have to reschedule a meal with a vendor he shouldn't have planned for a custodial Sunday.

"Let me see your driver's license." Command, not request.

He set the overnight bag on the hood and reached for his wallet. "Sure. You gonna run a screen on me so you know I'm a safe driver for next time?"

She motioned for him to hold his license still while she snapped a photo of it. Maybe later he'd ask himself why he was following this woman's grumpy dictates.

"You're never driving her again."

The declaration was firm and her jaw was jutting and he was too polite to get into a fight about it all. He slipped his wallet back into his back pocket. "Sorry, sure. Whatever you say."

"Are you mocking me?"

"Would I mock your mama, little Hannah gal?" He pulled a long face, eyebrows up and chin tucked down.

Rachel huffed and swiveled so she was between him and her daughter. "She doesn't like strange men."

Hannah leaned around Rachel and pointed at Theo, smiling like he was the latest craze in animated unicorns. He wiggled his ears, not because he thought the toddler would notice, but because it would irritate her mom.

Hannah giggled. Rachel glowered. Theo laughed.

"I'm sorry. You're very stern, and I'm cowed, I promise. Although it's hard to take you seriously when you're wearing all those glasses."

Her free hand covered her forehead and he tried to hold back a snort at her growl. She paused a moment, then whipped the purple star lenses off her face and the other two pairs from the top of her head. Her eyes were bluer than her daughter's, and at the moment twice as large. He wasn't sure if she was enraged or embarrassed, but either way she was enthralling.

Theo held out his hand. "Can I help you with those?"

"It's fine. I don't need help." She glanced back at the store, lifting the fistful of eyewear. "We're heading inside anyway. Let's go, okay, Hannah banana?"

He let her walk away, but called out before she was stuck juggling glasses and child to open the convenience store door. "Rachel?"

Her pivot towards him was as slow and rigid as she could manage, he guessed, given her burdens. "Theo, was it?"

He hefted the overnight bag. "Can I carry this in for you?"

Those blue eyes narrowed. She hitched Hannah more firmly on her hip. He debated, too late, the wisdom of baiting her. Her one-word answer was a slingshot of civility. "Please."

She turned back towards the store, and the face he made as he approached them was probably responsible for Hannah's renewed giggles.

HER NOW-WET SOLES squeaked and stuck on the linoleum as she carried Hannah to the checkout. *Squee, squee-pop, squee, squee-pop.* The stranger who'd propelled her daughter in a two-ton vehicle stalked after them. She ignored him in favor of burying her nose in toddler curls. Seemed Sergei had managed to parent long enough to give her a bath over the weekend.

The star-rim glasses got caught in her own hair as she shifted Hannah to the other hip. If the stalker man—Theo—hadn't been so late, she wouldn't have even looked at the sunglasses. After wearing merchandise straight out of the store on top of abandoning Hannah's snack on the counter, she'd rather buy all three pairs than fumble excuses for herself. So there went forty not-so-spare dollars, and Sergei's buddy was still lurking when she turned to leave.

"Excuse us." Because Aunt Johnston's lessons in politeness bubbled up when she couldn't let loose in front of her child.

"The bag?" He hefted it like it was a game-show prize.

It was her favorite one, with room for every possible contingency. She wouldn't pack it for Hannah's overnights with her father, except Sergei refused to keep clothes and diapers for his daughter on hand. He claimed it was because she grew too fast for him to keep track of her sizes. Rachel's friend Gillian claimed it was because he would never take on the emotional labor of parenting if there was the tiniest of loopholes available.

Gill was the most cynical person she knew. And in this case, certain to be right.

Rachel worked on stuffing the juice and sunglasses in her purse. She gave herself a half-second to close her eyes, then reached for the bag. "Thank you."

He sidestepped so the door was clear. "Anytime."

Big surprise, he followed them into the parking lot, and to her car. Not to Sergei's, a whole four spaces away, but hers. Just stood there watching as she jiggled the key in the lock—a pattern she could do in her sleep, but wasn't so easy when her arms were laden with daughter and bags and Effie, the most vital stuffed elephant in Texas, threatening to slip past her elbow and straight into an oily rain puddle.

She felt a tug, and swiveled her neck to see Effie being danced behind her shoulder, which meant Hannah leaned into her instead of away, which made balancing the straps on her other shoulder easier. Which meant she got the door unlocked and could sling purse and diaper bag towards the passenger seat.

He used the wrong voice to make Effie trumpet. Way too low and not nasal enough. Pathetic, for someone who claimed to be a parent.

Aunt Johnston's voice niggled at her, which Rachel preferred to Sergei's insidious grasp on her subconscious. "Thank you."

Something about the way he bit the inside of his cheek as he handed Hannah her elephant told her he wasn't fooled by her polite words. She slid inside the back seat to buckle in her daughter, as content as it was possible to be about how very clear her dismissal had been. When she emerged to take the driver's seat, he was gone.

CHAPTER TWO

BEMUSED, Theo retreated to Sergei's car. Serg hadn't told him much about his ex. Certainly not about the vicious spark in her big blue eyes, though he could have guessed from the way her daughter used those same eyes to tell the world how little she thought of it. Kid cracked him up; she was so suspicious all the time but full of belly laughs and chatter in the right circumstances. Just try to take her stuffed elephant away, though, and she summoned the furies. Theo suspected the mama could access her own underworld vengeance deity to protect little Hannah. He grinned. He'd been maybe an inch shy of the line past which she would have completely laid into him. It stirred an impish desire to edge closer. To see her all full of righteous indignation. Talk about passion.

Serg hadn't mentioned the passion.

"Fool," he mumbled to himself, glancing back at her old sedan. As if Serg would have said, "*Re*, take my kid back to her mom, and by the way, she's hot. Whatever you fantasize is the tip of the iceberg."

He was in nonsense land, thinking about Sergei's ex and sex. Not compatible thoughts. He had to work with Serg, day in and day out and plenty of long nights in between. He'd only hired him a matter of months ago, but he'd got on with Sergei Matsouka from the outset. The Greek-American network threw Serg's resume his way the minute he made noises about needing a new restaurant manager. The man was gregarious, open, full of ideas. He had a good attitude most of the time. Seemed foolish to test that attitude by making moves on the man's ex.

He started the car, picked a playlist off his phone. Sang along as he backed to a free gas pump. He likely could make it back to Elixir without filling the tank, but Sergei had passed over a couple of twenties along with his kid when he roped Theo into dropping back Hannah.

Twisting to insert the nozzle, he noticed Rachel hadn't yet left. He propped his forearms atop Sergei's roof and gave in to the temptation to watch as she sorted through the bags on her passenger seat. When she turned to pass something to Hannah, she spotted him. He gave the best shrug possible given his posture. Didn't hide his interested grin. She shook her head once and cranked her car's engine. He stopped singing. He wasn't as tuneful as Orpheus, but it hardly mattered. Rachel Groff was not his Eurydice. More like the three-headed Cerberus ready to attack anyone threatening her realm. And Theo didn't need to seek out any more scars in his life.

Sergei sent back dirty laundry. As if his mom wasn't still washing all of his own clothes. Rachel balled up Hannah's overalls and t-shirts and lobbed them at the hamper. No used diapers this time. What a victory. In fact, she found a drugstore bag with a torn-open package of diapers smushed at the bottom of the bag, under the sandals and storybooks. She passed the shoes to her girl to return to the cubbies by their front door, and carried the bag to the changing table.

The crinkle of paper sent a jolt through her. The sound had

smacked at her gut too many times. Washing Sergei's jeans, hanging his jackets, pretending she needed to find something in his glove box because after the second or third or thirtieth time, it turned into a sick game. He 'forgot' to throw out incriminating receipts. She accumulated them, trying to read a web of certainty from their evidence. Blaming her dyslexia for her failure, calling on friends for backup. And when she brandished a fan of smoothed-out receipts, line items circled, asking what and who and why the brunch with two coffees, the boutique, the gas from a station eighteen miles away, he sneered. He reminded her how important he was. How it was just like her to be so pathetic. How he shouldn't even expect her to understand all he had to put up with from her.

Too many times.

Doing her best to not read it, Rachel ran the receipt along the edge of the changing table to press out the wrinkles, snapped a picture, opened a text box.

RACHEL: Stop me if I don't need to read this.

GILLIAN: You already know the answer to that.

SERENA: Is this related to Sergei?

GILLIAN: And YOU know the answer to that, too.

NATALIE: That unmitigated ass!

Rachel let the first few replies flow up her screen so she could no longer see the photo she'd taken.

GILLIAN: We all know he's the mold on a pebble picked out from beneath a horse's rear shoe, but that's no reason for R to be looking at his receipts again.

NATALIE: Fine, sure, but why do you have it, Rachel?

She explained about the diapers, and her case looked weak. Before anyone replied, she threw in Sergei's springing Theo on her with no warning. A second later, Gillian phoned, incredulous.

"He what?"

Rachel double-checked Hannah was still turning all their pairs of shoes into a train. "I mean, Theo's the owner—not the brewer, the other one—so Sergei knows him. Hannah seemed to like him."

"Do not make excuses for that man. He can't hand your daughter off to any random lackey. She's two!"

"I'm not saying he can. I'm ... okay, maybe I am. And I don't agree with what he did." She dialed back her defensive tone, partially for Gillian, partially so Hannah's ears wouldn't prick up. "I don't. I do not. I laid into the guy, but you're going to help me write a no-wiggle-room letter to Sergei."

"And his lawyer."

"And both our lawyers. Anyway, what's on the receipt?"

Gillian's silence stretched. Could be she was talking herself into accepting Rachel's promise of delayed wrath. Could be she was zooming in on the picture to decipher it.

Could be there was something gross Gill wasn't sure how to interpret.

The phone vibrated and she pulled it away to check the incoming text from Natalie: "Condoms, Lucky Charms, and something from Revlon."

"Wait," she asked Gill. "Does that mean he bought someone else mascara, or that he sent someone else to buy diapers?"

"Who cares? What impact does either scenario have on your life?"

She sat with the question. Not an hour before, she'd been high-fiving herself for putting unsuspecting Theo in his place. Or, if not his own place, any place far from Hannah. Taking her pluck as proof she had her boots on the correct feet, as Aunt Johnston would say.

And a maybe-not-even-Sergei's receipt kicked her straight back into her swirl of anxiety.

The hypothetical condom and makeup use no longer impacted her. Gillian was right; Rachel told her so.

"Good." Gill's smile brightened her voice. "Put the receipt in the trash."

"Recycling," she corrected, heading into her kitchen.

"Trash. We are being symbolic here. That thing is toxic, and it's not going to infect your apartment. Straight into the dumpster."

"We're not wearing shoes."

Hannah slotted her feet into Rachel's sandals. Time to change the subject before her daughter used her exploding vocabulary to parrot Rachel's attitude. She had enough trouble shutting down her inner voice, and didn't need an external chorus.

But as she crumpled up the receipt to shove it deep into the garbage, it crinkled again. So before she asked Gillian how her grading was going, she said, "And if he's been feeding her sugary cereals again, I'm going to spill spaghetti sauce all over that ugly dress his mom sent and make sure she's wearing it for his next weekend."

CHAPTER THREE

MARY LYNN'S distinctive rap on her door brought Rachel and Hannah both from the kitchen.

"I've got baked spaghetti in the oven," she said. "Will you stay to eat?" It was Mary Lynn's recipe, one she'd convinced Rachel to try when Hannah was in one of her cheese-and-apples-only phases, and it had fast become a staple.

"Thanks, love, but not today. I'm picking up a shift tonight."

Rachel raised her eyebrows, but didn't comment. Mary Lynn hated working Saturday nights, despite the higher turnover and bigger tips. She disliked crowds, so slow weekday afternoons and the occasional Sunday after brunch were her preferred schedule at the steakhouse where she worked. She always said it gave her a sufficiency, and the cash she earned babysitting Hannah was for all of her indulgences.

Mary Lynn flapped a wrist at her before snugging Hannah into her lap. "You hush. I have my reasons. And I have my Xanax, so I'll be fine."

"Okay. Do you want us to drive you?"

"Would you? That suits me well. I'll have someone drop me home after."

"No worries. We're happy to."

Her friend told Hannah to bring out some puzzles from her room, and let her round features settle into seriousness once the girl was off her lap. "I'm moving."

Rachel threw herself involuntarily against the back of the sofa. "What?"

"I'm sorry. I thought it was best to blurt it out while the coast is clear. None of this 'I have good news! But it's bad news for you!' hedging. So. Yes. I'm moving to Brenham."

"Brenham?" She liked the town fine, but it was over seventy miles away. Mary Lynn had knocked on her door the day after she moved into the apartment, and started filling in as babysitter a couple of weeks later. The occasional nights out when Hannah wasn't with Sergei, and a few hours in the morning if Hannah was too sick to go to daycare but Rachel couldn't reschedule all her clients. Sometimes she would wander over from next door and announce that she needed some baby time, hand Rachel her own grocery list, and send her to the store where she could wander the aisles without wrangling and placating and negotiating with her cart-bound child. Mary Lynn was a central pole of the tent that sheltered Rachel's life as a working mother.

"Brenham."

"Okay. I've taken a deep breath. Fill me in."

"You remember Goldberg?"

"The caterer?" He sometimes hired waiters from the steakhouse to cover large events.

"That's the one. He's been—don't look scandalized at me, young lady—he's been paying me calls. And he's a rascal. And I love him. And he's selling the business, and we are retiring to his land outside Brenham, and living in flagrant s-i-n and my mother's ashes are positively spinning into a tornado inside their urn."

Rachel's hand was insufficient to contain her laughter, which was fine. Hannah thought she'd made a joke by putting the train puzzle piece in the space for the tractor, and filled the room with her belly laugh.

The women turned from watching her to smiling at each other. Rachel pushed back all her thoughts about how much more comforting it was to sink into the arms of this woman she'd known for not even two years than it was to hug her own mother. How much bigger a gap Mary Lynn's moving would leave in Hannah's life than did the remote grandparenting she got from her family of origin. She sniffed.

"So I'm working extra shifts, because I want to pad my nest egg. Goldberg says he'll always take care of me, but I'm an independent woman, right? You've taught me all about self-reliance." Her cherubic expression twinkled diabolically. "I'm bringing feminism to the farm."

Rachel squeezed her hand. "Poor Goldberg won't know what hit him."

"That's the idea."

"I approve."

Mary Lynn shifted to lean over the coffee table and help Hannah rotate the airplane piece so it would slot into place. Her voice quavered when she asked, "You'll bring my girl up to visit, right?"

It hurt, suppressing the tears so her daughter wouldn't fret. "All the time."

"I hope so. Goldberg promised to replace the old mattress in the spare room, so you two can stay over. And his son baby proofed the place already, but I'll check it all, since his grandkids are older. You never know what's been let slip."

Rachel shook her head. "Don't fuss. You sound too sad, and this is a happy thing. Such a happy thing."

"I can't believe I'm going."

"I can't believe you were seeing Goldberg behind my back."

"Well." She blushed and turned her head.

"Mary Lynn!"

She patted her salt-and-paprika curls into place and played at being demure. "Like you said, it's a happy thing."

"Well, good job, Goldberg. I'm glad he's worthy of you." Rachel glanced at the clock and stood. "I'll turn off the oven. The spaghetti can sit while we drop you off. Are you ready?"

"As soon as my girl and I are done with this puzzle, right, Hannah?"

Hannah pointed at the jungle and the dinosaur and the alphabet boards. "And this puzzles and this puzzles."

"You negotiate. I'll grab my keys." Rachel left them to it, not contemplating all the ways her life was easier because there was someone just next door who she trusted to keep her daughter safe and loved.

"THEO? What's with that table full of kids?"

He glanced up from the tax report. Sergei was leaning against the threshold, pulling one of his quizzical faces. "No school today," he said.

"So people are sending their kids to the bar instead?"

He sorted. "Sure, it's the new fad."

"Seems like that would be against our licensing."

Theo grinned. "Look at you, remembering we have regulations."

"Funny."

"The kids belong to Marti and Shawna and Pat."

"So now we're free daycare?"

Theo clicked his pen closed and slid back in the chair. "Are they causing any problems?"

"They don't hold much appeal for the normal lunch crowd."

"Well, the option was let them bring the kids, or lose half the shift on a busy holiday. Marti said no one had backup care, so I told them if their kids would stay at the table and stay calm, they could bring them in."

"Generous of you."

"If they're not disruptive, and the wait staff are getting their work done, it's better than us covering their shifts."

Sergei's cheeks bulged and he blew a huff of air. "Sure, fine. Your call. I guess next time people will schedule themselves to work whenever their schools are closed, so they can let you feed and entertain the kids and pay them at the same time."

The guy brought Hannah in for dinner most every Wednesday night. And palmed her off on the staff if Depy wasn't around when he got busy. "Not everyone has grandma available for fill-in child-care you know."

"Behind you." Marti was trying to pass with a tray of drinks.

Sergei glanced her way, but didn't shift over. "That for the kiddos?" he asked.

She nodded, shooting a glance Theo's way but not losing her wary expression.

Sergei reached to take the drinks. "Let me deliver them. I want to meet everyone." He nodded his head towards the kitchen. "Why don't you grab them a couple of baskets of fries, too? And some spanakopita."

Marti's eyes widened and she said, "You got it. They'll love that, thanks."

Before he sauntered off to interrogate the kids about their names and the games they were playing and their summer plans, Sergei shook his head at Theo. "Try and warn me next time this place is going to become rugrat central, okay?"

———

RACHEL COASTED to a stop at the gate to the complex, walking the bike forward a step so Hannah could reach the keypad. Her girl remembered her promise, looking to Rachel for permission before stretching her fist out and extending both pointer and thumb in that not quite dexterous way she had. She knew the first number was two and pressed it before letting Rachel guide her finger to the rest of the entry code. With a squeak, the gate began to swing open, and Hannah squeaked at it in return.

"Good one, Banana. Do you want to walk to the door, or ride?"

"Walk!"

Once they were in and the gate closed, she checked for traffic and propped the bike against her hip as she unbuckled the straps keeping Hannah in her seat. "Hat off now or inside?"

Hannah clamped her hands to her puppy-festooned bike helmet, which left Rachel maneuvering her arms one at a time through the straps. Lifting her daughter to the ground, she turned her towards the staircase and navigated the bike to a rack by the mailboxes. She kept an eye on the toddler mounting the steps as she locked the bike, fetched her mail, and shrugged their backpacks onto her shoulders. Hannah was getting faster. She'd planted her feet on the fourth step by the time Rachel got to her. It wasn't a handholding day, it seemed, so she stayed behind Hannah, ready in case she was needed. As always.

"Dinosaurs and trees for dinner," she said, but Hannah was too focused on the lights flashing on her sandals to answer. Rachel flipped through the mail. Mostly ads; very little to distract her from the padded envelope she'd stuck at the bottom of the stack.

She didn't need the glimpse of black-spider writing on the front or the profusion of sickly dessert stickers on the back to tell her it was another offering from Yia Yia Depy. Since moving out, every hand-addressed package she'd received had originated with her former mother-in-law. Her sister and parents followed a schedule of generosity. Hannah had several gifts from them each birthday and Christmas. They even paid for the companies they ordered from to gift-wrap everything. Her friend Natalie had once called the resulting pile of matching colorful rectangles antiseptic, but Rachel disagreed. She preferred the computer-generated gift notes to the randomly arriving and faintly intrusive packages from Depy.

Each one reminded her that Depy had her address. For good reason, yes, but Rachel did not want Sergei finding it. Did Depy keep the info in her battered old floral-fabric-covered notebook under the living room phone cradle? On the legal pad under her keyboard which listed all her passwords and social security number? Slipped into her overstuffed wallet with all the receipts and coupons and pictures of Hannah from every stage of her life? She'd lived with Depy too long, those newborn months post-divorce when she had nowhere better to turn. She knew the woman's habits as well as Sergei did. And she knew it was because he understood exactly where to find her address that he'd capitulated when she refused to tell him where she was moving.

Depy would do nothing to prevent her precious perfect asshole of a son from finding the address if he wanted it.

So every package the woman mailed hit her like a veiled threat: here's an over-embellished dress, and also a reminder that Sergei could be yelling through your closed and locked and chained door within minutes.

She let Hannah yank on the envelope's red pull-tab once they were inside the apartment. Dusty grey padding fibers flew everywhere, like airborne contaminants infecting the security of her home. She would ask Depy to use bubble wrap instead, but that was tantamount to admitting that the shredding envelopes bothered her. And Rachel was not in the business of admitting that anything the Matsouka family did bothered her.

Hannah, true to her toddler nature, ignored the enclosed outfit —bismuth pink coveralls with lace ruffles on the seat and a coordinating pink tee emblazoned with 'PRETTY GIRL' in black bubble letters—in favor of picking at the stickers on the envelope. Rachel tossed the clothes in the basket she kept by the door with things ready to pack for her daughter's next overnight with Sergei. Handing Hannah a red marker so she could deface the envelope, she sank into the sofa cushions and opened the envelope Depy had labeled with her name.

No note, unless the scrawled 'Hannah' on the memo line counted.

The list of things she could do with two hundred dollars unfurled in her imagination. It was an old-fashioned scroll, closely written, and spread across the room, out the door, down the stairs. Cars in the parking lot left tread marks across the scripted rows of options. Phone bills and student loan payments and a kid wardrobe that Depy had no hand in and a decent haircut and a comfortable saddle for her bike and flowers for the daycare teachers and a motel room at the beach and a bedroom fan and at the top of the list and the bottom of the list and on every other line of the list, savings towards someplace she and Hannah could live without factoring in Sergei's child support excuses.

It was past time to start dinner. Rachel countersigned the check and opened the bank app on her phone. Navigating to the remote deposit screen, she tapped all the right places until Depy's check was lodged in the account she'd nicknamed 'H's College Money.'

"Let's go chop up dinosaur trees," she said, and waited while Hannah maneuvered the cap onto the marker. Her girl bounced up and took her hand, tugging her into the kitchen while singing her version of her favorite dinosaur song.

Rachel joined in the chorus, and they didn't stop trading tunes until dinner was ready.

CHAPTER FOUR

"I NEED HER ON THAT TWENTIETH," Sergei was telling Rachel as Theo approached. He didn't quite mean to butt into the end of Serg's regular Wednesday evening time with his daughter. But also he'd kept thinking about Rachel since that encounter at the gas station, and now she was in his brewery. So he ignored that he was interrupting, and approached.

She didn't glance his way, just narrowed her eyes at her ex. "Did you put it on the calendar?"

Sergei tossed his head, which Theo had picked up on as his go-to impatience gesture. "You know I need her every July twentieth."

"You should have put it in the custody agreement, then. Or at least bothered to add it to the calendar. The deadline to claim extra summer days passed weeks ago."

"Don't," he stopped to kiss at Hannah's neck, making her squeal. Lowered his voice. "Don't invent problems because you can. I'll call my lawyer if—"

She took Hannah from her ex and pivoted. Spotting him, she moved the two steps to bring them close. Theo scanned her face, searching for signs she needed him to offer an out from the heated conversation. Or a hug. He'd gladly offer her a hug. What he didn't expect was that she'd snug Hannah into his arms and ask him to carry her away for a minute.

He hitched the girl up onto his shoulder and nodded. As Rachel turned away from him, Theo glanced at Sergei, who shrugged. He started away, but Rachel's voice was combative enough for him to hear her say, "Yes. Call your lawyer. Go for it. Be sure to tell him how much back support you owe while you're at it."

He got Hannah over by the kitchen before he could hear more. Not his business. Not. And if Rachel or Sergei either one needed him to be involved, they could make the ask directly.

Or he could stop thinking up scenarios that would put him in the middle.

"Juice or water or milk?" he asked Hannah, and set about getting her a snack. He'd seen her smush several bites of his chocolate-banana pie into her mouth over dinner, so he skipped the cookies, stacking a pita and a scoop of hummus and some olives in a bowl.

A few minutes later, Rachel found their little alcove. She smiled, shoulders dropping into softness, as she spied Hannah playing spyglass with an olive. Andres still did the same thing sometimes. He'd done it himself, according to the pictures from his childhood. Maybe a Greek kid thing, maybe a food with holes in it thing. Either way, it was cute.

He stood to offer Rachel the seat beside her daughter. She drew him a couple steps back, though, and offered up a complex, eyebrows-raised smile.

"Thanks for taking her."

He didn't squeeze her shoulder. He didn't lean down to kiss her cheek. Or her mouth. He didn't suggest a date, or that he could follow her back to her place after she had a chance to put Hannah to sleep.

But he didn't keep his mouth shut, either. "No problem. Seemed like you two had things to discuss."

She rolled her eyes. "Yeah. You could say that."

She stopped. He didn't want her to stop. "So, what's so important about the twentieth of July?"

"Name day for Iliana." Rachel nodded at her olive-smashing daughter. "She's Hannah Iliana Groff."

"Groff and not Matsouka?" He wouldn't have pegged Sergei as someone placid about his child not carrying on his name.

"We were divorced before she was born. And yes, it irritates him. But I let him give her Despoina's mother's name, and now they flip out if they can't have her on her name day."

Back in February, Depy and Sergei had both given him gifts on his name day. His own parents, they said, had almost forgotten to call. They were on a Valentine's week cruise, so it wasn't like he'd expected to hear from them. Either way, a call was better than the years upon years of discounted heart-shaped boxes of candy he'd grown up with.

"My family name days are more low-key," he told her. "But even though it's not a big production, they still make some sort of celebration. I've got one set of cousins who go all out. Balloons, bands, ponies, parades."

"Parades?"

He grinned. "Okay, maybe not parades. And a pony just the once, I think. But name days are a big deal to Greeks. I guess it's hard on Sergei and his mom to wish Hannah many years if they can't surround her with flowers and trinkets in person."

Rachel's shoulders were rigid again. She dipped a napkin in his glass of water and began wiping olive debris off Hannah's hands. "I was embroiled with Sergei for over six years. I know how name days work in Greek-American culture, Theo."

"Oh." He watched to see if shutting him out was deliberate. He had the sinking feeling it was. "Right, of course you do. I wasn't trying to—I mean, I thought, you know, from their point of view...."

She had Hannah on her hip, bag on her shoulder, and all defenses in place. "No one needs to tell me about their point of view. They have that well under control. Thanks for keeping her from overhearing us."

"Rachel, listen."

"Gotta go. Say bye, Hannah."

He forced a smile as he caught the girl's blown kiss. As he sank back down at the messy table, he held on to her imaginary affection, and the all too real sense that he'd blown his chance to show Rachel that whatever her problems with Sergei had been, he himself had sprung from a different source.

<hr>

ONE OF THOSE motherhood side effects no one warned about: habitual early rising. Like, ridiculous amounts of early, sometimes. Also, snapping into full alertness as soon as the internal clock buzzed her senses. Not a peep from Hannah's room, so Rachel stretched and snuggled up with a pillow. Five whole minutes to stay sunk into her mattress, before cereal and clean up and clothes and cycling to daycare.

Scrolling her phone, she caught up on the group text from the night before. Serena and Natalie one-upping each other with pics of unsuitable wedding dresses. Gillian threatening to block them both. A stream of emojis from Serena, followed by a snide poem courtesy of Nat's fiancé Evan. All so much like the good-natured bickering back when they'd shared an apartment in college. The sense that they'd always be in each others' corners, even if they couldn't decide on the most effective use of that corner's space. She'd come into the roommate situation as the outsider, still at sea trying to navigate the huge university after a couple of years of small town community college. Gillian, Serena, and Natalie absorbed her, lifted her up, guided her both logistically and emotionally.

And she loved the gals. Hundred percent pure love and appreciation for their friendship, their acceptance, the way they, as individuals and as a group, looked out for her and for Hannah. God knew she wasn't going to say no to anyone looking out for her in life, not after all those years of second place and leftover and afterthought and rejection.

So her love was true, and she never wanted to take away from any of them. But first Serena and Dillon got engaged, then Natalie and Evan. Both worthy men, both great fits—for her friends. She wouldn't want either guy herself. Dillon too restive like her; they'd never be quiet together. Evan too focused on achievement and externals. He was sweet, goofing around with Hannah, and would probably start his kids' college funds the day their social security numbers were established, but Rachel couldn't imagine him holding Hannah's hand and talking her through the death of a pet or the casual cruelty of a kid at school.

What donned steel capped boots and kicked at her sternum wasn't envy of her friends' specific relationships, but jealousy that their lives held the possibility to jump into romance without considering anyone but themselves.

Seven months pregnant when her divorce was finalized. Dating wasn't on the radar for close to a year—life was too full of diapers and getting back to work and finding a place to live independent of Depy. Of separating heartbreak and anger and healing from the intense process of falling madly in love with her infant.

Her heart healed. She chiseled away at the Matsouka family obstacles until she'd sculpted a shape for her life that was independent of Sergei and his mom. Those final shards weren't easy to smooth out, but she had a plan. Goals. She'd even drawn herself a picture, one day when she and Hannah were coloring. Hannah told her to make a flower box like the one they'd planted on their balcony, so Rachel colored in the planter, and several daisy-like shapes. She'd been contemplating adding some tulips, since they were the only other flower she could draw, when Hannah stopped her to count the petals. Rachel watched her point and mangle the order of numbers, and silently tallied the petals on her own.

There were nine flowers and eight loops of petals per flower, because she wasn't artistic but she was methodical about the few things she did draw. When Hannah went back to her coloring page, Rachel added one more daisy. And though she knew the number almost to the penny, she logged into her bank app to check her savings account. She had three thousand four hundred saved towards the cushion of eight thousand she needed to ensure she and Hannah could survive six months without losing their apartment, if she ever lost her job and Sergei stopped paying child support again. Instead of letting herself remember the ten thousand she'd saved before Sergei left his last job, she drew a tenth flower in her box and colored in thirty-four of the petals.

She kept her garden pegged to the freezer with a couple of the shrinky-dink magnets Hannah once brought home from craft day. Every time her balance climbed, she filled in another petal. Twice she'd had to squeeze spare petals onto completed flowers—Hannah's rotavirus meant time off work and way too many meds, and she'd let herself go over budget for Natalie's thirtieth birthday gift.

But no matter how contrary she got about life as she budgeted and bargained her way to financial security, her garden was growing. Almost two-thirds of the petals were colored in. She—unlike her ex—wasn't in arrears to anyone.

It cushioned the kicks of jealousy, knowing her safety net stretched tight beneath her and Hannah. Because dating again—and Rachel liked the occasional date, she refused to dislike it, no matter what it had led to with her past relationships—wouldn't stop being difficult thanks to her permanent label 'single mother.' She'd seen the dismissiveness online and in person. No one felt like adding a toddler to his pro column. And she refused on principal to view Hannah as a negative. So no matter how independent and positive and strong she was, Rachel couldn't just go meet a man and start a relationship. Hooking up, yes. That, as Serena pointed out when Rachel first ventured out of her apartment to sample barhopping with a babysitter at home, was easy.

The post-bang follow-up conversation though?

Wanna do this again?

Sure. How about Friday?

Maybe, I have to check with my sitter.

You have a kid?

Yep, a one-year-old daughter.

And there it stopped. Sometimes she got platitudes about being a single mom. Sometimes she got vague compliments about a child the guy hadn't met. Sometimes the honest recoil and backing away. Her protests about not looking for anything serious never mattered, so she stopped bothering, and then stopped saying sure to the re-match. Now with Mary Lynn turning in her thirty-day notice to move, she wondered when she'd bother to find someone new to babysit on nights she had custody.

Better not to text that thought to the love-struck brides-to-be in her friend group.

Anyway, she wasn't tied to the idea of a relationship. Being single? Plenty of perks. And Sergei's whole self was an object lesson to single people yearning for a partner.

But damn would it be a freedom to go through the new coupledom explorations Serena and Natalie had—tussling over how they like their coffee, debating when and how much to tell their families. Taking it slow or fast or whatever happened to suit, getting het up over concerns like moving the furniture or mean-spirited sisters.

Not "Your flirty texting game is cute but I can't play and coax broccoli into my kid at the same time," or "I spend ninety percent of my non-working time potty training a toddler, so I can't drop everything to bop out to the beach with you this weekend," or "Stop asking; sleeping over is never an option."

Her baseline was different. She'd never think of Hannah as a hindrance—well, maybe the potty training, but not otherwise—but, oh. The eternally lost freedom of irresponsibility.

Flinging back the covers, she got up to attack the to-do lists of the day.

CHAPTER FIVE

"You're here, finally." Sergei was halfway across the pub, which was full of customers, but that didn't stop him from booming over everyone's heads as soon as she cleared the threshold. He put his whole arm into waving her over.

Big surprise. Sitting half-hidden until she'd waded through the crowd was Depy. Her former mother-in-law made a meal out of standing to plant powdery kisses all over Hannah before Rachel could back away from her. Back in the exhausting post-divorce, post-birth months, when living at Depy's house was the least of several evils, she'd failed to make peace with the woman. Relied on her, yes. Trusted her to keep Hannah safe and loved, yes. Agreed about her nine thousand theories of childcare, not even close.

Over several colic-pacing nights she'd investigated the laundry room and kitchen and cleaning supplies, trying to pinpoint the particular combination of scents that lead to Depy always seeming a bit musty around the edges. She'd never found it, and never quite gotten used to it, though she was ready to admit that her feelings about Depy and her ex-husband fueled her reaction more than actual sensory objections.

At least there was no denying the woman's devotion to

Hannah. And the adoration was mutual, much to Rachel's mingled relief and frustration. Now, losing Mary Lynn, she resolved to appreciate someone else putting Hannah at the center of the world. Or, close to the center. Depy would always value her son above everything.

Almost always. Only when Sergei's behavior during the divorce threatened to put a permanent wedge between Depy and her soon-to-be-born grandchild had the woman put her foot down with him. Now Depy kept him following the visitation schedule, and in time he'd figured out how to be a decent father. If not a decent ex. Plus, Hannah adored her papa, and the thing Sergei loved most in the world was the adoration of others. In return, he was charming and focused and capable of behaving like a prince.

Just like he'd once been with her. So charming, so infatuated, so ready to bask while she worshipped him.

The problems came when mutual infatuation faded to what should be some kind of mature partnership. She'd gone through it herself, and seen him do the same with girlfriends in the years since they'd separated.

She'd even been jealous of those girlfriends, the ones with the backbone to stand up to him when he smashed the pedestal he'd built for them and used the shards to hurl abuse their way. Those other women—Depy made sure she knew about all the other women—didn't stick around while Sergei belittled them and used his pitying tone to explain how they weren't book smart, and they ought to buy clothes that didn't make them look so frumpy, and they should let his mother show them how to starch his collars.

Depy never shared those stories, but Rachel could sense them from the way Sergei's charming facade began to slip a few months in to any relationship, He was less reliable with Hannah drop-offs. His texts about the schedule got snippier. He stopped posting pictures bragging about Hannah on Facebook. It didn't matter that Depy and Hannah still idolized him; a single blow to his armor and he treated the whole as if it was about to rust in place around him.

It took her three of his failed post-divorce relationships to learn that she had to stop scurrying around with an oilcan and polishing cloths trying to keep his armor shiny for him. He would have to squire himself. Or let Depy do it.

Rachel's job was to be all the parent Hannah would ever need, because at some point, Sergei was going to decide she wasn't enough of a reflection of his glory. Hannah would need a place where she could always be herself, even if her self wasn't in the mood to heap adulation upon her father. It might not be until she was seventeen, or it might be when she was seven, but at some point, it would happen. And until then, Rachel would monitor Hannah's post-visitation moods for signs that Sergei was giving Hannah the broken pedestal treatment.

It was another reason she was forced to be grateful for Depy. Depy was many things, and many of those things fed into Sergei's outsized self-regard, but she was Hannah's champion. Rachel could trust her to shield Hannah from any of Sergei's direct insults. Even if he snuck in some of his insidious tearing down of the girl's self-worth, she would be protected, thanks to Depy.

Who smelled musty around the edges.

"Hannah, you're getting too big for Yia Yia. Come sit on my lap because if I hold you in my arms they will break from the strain."

She refused to roll her eyes. "So the reward chart and stickers are in the bag. You got my email about the schedule?"

Depy shook her head. "Yes but those newfangled tricks are all wrong. I will tell when my Hannah is ready for big girl panties."

"We don't say that phrase." Depy deigned to look at her, so she clarified. "'Big girl,' I mean. Potty readiness doesn't relate to size."

"But she is a big girl. Aren't you, Hannah? Aren't you Yia Yia's big girl? Your mama doesn't know a big girl when she sees one?"

The woman might set back every milestone she and Hannah had reached, but Rachel didn't need to stand there and watch it happen. Sergei, giant surprise, had slipped off somewhere. So she kissed Hannah and retreated to the bar, needing a glass of water and a moment to herself before leaving her daughter in Depy's know-it-all hands.

***

"Ron, got a minute?"

The brewer turned from his whiteboard, lifting his chin in affirmation. "What's up?"

Theo stepped into the walled off section beside the fermenting tanks, sliding to the left of the door to catch a bit of the breeze from the floor fan. Despite the buildup of heat on the brewery floor, Ron refused to set up a desk in the brewpub's front offices. It gave Theo more room to spread his work out, but doomed him to hunting across yet another area for the packing lists that Ron shoved on a clipboard and Sergei stacked in a cardboard box under the bar.

Such was the life of the CFO. "Hey, did Javi check the delivery of the 2-row and red wheat this time?"

Ron gestured at the clipboard hanging on a nail by the door. "Told him to."

Pulling the wedge of receipts free, Theo said, "Thanks. Listen, I need to see if we can move up the monthly meeting. I'm heading to Fort Worth early. Annalisa wants to take him on this schools-end campout Saturday, so I'm going Thursday-Friday this week and extending Father's Day to the whole weekend." He straightened the paperwork, shuffling the pink half-sheets from their malt vendor to the top so he could verify that the dockhand had counted the sacks before storing them on the pallet rack.

Ron, who'd been consulting his calendar, said, "I wanted to bring the summer ale to the meeting. Won't be ready before Thursday. Can we do it the next week?"

"I'll check with Sergei."

Ron grunted. "He'll care?"

Straightening, Theo rapped his knuckles against the door-frame. "Monday after lunch, then. I'll let Sergei know."

He passed through the swinging doors beside the back bar, and just about smacked into Rachel. She was settling Hannah's overnight bag onto a stool, eyes trained on where her daughter danced in Depy's lap.

"Oh, sorry."

She spun to face him, backing up a hasty step and increasing their personal space more than Theo thought was strictly necessary. She looked grim, brackets alongside her mouth and shoulders slumped like they still bore the weight of the duffel. "Theo."

He waited, but that seemed to be the extent of her comment on his presence. Not that there was anything remarkable about his being in his own business. "You doing okay?"

She shrugged, turning back to watch Hannah. There was something coiled about her, Theo thought. A spring ready to bounce, a catapult ready to fling. He skirted around her, watching Sergei's interactions with his mother and daughter. The man was scrolling through his phone, which come to think of it he was doing a good quarter of the time Theo saw him. He'd condensed as much of his job as possible to fit on his phone—another reason Theo was able to spread out in the brewery's office. Hannah reached over for a fistful of Sergei's shirt, and Depy unhooked her fingers before sweeping the girl up for a series of kisses.

Rachel wrapped her arms around herself.

"Do you...?" He trailed off, relieved she hadn't seemed to hear him. Her tension wasn't any of his business. And none of his ideas for how to help her relax were, he had to remind himself, wise ones.

But then Sergei stepped away from the family tableau, lifting his phone to make a call. He plugged his other ear with his free hand, squinting down at his squealing child.

Rachel's indrawn breath was sharper than the well-honed blades on the industrial blender. She turned back to him. "Do I what?"

He was stammering for an answer that would be nothing but

kindness and banality, but maybe his cheeks had flared or his Adam's apple had bobbed or somehow else she saw that he hadn't started the question with pure intentions. She stared. He closed his mouth. She nodded.

"I do."

CHAPTER SIX

HE CLEARED HIS THROAT. She watched it bob and contract. "Sorry. What?"

"You were about to ask me if I wanted to get out of here. I do. Let's go."

It wasn't but a moment before he glanced away, but hellfire if she wasn't scorched by the blaze. He waved the sheaf of mismatched paper in his hands, a flimsy fan against the flames between them. He focused on the receipts and said, "I need to...."

She looked at him. At his creased brow, his parted lips. At his body.

He met her eyes and hushed. Then: "Give me a minute and I can follow you."

"Good plan. I'll be in the parking lot." She rolled her shoulders back and pasted on her Mama smile before returning to Hannah for a final hug. "See you tomorrow, Hannah Banana. Have good giggle times with Daddy."

"Depy," her girl said, reminding Rachel that Sergei hadn't yet kissed their daughter hello.

"And with Depy, yes. Bye-bye." She caught the kisses, blew some in return, and on the way out resisted body checking the squid slime whose one good service to the world was fathering her amazing daughter.

She was getting out of here. And, odd and bubbly and unexpected as it was, she wasn't getting out of here alone.

———

THEO'S NECK was a marble column, immobile, not about to twist, twitch, turn toward Sergei. Rachel glanced back—to Hannah, to her ex; Theo wouldn't speculate. He kept his gaze forward, his senses stuck on the woman who'd just walked away from him. The firm quiet thock of her shoes on the painted concrete floor. The bounce of her curls. Something a touch antiseptic in her scent, a whiff of hand sanitizer. It smashed a crisp image of Andres through him, showing off his kindergarten classroom the Friday Theo drove up early to attend the Parent's Picnic. His son's gap-toothed chatter boxing and the downy hair on the nape of his neck and the heart-shaped birthmark on his wrist.

He shook his head to clear it, and found himself watching Rachel walk out the door.

Damn if there wasn't a swing in her hips as she strode away. He succumbed to temptation, glanced at her family. The Matsouka family. They weren't paying her the slightest whit of attention.

Sliding into the office, he dropped the receipts in his basket, double clicked on the company's calendar, switched the date for the meeting, hit the sync button. Normally he'd have mentioned the change to Sergei, but normally he hadn't just been pierced by the summer blue eyes of Sergei's wife. Ex-wife.

He managed to not slam the office door as he left. Lifted a hand in farewell as he passed the bar. Did not sprint from the front door to his car. She was standing a couple of spaces over, next to her rusty sedan. Standing didn't quite cover it. She rocked a bit, her head bobbed, her jaw shifted, she glared.

He grinned.

Do not, Theo told himself, *draw this woman into the shadows between cars to explore the meaning of that look.* But every muscle in his torso strained to move. He held himself all the stiller. Found his voice. "Dancing?"

Her chin tilted further back. "You want to go dancing? It's not even lunchtime."

"Or grab tacos? A movie? Kayak along the bayou?"

Her eyebrows went up. "Kayaking?"

He resisted stepping closer. The pulse on her neck shimmered, and he bit his cheek. Exhaled. "Only a suggestion. I'm open to all possibilities. You looked in there like you needed to blow off some steam, but could be my way isn't your way. So whatever you want. I'll follow your lead. No expectations, no demands."

Her killer blue eyes caught a splash of sun as she straightened off the bumper. He made out shades and variations in her iris. A muddy greenish color around the contracted pupils, a dark marine band at the rim. Disconcerting, that, to a man who pretty much only looked deep into brown eyes all his life. The blue hues drew him in, though, instead of shutting him out. He matched her chin tilt.

"Serious?"

He did not lean her way. His feet were planted firm to the asphalt. He nodded. "Serious."

Her surface tension broke like an oval stone had skipped across the lake of her emotions. The ripples were quiet and entrancing and made him proud he'd found the right words.

SHE WRIGGLED HER SHOULDERS, feeling suddenly disarmed. "You know what? I'd love to kayak."

Not going to ask herself what she was doing. Who she was doing it with. It wasn't like she was taking her life into her hands, spending a sultry summer hour or so with paddle in hand. Even if the guy she navigated with kept her brain buzzing with questions.

One thing Rachel was good at—was forced by history to be

good at—was recognizing bad gut feelings. She couldn't deny that interacting with Theo set her up with some feelings. But they weren't bad ones.

They might even, if she were a tad less cautious, count as being good.

He gave her directions to the part of Buffalo Bayou Park where they could rent a hull. He nodded when she said she had errands to run before she could meet him. He said everything that was chivalrous, and never quite lost the intent look she interpreted to mean ... well, all kinds of interesting things.

History and habit meant she didn't often run into these slivers of being intrigued. And Theo came with more than anyone's fair share of marks against him: Sergei trusted him, they worked together, they looked like they could be brothers. But up against all that was this sliver of interest. It was a green light, faint but true. She decided to take it. To run with it. At some point—not today—she might even take it out and let it glow long enough to shed some illumination on what on earth she was thinking.

"So, have you done this before?"

"I grew up in Colorado."

"I'll take that as a yes?" He smiled at her smug expression.

She nodded. "Until I moved before high school, I had my own boat. We all did."

"Where did you move to?"

"Up by the panhandle. Plainview. My sister was headed off to college, and my parents took the opportunity to downsize. So I moved in with my aunt and uncle to finish school." She rattled off the information as if she's said it a thousand times, and there was nothing questionable about it.

Well, the point of the excursion was to give her an escape. Digging into her family dynamics was no way to accomplish that.

He gestured to the rental building they were approaching. "Want to double up?"

And damn if she didn't glint up at him like he'd made a double entendre.

And damn if he didn't glint right back.

"On the kayak? Or should we get singles?" He'd intended the double, else he'd have brought along his own boat. But again: it was Rachel's escape. She called the shots.

"I'm fine with doubling."

He slid a waiver form her way and handed his card to the kayak guy.

"Let me..."

"No." He stopped her, mid-reach, from dipping into her handbag.

Warm skin. Soft.

He cleared his throat. "Sweet of you, but no. My idea, my treat. I'm overdue for some time on the water, and glad for some company."

As she moved to retrieve the pen she'd dropped to the counter, her forearm slid under his fingers. Very soft skin, and extracting himself before he tangled their fingers together was an effort.

Forms, signatures, storage bag, vests, paddles, and finally, zigging down the path to the water, separated by the precise length between the stern and bow grab handles.

At the launch spot, they slid the bow into the bayou. "You want to sit in front?" he asked, one hand on the rear cockpit and the other balancing his paddle on his shoulder.

She waggled her eyebrows, but without much heat. They both were tracking a group of canoes floating a few dozen yards away. Each held three or four teens or young adults, laughing and calling and delighted with every aspect of themselves. "You're fast, right?" she asked, turning back to him.

"Like Hermes himself."

For a moment, all she gave him was a blank face. He didn't know if he should explain or apologize. She shook her head.

"Trying to remember if he ever got himself in trouble with any of the Oceanids. Best to hope not."

With that, she laid her paddle across the back of her cockpit and hopped into the kayak. He shoved it another foot into the water before taking his own seat, and together they pushed off. Within two minutes, they'd passed the canoes and the only sounds were the wind, the call of birds from the tree-lined banks, and their paddles stirring up water as they dipped, in unison, to propel themselves through the cool, mud-brown water.

HADN'T PEGGED her for a knower of Greek mythology, had he? Never mind her scatter-shot education and preference for movement over books. She'd lived with either Sergei or his mother for six years. Depy stocked her shelves with Rick Riordan well before Rachel scraped together the funds to move to their own apartment. When they moved, Hannah's pile of storybooks about the pantheon came along. Rachel knew her Olympians.

"Hey." Theo sounded determined, like he'd noticed his assumptions about her and wasn't into letting them float along on this journey.

Theo. God. Ha. "What's your full name?" she asked without turning around. Let him squirm.

"Theo Melis."

"No, I mean, is Theo short for something?"

"Oh, don't ask that. Look, there's sometimes a heron or two in that inlet up ahead."

She glanced back at him then. "Nice try. Spill."

"Or what? You'll spill the boat over? You'd get yourself soaked, too."

He squinted into the early afternoon sun—they were paddling upstream so they could turn and laze back after their arms got tired or their rental hour was near up, depending which came first. His face held all kinds of angles and lines picked out in the brightness of the day. His cheekbone and his beard and his lips and the trapezoid of forehead between his hair and his brow. It made him very much himself in a way that felt comforting.

She brought her elbow up sharp so the paddle kicked a spray towards his chest.

"Hey!"

She laughed. "Better tell me your name, then."

He flipped his paddle over so the concave side was up and skimmed a scoop of water forwards, but it only sent a few drops onto her arm. "Nice try."

"Fine. You win. This time."

"And to the victor, I'm told, go the spoils. Which would be your full name."

"Never call me this. Especially in front of anyone else. They'll think it's funny how I flinch and I'll have to carry around bottles full of bayou water to squirt at people who laugh at me."

She knew the color was more to do with silt and dirt than any pathogens, but the thought still made her shudder. They were passing under some vines dangling in the water and up ahead she spied not only the promised white heron but also a pair of dragon-flies playing their own games with the sunlight on their faceted wings.

"I promise."

"Okay. Fine. I'm Theodoros Andreas Melis."

She grinned, which he probably could guess at even though he was looking at her spine and her helmeted head. "So that's gift of God, right? And what else?"

"What are you, some sort of etymologist?"

"Ha. I have a client in one of my groups, Teddy, she loves to tell people what their names mean. She's properly Theodora, so I guessed you're the same as her."

"And I suppose if I don't tell you, you'll go ask her?"

"First thing Monday, yep."

He groaned. She flashed him a smile over her shoulder.

"Okay, fine," he said. His voice was only playfully reluctant. "Melis has to do with honey."

"Because you're so darn sweet." Her voice was plenty tart as she teased him.

"Right. And Andreas is a form of Andrew. That's where we got my son's name, Andres."

"I know you know its origin. Or do I have to ask Teddy?"

The hull tilted to the left and on instinct she leaned to the right. The move saved most of her sleeve from the arc of water Theo splashed up at her before straightening and taking hold of his paddle again. "Manly. It means manly, okay? Now, should we turn around here or do you want to go all out to that bridge first, and then float back?"

It hit Rachel that she hadn't locked her jaw or ground her teeth in the least while thinking about Greek gods. Not spent any time trying to imagine when Hannah was next due for a potty run and if her father or grandmother would be doing a thing to help her stay on track with her toilet learning. She was grounded in the water, everything else floated away.

"Oh, bridge, definitely," she said, and as one, they set off towards their goal.

CHAPTER SEVEN

"So, listen," Theo began. And then he stopped. What an awkward thing to say. They were the only people within earshot, and he was talking, so what did he think would happen when he spoke up, that she would get up and dash to the other side of the plaza?

And now he'd officially let the silence draw on too long. To cover, he slurped some of the juice about to drip off the bottom of his popsicle. After returning their kayak and gear, they'd picked them up from a food truck in the parking lot, then retreated to an empty bench in the shade. Glancing up, he caught her watching his mouth, which made him feel less like a flounder. He licked his lips. "I'm heading up to Dallas on Thursday. My ex switched the schedule so she could take Andres on this campout, but she's giving me an extra couple of days next weekend to make up for it."

"Why didn't you do the camping? You like all this outdoors stuff, right?"

So, she was paying attention to a few things about him, too. Good. He wanted to give her a great deal to pay attention to. "Annalisa's the real outdoorsy one. She got me into kayaking, but I pretty much dropped the rest of her whole hiking, camping, tents and campfires thing once we split. Golf. She definitely got golf in the split."

Her cocked head and silence were maybe a signal he'd let something slip. She didn't ask for details, though. He forced nonchalance into his voice. "Besides, she helped organize the trip. She said I could join them, but then we'd have to share a tent or Andres would have to bounce between us, and neither of those is what you'd call an ideal solution."

She nodded, then nodded again, a little abstracted. "You two—you and Annalisa—how is it? Are you...?"

Rachel trailed off, glanced off, fiddled with her napkin.

"Amicable, yeah. Pretty much. I don't think we'd either one say we did that cliché thing, you know, have a kid to fix our relationship?"

She nodded.

"Oh. That wasn't you and Sergei, was it? Did I say something crass?"

Rachel's smile, when it caught the dappled light and was enhanced by her flush from kayaking and the raspberry-lime popsicle, made him feel like he'd somehow invaded a watercolor painting. "Not hardly. There was nothing to fix, and Hannah just complicated everything. Not that I minded, in the end, of course."

"Sure, how could you? She's aces."

"She sure is."

He grinned right back. "So is Andres. He steals my breath away, you know?"

She did. He could see it in the flash of her blue eyes as she nodded.

"The line I give, and I had plenty of soul-searching with a therapist and even she agrees now it's true, is that the problems with Annalisa and I predated Andres, and that our marriage was built on the feeling that it was time for us to check off these life events. We were already dating, so we took it to the next level without being sure we were with the right person. The stresses broke us apart before we had time to fix them." He stopped another sweet cold purple drop from escaping the popsicle onto his hand. "Though I'm not sure we could have acted soon enough or done enough work to salvage it."

"Mind my asking, how long ago was your divorce?"

He closed his eyes as he counted back. "Three years, three months."

She nodded. "Around the time you opened the bar?"

He suppressed a laugh. She was quick. "Yes. And yes, that had something to do with it."

Either she wasn't interested, or he was pretty clear about not wanting to talk about it, but she let him change the subject to her job as a recreational therapist.

"For the most part my clients are recovering from strokes or mobility-related injuries. We do movement and dance, some crafts, sports. I think I'll see about setting up group kayaking outings, if I can find a launch without so many steps down to it."

They got talking about logistics of Houston's waterways, and before he was ready, they'd washed off the residual stickiness and sauntered to their cars. He leaned against his bumper, thinking how Rachel was a creature made for sunlight.

"This was a good idea. It was just what I needed, thanks."

He shrugged. "Any time. I mean that—I had fun, too. It's a nice change to not be on the water alone."

"Well, it was sweet of you to notice I needed an outlet. And all my cares floated off downstream—or down bayou, I suppose. To the Gulf, either way. I'm not going to spend one more second this weekend wondering if Hannah's potty learning will be destroyed by Sunday night."

He laughed. "That's what I was diffusing?"

She was quick to temper, too. "Are you telling me I was over-reacting?"

He held out a hand. "Peace. We didn't get Andres out of pull-ups until after his third birthday. I still have stress dreams about reward charts."

To his relief—and pleasure—she took his hand and used it as

leverage to pull up onto her toes as she leaned in to kiss his cheek. Lips softer than her fingertips. "Peace. See you later."

He hoped she meant her words, meant them even though he'd never managed to bring up making plans for another date. He hoped the quickness with which she hopped into her car and pulled out onto Allen Parkway indicated only that she was a woman unburdened by stress, and not that she was eager to leave him, standing in the dusty-hot parking lot, alone.

THAT MONTH'S Sunday dinner with the gals was at Serena and Dillon's. As they finished their meal, Rachel kept finding her gaze drawn to the framed game board mounted on the wall opposite her.

After eating, she spoke up. "I want a do-over."

Her friends, in unison, turned to look at the fortuneteller they'd concocted, back when all of them were unattached. Natalie's not-yet-ex had disappeared on her, and Serena masterminded the game board as a combined distraction and comfort. It was a grid of predictions about their true loves, like they were back in middle school fantasizing about the future. Hair color, eye color, what car he drove. How he'd perform in bed, because they were adult women not seventh graders and they had important criteria at stake. Once Serena indulged all her graphic designer impulses to beautify it, they'd all rolled dice to determine their romantic futures.

It would have been simple silliness, except that Serena and Dillon proceeded to fall like skydivers for each other. And now Natalie had Evan, who was making obvious faces at Nat and saying, "The die never lie, Rachel."

He and Dillon fist-bumped. "Damn straight," Dillon said. Then, "Ouch. Sorry, Rachel."

"I will start banning you two from dinner if you can't watch your language around Hannah," she said. And fist-bumped Serena to thank her for kicking her cursing fiancé.

"It's my house," Dillon said, as if that could keep him from being banned.

Serena, on cue, said, "My house."

"A plague on both of yours house," Evan said. "Why do I have to get banned when he's the problem?"

"Because neither of you understands why Rachel gets a do-over with the game board. Go do the dishes or something," Natalie said to both men. She cleared space on the dining table while Serena stood to lift the game board from its hook.

Dillon started to collect plates, but Rachel stopped him. "I need a die."

He handed the stack to Evan and started towards the living room.

"Make sure it's not twelve-sided or anything," she added.

Dillon turned around, eyebrows raised. "Not every sci-fi fan plays D&D you know."

Rachel smirked and went back to helping Hannah wipe her chin.

Crossing his arms, Dillon leaned against the doorjamb and leveled a resigned look at Serena. "You told them?"

"I tell them everything."

"That she does, Rocket Man," Gillian sing-songed. Serena had rolled for the rocket ship in the fortune-teller's 'Sexytimes' column. "One six-sided die, please."

He was a good-natured man. As was Evan, but his recent revolt at being treated as the eternal baby of his family made him less fun to tease than Dillon, who still relished the role of little brother. And much as she admired Evan and Natalie's relationship, it was still newer to her. Part of the Sergei fall-out was that Rachel was far less trusting about men in partnerships than she once was.

As if to prove his worth, Evan brought her a damp paper towel to help with Hannah cleanup. So maybe the game board's success rate boded well. But Rachel's own original rolls had conjured up Sergei. Or someone exactly like him.

In other words, everything she was never falling for again.

And sure, she knew all about confirmation bias. Libra horoscopes only had some eerie accuracy as long as she filtered out the stuff that didn't fit her life. Just look at Dillon. No sign of either a motorcycle or a dog, both elements Serena had rolled for back when she'd first started seeing him. That didn't stop her seeing a touch of fate or magic or some such in their union.

Dillon delivered a handful of dice and took the rest of the dinner detritus through to the kitchen, where Evan was scraping plates into the compost bin. Rachel lifted Hannah out of her chair and sent her toddling after the men, then centered the game board on the table between the four friends. "It's not that I'm looking for a new husband or anything."

"Sure. We know." Natalie handed her a sparkly purple die.

"Let's say last time your cosmic forces weren't aligned right, because it was too close to the divorce," Serena said.

"Right. Slimy Sergei tainted my rolls."

"Typical of him." Gillian hadn't even snorted at their hint of mysticism, which is how Rachel knew her friends were not so secretly hoping she was ready to try a serious relationship again. That, and the fact Gillian kept passing along lipsticks she claimed weren't her color once she got them out of the store.

Well, good for them. She had reservations.

Reservations that hadn't kept her gaze from straying to the game board all through dinner. So she trapped the die between her palms and rubbed for luck. Her chest had that irritating tightness, the kind she had to breathe through when her therapist asked if her thought patterns were giving Sergei power over her actions. She blew on the die. "First roll."

"Hair color," Natalie said, and her voice was steady and encouraging.

Opening her palms and letting the die drop straight onto the table, she lifted her chin and looked at Serena. Serena smiled and glanced down. "Three. Brown hair."

"Same as last time."

Gillian picked up a black die with green pips. "Well, statistically, that's the most common anyway. I'm still searching for my bald man."

"Wait long enough or expand your age range enough and your odds will improve," Serena said.

"Or hang out near barber shops," Evan added. He had Hannah on his hip and an arched eyebrow. "And brown is the second most common hair color. Those of us with raven locks prevail, don't we, Hannah?"

Her daughter thunked her head against his chest and rubbed her eyes.

"I'm thinking of taking sleepyhead here for a walk around the block."

One quick heart thud, and Rachel swallowed so she could nod.

"Unless you'd rather I didn't?"

"Rach—"

"No, it's okay." She placed a palm on Natalie's outstretched arm, and then took in Evan's ease with the toddler. "It is. You're sweet to offer, thanks."

"Want me to go with?" Dillon asked from the kitchen.

She and Evan said no at the same time. "Let me take her to the potty first," she added.

Shut in the bathroom, coaxing the tired girl through her routine, she could hear murmurs of conversation from the dining room. Evan sounded worried, and so did Gillian, then Dillon made a joke of some kind. She hoped it broke the tension. She hoped it wasn't at her expense.

Hoisting Hannah, she rejoined them. "I doubt you'll get as far as the driveway before she conks out," she told Evan.

"Nat can track my phone if you want to watch our progress," he said.

She kissed him and Hannah both on their cheeks. "Being

ridiculous can also get you banned from dinners, you know. My hesitation isn't about you. It's just a mom thing. A mom with maybe a couple of issues thing."

He squeezed her shoulder before heading out. It made no more sense as reassurance than anything he'd said, but still, she turned back to the game board with a full, genuine grin. "And now for eye color."

CHAPTER EIGHT

THEO DRUMMED fidgety fingers on the countertop. He'd spent the day baking desserts for Elixir, which should have been soothing but left him restless like he'd substituted cardamom for cloves and had no idea how the recipe would come out. None of the pies themselves seemed off; he was the one without all the right ingredients.

He pulled out of clean rag and began wiping down his stand mixer. Thing was, yeah, he liked Rachel. She was sexy, complicated, bright, an excellent mom. Hot. Something about her coiled strength made him think it would be fuck ton of fun to be around when she decompressed.

And her ex was his manager. A friend of a friend of someone's relative, in the way things worked in their community. Four résumés landed on his desk the day after someone at church heard about the open manager's position. Of those, he'd picked Sergei, and neither he nor Ron regretted it.

He didn't care—he didn't think he cared—what the deal was with Sergei and Rachel's marriage and divorce. In general, knowing their outline meant it wasn't too hard to shade in the picture. Married young, discovered they one or the other or both had problems they couldn't surmount, ended the marriage and figured out a way to co-parent despite whatever had gone wrong. Not a lot of closeness between them, but nothing alarming.

None of it impacted Sergei's ability to do his job. Or erased any of the awkwardness that came with telling someone on his payroll, "I'm into your kid's mom."

It also didn't mean he could avoid ever talking to Sergei about it, should his half-baked ideas about Rachel rise into reality.

The kitchen timer chimed. He extracted the blackberry-raspberry pie, slid in a tray of baklava, and decided to leave the washing up for another time, when being around the sweet spicy scents of his kitchen wouldn't prompt such maudlin and too-hasty ruminations.

By Wednesday, he'd invented an excuse to ask Sergei if he would have Hannah at Elixir. Cobbled together some cheese and honey pastry bites, based on a hand pie recipe he'd run across. Claimed he wanted a kid's initial reaction. He knew Hannah liked his baklava, but these had a more savory flavor profile. Theo thought it could be added to the children's menu. If Hannah didn't throw them on the floor.

"Are there nuts in them?" Sergei asked.

"Hannah's allergic?"

"No," he shrugged, "I don't think so. Her daycare is nut-free."

"But she can eat tree nuts, right? She's had pistachios here."

"She has?" He glanced at the daily specials board at the end of the bar, as if it held the history of his daughter's menu choices. "Right. Sure. She can eat tree nuts."

Theo wasn't getting the answer he needed. If Hannah would be at the pub, Rachel would drop her off, and he could aim to waylay her and ask if she wanted to go out again sometime. Catch a movie or grab a meal. Or spend the next couple of hours naked with him. "So it's okay for me to test these out on her tonight?"

"Right. Sure thing. But I'll have to check with her mom." He didn't sound eager for the encounter.

Theo tried to channel casual disinterest. "Want me to ask her about it?"

"Who, Rachel?"

He nodded.

"Sure. That works." Sergei checked his watch. "She should be here in like forty minutes. Do me a favor? Find out about the whole nuts thing without telling her you asked me first?"

He wasn't going to play with his gift horse. "You got it."

NO MATTER what Gillian might accuse her of, Rachel did not reapply her lip-gloss before unlatching Hannah from her car seat. Well, she did, but it was because they were dry, not because Theo might be inside when she dropped Hannah off. And they were only dry because it was that kind of weather—an odd lack of humidity for a Houston summer. None of that had to do with Theo's brown hair and computer-related job and the possibility he had a goldfish swimming around somewhere.

Not that she was looking for permanence of any kind, like Serena and Natalie had found rolling dice for their relationships. Just ... something a step up from occasional hasty single encounters between near-strangers. She'd had, for now, her fill of those.

She paused in the doorway of Elixir to let her eyes adjust, and to hunt down Sergei. In the dim light, it was natural she'd mistake the man over by the bar for her ex, with their same build and his back to her and all. Never mind that her stomach's slight flip was so different from the distinct knot she got whenever she had to walk up to Sergei. Hannah, at least, seemed to know the difference between the men. She lunged at Theo as they approached, and he caught her up easily, settling her on his hip with a ready laugh and a kiss to her forehead.

Rachel decided her body language must explain it all. No matter how she worked to keep an upbeat tone about Hannah's dad, her daughter must pick up on nonverbal cues, and that's why every handoff to Sergei was a struggle. But with Theo, there was none of the clinging, or the repeating of 'no no, Mama,' or the occasional and dreaded toddler tantrums. She went to him as readily as she did to any of Rachel's friends, or to Depy. It wasn't that she didn't love Sergei. Rachel had lurked in parking lots spying on them often enough to know her daughter was all smiles as soon as the door shut behind her. So she'd already suspected the bad handoffs were her fault, even without the periodic comments from Sergei telling her so.

Add another thing to the list of 'ways Mama's decision to divorce screwed up Hannah's life.'

"Hey," Theo touched her upper arm gently. "You okay?"

"Sure."

He pressed a little harder, both with his fingers and with his words. "Seems like you're shaken up or something."

Rather than enlighten him about all the ways she was failing at the most essential responsibility of her life, she backed up and narrowed her eyes at him. "You think every time I come in here upset now you have to swoop in to my rescue?"

His deep brown eyes widened. "I wasn't trying to talk you into anything."

She looked at her daughter, kicking and content in the cradle of his arm. Told herself to dial down her stress levels so Hannah wouldn't cry when she left. "All right. Sorry. How are you?"

"Good. Fine. Happy to see you again. I was going to call but I don't have your number."

She maintained her pleasant face. Reminded herself she'd had a good time with the man, and anyway, he wasn't to blame for her bad parenting. "I didn't think about that." Not that she'd called him herself. Hadn't planned to. Didn't cross her mind to imagine doing anything further with him.

"Hey, little H." Sergei came from behind her and lifted Hannah from Theo. The men exchanged a look she couldn't quite decipher.

Theo turned back to her, nodding. "So, you know I make the desserts here?"

She shook her head.

"Yeah. Well, the baked ones. And I have a new one, a savory variation on baklava, I want to add it to the kids menu."

"Right?" She wasn't sure how it mattered to her.

"I thought I'd see if Hannah would be my taste-tester. If that's okay with you?"

He looked super eager. She sensed something subterranean happening with his mood. "Is it any good?"

"Yeah, I mean, I think so. Want to try?"

Now the man was gleaming, body canted towards the employee area. She shrugged and followed him, leaving the diaper bag on the nearest table. Sergei hadn't bothered to collect it from her, and she reminded herself he was only incompetent when she was in the mood to insult him, not in actual fact. He could figure out where it was if he needed it.

Theo rambled on about savory and sweet and some old cook-book he'd found and the windowpane consistency of phyllo. And here she'd thought he was all about reports and meetings and spreadsheets and that sort of thing. So much for her roll of the computer for the 'Jobs' column. She'd been imagining his work life kind of the way her manager's office was, a cluttered desk and lots of emails about proper formatting for case reports and color-coding or whatever.

Not that she'd been imagining his work life. Just, she'd gotten an impression, based on Generic Managerial Type, and was a tad taken aback—a tad charmed—by this dessert-obsessed side of him.

"You're not allergic to nuts, are you? There's a walnut paste layer in here."

She shook her head and took the little pastry from the plate he offered. The man was almost giddy. It was absurd. And added even more to his charming side. She let herself forget her well-earned suspicions about men with charming sides.

Especially when his baking was yum. "Can I have another?"

"You like it? Serious?"

"Serious." She reached for the plate, which he thrust her way with a start of haste. And then he took one for himself, and was all deliberate about setting the plate back down, and she wondered if there were laws against anyone being quite so charming on a random Wednesday evening. The cosmos should protect against that sort of thing.

He cleared his throat, lifted half his mouth in one of those wry smiles like every rogue on TV, asked, "So it's okay for Hannah to eat these?"

"So long as I don't eat them all myself first, sure."

His gaze flickered away, then back at her. "Confession time."

"You've got a confession?"

"Yeah." He rubbed his neck. "Two, I guess."

Sometimes she swore she could feel each vertebra stack up as she straightened. She grabbed a napkin and wiped phyllo from her fingers. "Oh. Kay. Go on, then."

"Right. So, I made these as, well, kind of an excuse for waylaying you today."

She didn't answer, no matter how expectant a pause he left.

"I was hoping to ask you out, but I didn't want to be, you know, obvious about it. I didn't want to complicate anything with you and Sergei, or, I should say, I didn't want to decide for you how we should be around Sergei. If there's going to be a 'we', which, I'm not taking you for granted. I'm very good at this, aren't I? I'm trying to say I'll respect your boundaries, whatever that means for you. Dating me, not dating me, making out with me on top of the bar." His smile held maybe more hope than self-deprecation, and his eyes seemed to be full of pleas that she speak up.

She wiped her mouth, and noted the sheen of her lip-gloss on the napkin. Balling it up, she lobbed it towards the tall garbage bin by the door. A perfect shot—her trash sailed into the bin's depths. "That last one isn't super likely."

His own vertebrae shifted, sinuous, as he swiveled towards her. "So the others might be?"

"What's the second confession?"

"Oh." He slumped. "It's not that dramatic. But it would feel odd not to mention it. I asked Sergei if I could give one of these to Hannah, and he asked if there were nuts in them. He said he knew daycare was nut-free, but didn't know if she was."

There went her spine, fusing again. "Excuse me?" Not that she hadn't heard him.

He winced. "I know. Don't—well, do what you want. I offered to find out if you'd mind Hannah trying them, and he asked if I could find out if it was okay without first telling you he didn't know, and technically I did. Find out first, that is. But probably he meant for me not to tell you at all. Not 'probably.' I'm sure he didn't want me to. But that's kind of bullshit, and how would it be decent of me to hide that from you one minute and ask you out the next?"

Two factions battled over her reaction. Stay still, the better to be charmed by his aggrieved babbling, or storm off to pluck her child from the arms of a man who couldn't be bothered to remember the most basic facts about her. "Her friend Rishi has a peanut allergy. But the daycare is peanut-free in all classrooms regardless."

"Hey."

"Hey what?" The more she thought about it, the stronger the storming off to yell at Sergei impulse was growing. Theo's cautious gentleness also veered too close to patronizing for her to stay glamoured by his charm.

"He's ridiculous."

"Rishi? He's two. I'm sure he'll conquer putting his shoes on the correct feet soon enough."

Laughing, he squeezed her hand. "You're breathtaking, Rachel. Your ex is thoughtless, but listen, I've seen him with Hannah enough to know he isn't—whatever dangerous thing you're imagining. Setting her down in the middle of the parking lot. Turning her loose in the kitchens to play with the knives and the ovens."

She rolled her eyes, but didn't retrieve her hand. "Thanks for the new mental images."

"So? What do you say?"

"About what?"

"Our whole dating thing?"

His charm was downright dangerous to her resolve. Her gut was beguiled by cheese pastries, and her fingers were warm against his palm, and she knew he was right. Sergei wasn't actively endangering Hannah. Or even passively endangering her. Brain weasels aside, she trusted him with their daughter.

Still. She wasn't sure about anything else Theo was offering. His intentions verged on romantic, all this talk of dating and of making public declarations and of advising her about dealing with her own ex-husband.

"Look, Theo—"

The door squeaked open and she turned to find Depy framed in the opening. Feet planted wide, eyes narrowed, arms tightening around Hannah's squirming to get down.

It was only when Theo let go that she realized she'd been tugging her hand away from his.

"Hey, Depy," he said, calm and even affectionate.

Not that her ex-mother-in-law was anywhere beguiled by that damn charm. "Theodoros."

Those months she and Hannah had lived with Depy after the divorce, she'd gotten more than intimate with all the woman's ways of expressing her displeasure. She'd even, in time, gotten good at rising above it. So she stacked up those vertebrae, ending with a lift of her chin. Turned her back to Depy long enough to meet Theo's eye-wide look. "Meet you in the parking lot?"

She wasn't quiet on purpose, or loud. If Depy overheard, she overheard. If she ran off to wail at her son, so be it.

Theo didn't even half-glance at the duo over her shoulder, to his credit, and good thing. If he had she'd really be questioning her impulses. He nodded. She grinned, and paused to grab a napkin and a cheese pastry before heading towards her bright beacon of a daughter.

Depy's grip had nothing on Hannah's determination to scuttle into her mama's arms. "Hey, Hannah Banana. Look here what Theo made for you. Want bites?"

By the time she'd carried the girl back to Sergei, she was covered in buttery flakes of phyllo that turned her goodbye kisses even sweeter than usual. Rachel handed over the child but not the napkin, and congratulated herself. For once, the transition wasn't teary.

When she headed into the parking lot to wait for Theo, she didn't feel one single urge to turn around and spy through the bar windows as father and daughter got on with their visit.

CHAPTER NINE

HE GRABBED the keys and checked to see had his wallet and some portion of his brain. He was inclined to sneak out via the dock, but that was ridiculous. Sergei wasn't paying him any attention, and if things went the way he was thinking, he might need to have a conversation with the man anyway. No point trying to hide if he was going to see as much of Rachel as he hoped.

Which reminded him to yank open the bottom left drawer of Sergei's neglected desk and snag a couple of condoms. "Better safe than sorry," the guy always said during orientation for new hires, offering them access to the stash alongside boilerplate about workplace relationships. He never saw anyone take one, but it hadn't been a week since Sergei mentioned that the supply was getting low. And the near-empty bowl suggested his employees waited until Theo was out of the office before helping themselves.

Any eon now, he told himself, it would be great to stop thinking about sex and Rachel and Sergei all at once.

TERRIBLE IDEA. *Doomed.* Decision fueled by frustration and flirt-

blindness and fear, even. Fear of sinking into a life made of nothing but motherhood; fear of managing that life with one of her safety nets moving off to Brenham; fear of Depy shuffling into the role of default co-parent; fear of how angry and helpless and powerless and mad and furious and useless Sergei made her feel.

Fear Theo was another man like her ex, and everything else— her sex-starvation, his smolder, the way Hannah burrowed her forehead into his neck like she knew something good and safe and trustworthy—was a trap. A ruse. A pit she may as well throw herself down now, to test the depths. And while she was down there, if she caught a flutter of a red flag from Theo, she could claw her way back to the nice safe surface of her life.

At least while she found out more, she'd get to have sex. The teeth he flashed her as he strode her way were a promise of nips to come. The width of his stance when he stopped in front of her invited her into his personal space. His direct gaze deliberately didn't track her body, a statement of his intent to scrutinize when he had her alone.

She'd played all these games before. She knew how to throw these dice, to collect these cards, to rack up these points.

So: doomed, yes. Maybe. Yes. But Rachel leaned a hip against her car and cocked her head. "I suppose I should ask you out for drinks, but it seems pointless. Considering."

He cut his eyes towards the brewery. "Pretty much."

She pressed her lips together to stop the flirt-high grin. That grin had an agenda and didn't care who knew it. It got things done, that grin. Done in the carnal sense. How many bar parking lots, how many hot-enough men, how many Saturday nights with nothing else on the agenda had that grin made an appearance? Not for ages, sure. She wasn't in high school any more; she wasn't still in college.

Sergei hadn't killed that grin.

On the thought, the pressure straining her cheeks drained. Her mouth deflated. She stopped thinking about her wilder years, banished every grim thing about her married days and those post-divorce nights with a newborn. Leaned towards Theo, who was frank and focused and who fired her up. And if she had to guess based on his reaction, the smile that overtook her then was sexy as fuck.

———————

HELL, she lit him up. He tried to find polite, coherent things to say. "So, no drinks."

She shook her head slowly.

"And you know I'm trying to ask you out, right?"

Her nod was even slower. His pulse kicked up in response.

"Rachel. I don't want to overstep, but you need to give me a clue if you want me to, you know, back off a little. My mind's got only one track right now. One very crude, slip and slide, ride me now track. I'm not trying to be coy about it, but I'm not an ass. I'm not making demands. I want you. But if it's no, or not right now, or something else, just say so."

"And like that you'll head back to work?"

He tried to cut off the inarticulate noise. "Well. I'd need a minute."

She let her eyes drop to his crotch, which didn't help in the least. "And if I take you home now you're not demanding sex?"

"Fuck. No. Of course not. No demands. It's your call."

"Not a single demand?" she asked, a tad taunting.

Damn her provocations. He edged closer. "I could be persuaded. If that's what you wanted."

"And you've got some free time?"

The report for investors. Ron's refusal to give up on the bottling machine. Approving the shift schedule. He palmed his phone, but didn't quite manage to look at the screen.

Her eyebrows danced. "If you've got calls to make, do it now. We'll be busy later."

He shook his head. Cleared his throat. "Nothing urgent. Plenty of free time."

"Give me your phone."

He unlocked it and handed it over. She glanced down then handed it back.

"Never mind. You type it; I don't like these keyboards."

He got over the stutter of panic that her 'never mind' was calling everything off, and added her address to his contacts.

"The rule is, never give that to Sergei."

"Okay." It hit him. "Wait, what?"

"He doesn't get my address. Depy has it in case of emergency. So don't give it to him, but do follow me to my place. Clear?"

He was nodding but the cogs in his brain were shifting in opposition to his head's movement. Dizzying. He should think with his cock instead.

How about that for something he'd never guessed he would have to tell himself to do.

BETWEEN MOM CAR and Mom purse, the very least she should have handy was a brush. Or anything not made of fuchsia sparkles to pull her hair into one of those casual chic knots Natalie could make blindfolded.

On the way out of the parking lot, she found a tube of her favorite tinted lip balm in the car door pocket. At a stop sign, she popped a couple of soft mints from her bag. But her foraging yielded no brush. No comb. A teal polka dot scrunchie. A couple of barrettes too flimsy for Hannah's hair, so she tossed them in the trash bag hanging from the gearshift.

Red light. She got methodical with her search. Nothing in the glove box, crumbs in the cup holders, useless crap in the center console. Finally, wedged under Hannah's car seat, a wet-hair comb with mostly intact bristles.

Good enough. She yanked it through a few of the tangled curls, made a face at her reflection in the visor, and put it all behind her as she led her asshole ex-husband's boss to her home.

For a while—maybe not long enough but for a while—he was in a divorce support group. Most of the members were parents. Not everyone. Enough that he got a sense of the usual kinds of custody arrangements, the usual types of communications. Some co-parents were excessively polite with each other, and some played Bribe Baby For Affection. Some got flighty about visitation schedules. But Theo couldn't remember any who hid their location from their ex.

It wasn't like she avoided seeing the man himself. She'd been talking to him half an hour earlier. He'd ignored Hannah and barely nodded at her instructions, but he didn't menace or shout or ... Theo didn't know what. Nothing he'd observed about their interactions screamed of mistrust. Sergei seemed far likelier to forget to pick Hannah up than to go throw midnight rocks through Rachel's windows.

Maybe it was her place that was messed up. Something askew about her living situation, something the would cause Sergei to ... and he was stuck again. He tried to picture Annalisa living in some way that would alarm him or start a fight. Neglect or seediness or drug paraphernalia strewn across the parking lot. Holes in the roof and rats everywhere and eighteen people in a two-room place. And even then, he'd want to know. Want to help her find a sanitary, safe place to live. And nothing about Rachel—or Hannah, who in some ways he knew better, after playing with her at Elixir a few times a month all year long—suggested they lived in condemned housing.

He followed her car. It was still dusted yellow with tree pollen, even this late in Houston's purported springtime. The bumper stickers were a mixed bunch: liberal politics and knitting jokes and her other car was a bicycle and even one for Elixir. As they idled at a red light, he plugged her address into the map.

Huh.

She lived closer to Sergei's place than either did to the gas station where they'd first met. Another three turns and they'd be at her door.

And yet she made a habit of exchanging custody another couple of miles down the freeway. Sergei sure as shit hadn't seemed to mind, beyond acting inconvenienced by the need for drop-off at all. Theo drove more than three hours each way every other weekend to see Andres, so, sure, it was all relative. And he knew where Annalisa lived.

Another turn, and he also knew where Rachel lived. A smallish, tidy but outdated apartment complex. Gates across the drive that stayed open long enough for him to follow her in. She waved him at a parking space and continued on to pull her car under a carport. Her lips pressed together, as he approached, holding in one of those shooting comet grins of hers.

"Come on, it's up this way." She brushed her warm, light fingers along his arm while gesturing to a set of stairs with the other hand.

Even in the shaded overhang of the carport, Rachel's blue eyes played color tricks. Little flashes of dark, hints of light. It kept him staring at them. Or she did. Her micro-expressions, her deliberate masks, her wary desire.

How long had they been divorced? How many people had she led to the apartment she kept hidden from Sergei? How much psychic weight had the man left in his wake?

Why hadn't any of the questions intruded back at Elixir?

She'd turned to him because she needed an outlet from the flack Sergei and Depy had sprayed when she dropped Hannah off. So it wasn't time to trade stories. To compare his months of post-divorce partner turnover to her, what? Single mom of a little one. Depy intruding in her business every day she could. When Andres was a baby, a toddler, it took him and Annalisa combined to manage all the playing, the supervision, the chores, their jobs. Forget about date nights, forget about time for themselves, forget about sex.

She gestured to a staircase, and Theo found he'd lost all the questions about her ex. Their steps were in sync, and the jangling of keys in her hand rang in time to his heart, and he'd gotten hypersensitive enough that the extra weight of the condoms in his pocket pressed against him. A promise, and a lure, and everything he'd been imagining since she'd barreled his way wearing star-shaped sunglasses.

THEO WAITED for her to unlock the door. A look on his face like she was worth waiting for.

"So, this is me."

"Hi, you." His voice was light. Not teasing or mean or bored. Just ... light. Some kind of burden floated off her shoulders as he spoke, like the shrugging off of her backpack once she'd biked herself and Hannah home from daycare.

She filled her lungs with buoyant air. "Hi."

"You're still okay with me coming in?" No innuendo, no judgment, no demand. As if any answer was fine, so long as she addressed his curiosity.

There went another weight. Like removing her helmet after a late-spring ride during rush hour traffic, when everything was grit and heat. Pretty soon she would be as unburdened like a Hannah-free Sunday morning, cool banks of energy reserves and a few hours free to fill as she liked.

And she wanted him for it. For his lightness. For having a voice the opposite of Sergei's. For checking in like her blatant invitation still left her the power to alter her plans. For that look, the one that said he hadn't changed his own mind, and wouldn't write her off if she had.

She could test him. Call him on it. Wait for him to be locked back on the public side of the parking lot before renewing her invitation.

"Hang on."

He stood still at her threshold.

She pulled out her phone. "Give me one second. Texting my friend."

"In case I've got nefarious plans?"

She unleashed a grin designed to mislead him about the sharp way his words tripped her heart. "Exactly. Telling her to check on me in a couple of hours, and alert Gillian to take custody of Hannah tonight if I can't."

He snorted. Snorted. Like a rhinoceros or something. "Good luck to her getting her away from Depy."

Her favorite animal was the rhino. So impervious to harm. So horny. She grinned. "You haven't met Gillian."

He narrowed his eyes. "She'd have to be pretty formidable."

Slipping her phone back into her pocket, she tilted her head up towards him. "I think elite security forces watch videos of her as part of their training. And she's got paperwork on her side. Depy doesn't stand a chance."

"Poor Depy. Good thing I'm not planning to disrupt you quite long enough to make you late getting back to Hannah."

One lock. The second lock. Her hand on the doorknob. "Not quite long enough?"

Now whose voice held innuendo?

Theo leaned at her. Just a half-inch. She had clients for whom that half-inch would be a major victory over their mobility. For Theo, it was easy. He didn't appear to struggle with control over his body at all. But he managed to lean that measly half-inch with all the impact of a full-body hug. "As long as you like, Rachel. You tell me. I'll follow your lead."

CHAPTER TEN

HER APARTMENT DIZZIED HIM. Or maybe it was the inept blood flow to his brain. Books and bright toy bins and a tidy but mismatched row of shoes at the entrance. Unremarkable furniture buried under knit blankets and a stack of folded laundry. His gaze roved, sending him impressions of a clean and organized and undersized space.

"It's not Buckingham Palace, but it's mine."

"Sorry." His knee-jerk apology had nothing to do with any defensiveness in her tone and more to do with worry he'd been giving her space a dismissive look.

Rachel's hand on his forearm cooled his blushes. "How grand a tour do you need before we get to the fun stuff?"

He slid out of his shoes and nudged them into line next to a green sandal. The other half of the pair was a few soles away. "I'm here for your needs."

She let her tongue slide over her lower lip, caught that lip with her teeth. Released a silent sigh.

He was riveted.

"Okay, then. Kitchen, living room, bathroom's at the end of the hall." She waved in general directions as she led him her way. "This is my room."

And maybe it was anticipation, maybe the contrast to the controlled clutter in the other spaces, but he felt as if he was entering an oasis. A brass bed with green and yellow bedding, three plants thriving along the top of the dark wood dresser, gauzy curtains. And in the middle of it all, not a mirage: Rachel.

"Cute."

She widened her eyes at him. "You are eloquent."

He rubbed the buzzed hair at the back of his neck. He shouldn't have let the barber use clippers; it left coarse prickles and he didn't want Rachel repulsed by running her hands over his scalp.

He wanted Rachel to run her hands over his scalp.

And his beard, and his body, and his cock. "Most of my words right now are beyond crude. If you want a civil conversation, let's go back to the living room. Or a restaurant. Or anywhere I'm not looking at you and your bed."

She stepped to him. Her hands were strong and capable, exactly the hands he'd have expected, with her job. Stroking down his arms, circling his waist. He stroked into her hair, wrapped fingers around her nape. She grabbed his ass. Their lips met.

Her eyes closed. She tasted of mint and her hair was a tangle of silk and, groaning, he teased his tongue against hers. Rachel hummed in response, and his cock firmed against her belly. She backed one step. Two. He followed, tight against her. Together, they slid onto the bed. He pressed her chest into his, running a hand down her spine while shifting so she straddled him. Still nipping at her lips, tasting her sweet softness, he slipped a hand under her shirt's hem and the satin of her skin set his fingertips aflame.

Her skin, her kiss, the eyes she opened to meet his, ate away anything he was going to say.

THE MAN HAD A MAGIC MOUTH. She could do hour-long infomercials about his kisses.

And they were just getting started.

"One thing," she said, lifting away and breathing heavy. "I'm out of condoms."

She'd passed all her human anatomy classes. She knew he didn't have more muscles in his lips than other people. But his were firm and strong and moved in opposition to each other, like the lower was still meaning to kiss her while the upper curved in self-satisfaction.

Somewhere behind the insistent tingling desire of her breasts a shard of curiosity prodded her to study his lips in motion.

"Now, aren't you glad I was never the scouting type?"

She glanced from his lips to his bright-spark eyes. Her fingers tangled to clasp with his as their hands met between them. "I thought scouts were the prepared ones."

"Nope. They were all off learning meritorious skills while bad boys like me snuck around thinking up devious ways to get laid." He slid her hands into his front pockets and canted up his hips to give her room to delve. She understood his goal, even grazed the edge of a foil packet with a fingertip. But thrusting up his pelvis also drove the ridge of his erection against her. She spread her knees wider to sink into the pleasure.

Theo fell onto his elbows, then flat on his back, bracketing her hips while she tilted into him. Those lips of his softened as he breathed out a moan.

It was too much. She was breaking into a sweat of need and panting and desperate action. She hooked a finger to draw out the condom, ran the heel of the other hand up his flies. Smiled at his louder moan. He unbuttoned and unzipped her jeans and started on his own. She peeled off her shirt and bra.

For a moment—two seconds, no more—as he was caught in the tangle of his Elixir-branded tee, his face was covered and memories of Sergei's body superimposed themselves. The broad inverse triangle of a torso, the black curls of chest hair. Had every man she'd fucked had those same nipples, or just these two?

But then his shirt sailed over her shoulder and he—Theo—stroked a thumb along her collarbone. Slid the other hand to the curve of her lower back. Swallowed audibly as he let his gaze roam her body. Everything as slow and quiet as river water coming to a boil over a campfire.

And as inevitable, given the heat.

She laughed her relief at finding herself right where she was, in her room, in her safe apartment, atop Theo. Dangling a condom in front of him. He snagged it and tossed it beside them as they finished stripping, and then they were right back to speed and hands and tongues and flesh. He was a man with good flesh, Theo. Warm and sure and tender. A touch too tender, until Rachel showed him what she liked. The firm pad of his thumb, the figure eight stroke that distracted her from her urge to explore his cock. His ass, his thighs, his entirely delicious abs. She collapsed back into her blanket as Theo focused in on her clit, clamped her feet against his calves in case he got foolish notions about abandoning her before she came.

He did not abandon her.

He did not stop stroking. His thumb obeyed her wishes, and he fulfilled desires she hadn't spoken aloud—unless Theo knew the language of groans and growls. Tongued her nipple, sucked, tugging a bit on her hair as he increased the tempo on her clit. Let her writhe. Her arms flailing, then hands landing in his coarse thick hair, and he grinned at her.

Maddening.

He maddened her. Slowed his movements. Made them lighter. Made her thrash as she threw herself at him, compensating for his failure of a thumb by doing all the work herself. Fuck that. She was a single mom, she knew about doing all the work herself.

But before she could twist her hips away and bring herself to orgasm, Theo said, "Condom."

Begged her, really.

So she bucked herself into his hand to make a point, but clawed the packet towards them and ripped it open, rolled it down his hot hard cock. They both were groaning, and hers turned into a gasp of bliss as he thrust into her. Thrust deep, but levered his body up so there was no need for his thumb to leave her clit. Smart, maddening man. He withdrew and slid back, slow, counterbalancing the torturous pace with his thumb's rapid pulse at her clit. Rachel's head spun and her fingers dug into his shoulders and she lost the last of her breath as she cried out and came.

He gentled again, fully sheathed in her, and traced tickle-sharp fingers up her sides. Waited for her half-open eyes to meet his smug look before leaning in for a kiss. Kiss. Meager word for the leisure and life and laughter and length of their lips meeting. Murmurs became words, and he asked, "Good?" Not self-satisfied, not curious, no. He was checking in, and maybe warning her, too, because when she nodded, Theo shifted apart his knees, braced his hands on her hips, and began to move.

Yes. Hell, heaven, all the gods and goddesses both full and demi, yes. He tried to focus on the soft blur of her eyes, slumberous but somehow still challenging, and ramped up his pace. Harder, more rhythmic, pushing forward and forward and forward until her eyes widened and her breathing matched his.

Both their voices half-coherent in rhythm, yes and god and oh and yes. Her arms flailed but then she got a grip on his ass and he was empty of finesse. No control at all. Nothing but the way she squeezed him tight, inside and out, and his thrusts slammed deep as he, as she, as they both moaned and came and panted and came and groaned.

She slid him to her side, a cool spot on her mattress that fast warmed to his radiating body heat. He mustered the energy to roll his head her way. "Wow."

Her eyes stayed closed but her smile broadened. "Ummm."

"I'll get water," he said, but let the torpor take his muscles until she nudged his ankle with her toe.

"Thanks," she mumbled.

He leaned in for a kiss before swinging himself upright. A quick detour to dispose of the condom and splash water over his flushed face, then he made himself at home in her kitchen. He found a tray between the fridge and microwave, and assembled a couple of sandwiches to bring back to bed.

"My hero." Rachel fluffed her pillows. She'd folded their clothes and donned a robe and tidied the bed. He froze in her doorway, a naked statue bearing sustenance. Even more out of place than the Parthenon Marbles in the British Museum.

Then she approached, and her robe gaped open, and she stroked up his flank before taking the tray. So he relaxed.

Except for the part of him fixated on the swell of her breasts.

She grinned. "If we're going for round two already, I'd better set this on the dresser for now."

He glanced at his watch. "I'm ready if you are."

"Good." She drained her water glass, and set it back with a distinct thunk. "I'm ready."

He had no right to be proud of himself that she didn't stop to fold her robe after discarding it. His chest filled with glory anyway.

Thorough sex, hasty sandwiches, dressing to beat the clock. With each second beside her, the feeling spread and became something too intense and too fragile for his own good. He didn't make the slightest attempt to curtail it. By the time they hastened out of her apartment so she could get back to Hannah, his mind was full of next time and hopefully also the time after that. It wasn't until they'd driven off their separate ways that he realized he still didn't have her number.

CHAPTER ELEVEN

"Why are you whispering?" Gillian asked. They'd met for their monthly lunch date, this time at a Belgian restaurant not far from the community center where Rachel taught her wheelchair patients to navigate obstacles.

"I'm not whispering." She glanced around again to ensure none of her seniors had ended up in the restaurant, then spoke more firmly. "I can be quiet without whispering. It's allowed."

Gillian leaned forward, sliding the small vase of daisies aside. "Why are you being quiet?" she whispered.

Rachel narrowed her eyes, but Gill just smirked. She sighed. "Fine. I took Theo home on Wednesday."

Gillian started. The wood chair leg screeched against the floor. Gillian winced, then slid back to the table. "Sorry. I was surprised."

"I noticed."

"In my defense, it's been three years since you had sex."

She regarded her friend, who seemed serious as all get out. "Gill, it hasn't even been three months."

"What?"

She tapped her fingers against the table as she counted back.

"Well, I know I'd finished my taxes, so maybe a little more than three months? But it was around then. Why did you ... hang on. How did you think I haven't been with anyone since Hannah? Even mamas got libidos, you know."

"I know." Gillian's cheeks hinted at a flush. Gillian, queen of the dating apps, proclaimer of sexual freedom for all, gifter of Rachel's post-divorce vibrator.

"You thought my last sex was with Sergei? Sergei?"

"Well, you haven't had relationships since the divorce." She tilted her head, frowned her brow. "Have you?"

Rachel smiled. "No, sweetie. I've been uncoupled. But I've picked guys up."

While their server delivered their meals, she worked on unraveling Gillian's misconception. "Not a lot, and okay, maybe I've been more private about it than you are with your hookups —I'm not judging, you know I'm not—but we roomed together for two years. How would you think I'd stop having sex after Sergei?"

Now Gillian was the quiet one. "I'm glad I'm wrong. Sorry for the weird reaction. It's a relief, if I'm removing all varnish here. I thought that sniveling turd of a louse had...."

The sheen of her eyes meant Gill wanted to march on Sergei with pitchforks, but lacked the spoons.

Rachel reached over and squeezed her hand. "You thought he broke me. You thought he'd sucked the life out of me and turned me into someone who only works and moms and needs her best friend to drag her out to a monthly lunch to remind her that she has more to her than that."

"No. No no no. I don't take you to lunch because of that. Rachel, don't think that way."

She raised her eyebrows. "Don't think that way?"

They laughed; Gill was the one who bristled most about people telling her how her mind should operate.

"Fine. Be autonomous in your thinking. But listen to me: I take you to lunch because I love you and I want to hang out with you.

And because someone has to listen to my stories about horrid men."

"Ohh." Gillian had the best bad hookup stories. Rachel slid to the edge of her chair. "Who was he and what did he do?"

"I thought he was a typical hot nerd type; we ran into each other at the library. But when we finished, still laying in his bed mind you, he told me he bet my students would be so jealous of him."

"No."

"Yes. And now I can never go back to the library in case I encounter more people with a Hot for Teacher fantasy, and that means I'll never finish my conference paper. So dealing with headaches like that, I never thought you were missing out by not hooking up. Though, I admit, it's true I don't think you get enough time to enjoy yourself on your own. But that's because you have a two-year-old, not because I'm trying to—to reprogram the way you operate. I love you exactly as you are." She lifted her own eyebrows, and went on with a wicked lilt. "But I thought you never had anyone to help you with your orgasms."

"Gillian!"

"Well, you never said. I thought you were off men."

She had to smile at the approval in her friend's voice. "You are such nonsense. Now I wish I'd mentioned it every time I hooked up."

"If nothing else, I wish you had, too, so I could be ready to rescue you if you needed me."

"Oh, that's Serena's job."

Gillian munched a fry, considering. "You told Serena?"

"We always put each other on alert when we go out with someone new. Or, now I gather I put both her and Dillon on alert. It's gotten a little unequal since they fused at the hip."

"Why not me?"

"First of all, why aren't you tethered to me to start with?" She pulled out her phone. "We're going to start tracking each other, then we'll feel better. And anyhow, I wasn't meaning to exclude you. It's something she offered, back when Hannah and I were moving into the apartment. At the time I didn't plan on dating for ages. You're right about the louse turd, or it felt that way for a while. But then I met this hot paramedic at work and thought, better to grab the moment when I had it, you know? So we grabbed the moment, just the one night, and I checked in with Serena before and after, and that turned into the system. I never thought about it like I was leaving you out."

Gillian finished setting the app up on their phones and passed Rachel's back to her. "I'm sanguine. You don't need to justify yourself. And I'm very glad Serena was on top of it. You told her about Wednesday?"

Rachel nodded.

"Good. So that leaves one bright glowing unexamined question on the table."

Rachel dug a tiny fork into one of her mussels, reluctant to meet her friend's eyes for a moment. She had a feeling she knew what the question would be.

And she was right. Gillian dabbed at her lips with her napkin and asked, "Why, after months and months of not mentioning the people you banged, but days after insisting on re-rolling the dice for your perfect man, did you tell me about Theo?"

HERMES HELP HIM, but he caught himself googling 'how soon until I call her' like a proper fool. He'd made pointed mention of going to Fort Worth for a long weekend, back before kissing goodbye in the apartment parking lot. She'd failed to offer any indication of what was next for them. He could have asked. He should have suggested something. Anything indicative of future plans. He wasn't clear why he was so keyed up over it.

Over her, sure. Rachel was ... great, in fact. Of all the available words, 'great' fit the bill. Bright and fun and direct and flirty and intriguing and in bed: electric. So, sure, he was a little keyed up over her.

Before sinking into the endless vortex of the r/relationships subreddit, he switched his browser to social media and searched for her, because that's what his last girlfriend had done between early dates: messaged him a dinner invite. It had propelled them into the next few dates, which led to a few months of exclusivity.

Except none of the Rachel Groff profiles were her.

Fine. Hermes was no help, nor was technology. He went in search of Sergei. Maybe the guy needed his help handling Hannah again.

And then he stopped mid-step, because he couldn't keep using a two-year-old to finagle his dates.

Theo diverted himself into a walk-through of the facility. Everything hummed along in that chill weekday way. A few large groups in for a late lunch, a few solo heads at the bar. All the staff seemed in control of their jobs. He couldn't get further resolving their expeditor's complaints about sauces until Ron answered his email. Nothing else tugged at his attention, and Sergei wasn't around, and every square inch of his office felt like it had shrunk by twelve percent in ungeometric ways.

He lifted a hand in farewell to the bartender and headed to the shed adjacent to the loading dock. A few minutes' effort and he'd loaded his kayak atop his SUV. An hour on the bayou would, gods willing, clear his head and leave him stuffed full of tranquility. And maybe some sort of plan, as well.

———

So MAYBE IT messed with her mind some when Gillian made connections between sex with Theo and a game playing at finding her life partner. Maybe it made her over cautious.

Never mind that her second set of rolls suited Theo the same way the first set had. It was all guesswork and confirmation bias anyway.

Any rules saying she had to get all relationship-minded with guys she slept with were outdated tools of the patriarchy. Rachel had long ago stashed all those tools in a tumbledown shed, thanks all the same.

And none of it influenced her decision to text Depy after she pulled into Elixir on Wednesday, asking her to retrieve Hannah from the parking lot.

She only did it because it was so hot out, and if she turned off her car to take Hannah in to Sergei, the interior wouldn't begin to cool again until she was almost home. They were in for a long boiling summer, including a multi-day road trip up to see her sister and parents. Any time she avoided overtaxing her faulty a/c, she felt she was preserving its lifespan.

Depy managed to keep her voice sweet even as she said; "I'm surprised you aren't sniffing after Mr. Boss Man in there tonight."

"There are spare panties in the bag, but she did a great job on the potty right before we left home, so if you stick with the schedule I emailed you shouldn't need them."

"Pah and bosh."

"Pah and bosh right back at you," she said, but light so it seemed like she was teasing. "I had to throw out those pink overalls you sent because Sergei didn't wash out the stain. Up to you if you want tonight's outfit ruined, too."

Depy pressed her lips closed, her favorite moue of disapproval. Probably she wanted to ask why Hannah wore the new dress if it was apt to get ruined. Too bad she'd pitched so many fits about never seeing Hannah wear the clothes she purchased.

She waved a final goodbye and backed out in her still-cool car. An hour and a half of nothing scheduled, and flying high on scoring points against Depy. What could be better?

Ignoring the traitorous image of Theo's naked ass that flashed in her overheated mind, she navigated home for some quality time with leftovers and her DVR.

CHAPTER TWELVE

Her non-custodial weekend to-do list was crowded to overflowing. A couple extra work shifts to bank against her upcoming road trip. A few hours helping Mary Lynn box up fragile items and load them into Goldberg's truck. Feeding Mary Lynn and Goldberg so they wouldn't fret over cooking after packing all day. Groceries and laundry and an oil change and getting to the gas station in time to fuel up before going inside to wait for Sergei to drop Hannah back to her.

All in all, not a second to spare. Not to wonder if she should have called Theo. Or to debate if Sergei sending Theo to the gas station again would make her mad. Or to answer any of the insinuations in Gillian's texts.

By Wednesday night, she gave up trying to fool herself. She likely couldn't even fool Hannah, who kicked her heels against her car seat a good half-dozen times, sparking her light-up sandals, while Rachel slicked on bright lip gloss then fluffed out her curls.

She winked at her kiddo in the rearview mirror. "You ready to go find Daddy?" She didn't add a word about Theo. That particular search was hers alone.

Months of Wednesday nights and every other weekends, a

hefty percentage of them involving hand-offs at Elixir, and she'd never noticed Theo. Not until he'd turned up holding her daughter, and she'd mistaken him for her toasted turdball of an ex-husband.

Now if she didn't quite seek him out at the brewery, she was aware he was there. Cognizant of his movements. Alert to the interplay of her pulse and his proximity.

Damned inconvenient, if she got right down to it. Hard to pretend someone was only there for casual sex if he inserted himself uninvited in all kinds of her thoughts.

She and Hannah hadn't cleared the vestibule before she was facing a whole bad dream, good dream, nightmare trio of faces. Depy, Theo, and Sergei all approached. Hannah tugged loose of Rachel's hand and wrapped her arms around Sergei's legs, which diverted him before they had to make polite conversation for their daughter's sake.

Another point in the 'when Mama doesn't treat Elixir like a house of horror, Hannah transitions are easy' column.

Speaking of scary, Depy was visible behind Theo's shoulder. She'd secured her wiry gray hair into her most disapproving bun, the one she fashioned to alert everyone to her dire mood. Even Sergei struggled to please her when she wore that bun. He'd trailed off mid-rant about needing an amniocentesis paternity test before the divorce was settled, merely because Depy collected her loose coil of hair and twisted it into the Bun of Displeasure.

It still marked the most in-her-favor statement Depy had ever made for Rachel.

But the woman was no longer her mother-in-law. No longer the provider of a roof over her and her infant's heads.

Rachel ignored the bun, and the bristling woman wearing it. "Hi," she said to Theo.

He rubbed the back of his neck. It was a feeble defense against the emotion-laden darts Depy was surely shooting at them both. "Hi."

"How've you been?" She knew her voice was over-bright. Not much she could do about controlling it.

He shrugged, which gave her a nanosecond of Depy being invisible. "Good. Pretty good. You?"

When she pressed her lips together to mute her helpless giggle, the smooth glide of her gloss nearly undid her composure. "Not too bad. Want to duck away from prying ears and chat a minute?"

A damn cute blush bloomed on his cheekbones, and Rachel held herself still to absorb the sight. His hand dropped to reach towards her, and he was nodding.

She passed him the diaper bag. "Can you give that to Depy?"

His shoulders shook off his laugh, and he turned. "Here you go, Yia Yia."

She muttered something too low and ungracious for Rachel to bother attending to it. Sergei was peering at the three of them like he was capable of solving the puzzle, so Rachel supposed his mother hadn't gone straight to him after last week, telling tales. Interesting, but not her problem. She swooped in to give Hannah a good-bye kiss and headed out.

She didn't have to look back to know Theo was following right behind her.

It was getting so he thought of the Elixir parking lot as 'their' place. So next time his cousin accused him of being an old romantic, Theo would call up the image of tire marks on pervious concrete bright with late-evening heat waves, and know Tomás was delusional.

She did shine, though, there with the sun bouncing off the hood of her car. "So I think Depy is on to us."

She snorted. "Clever deduction. You must win every game of Clue."

"Well, I don't like to brag."

If Tomás knew earning Rachel's smile endeared the parking lot more to Theo, his cousin would fall about with mirth. Good thing he wasn't a mind reader.

"So, listen." Too brisk, too devoid of flirtatiousness.

He answered as if it would never occur to him she might blow him off. "Always happy to hear what you're saying."

Rachel crossed her arms, shrugging. "You're right about Depy. I know it's your place and you can do anything you want, but I'd prefer if you're not right in the area when I bring Hannah in."

"Okay." He watched, but his quick reply didn't get her to lower her shoulders. "I get it, I do. She reminds me enough of my great-aunts to keep me on my toes when you and I meet."

She pursed her lips, but not in a sultry way.

"Hey," he said, going for tempting, "how about dinner? You have any plans now?"

"Are you trying to distract me?"

"No." He knew she knew it was a lie. Her shoulders shook, and she slipped her hands into her pockets.

"Don't be cute."

"You're the cute one. We established that." He watched, but she didn't even blink at his words. Not a hint that she'd been mentally transported back to her bedroom with him.

"I've eaten."

He glanced at his phone. It was early, but he didn't live with a schedule that involved getting a kid to daycare first thing every morning.

She shrugged. "I was hungry."

"Fair enough. How about we do something else? Or get dinner another time? Lunch, if that's easier. So you don't have to get a sitter."

"Theo."

"Casual. You said casual, and I'm being casual. Just, in a persistent way. Lunch is casual."

At least he'd gotten another smile. "Lunch is only casual if it doesn't mean all kinds of scheduling and dealing with the hospital parking garages and any number of other things."

"Okay. No lunch. Want to bring Hannah over to swim at my place? Andres will be down in a couple of weeks, we can let them splash in the shallow end together."

Rachel stepped back. "Are you feverish? Introducing each other to our kids is the very definition of not casual."

He laughed. "I've known Hannah for months."

"Still. That's not the same as a play date. And she's two; seven year olds don't want to play with two year olds."

"He's six."

"Still." Her lips pressed like that was the last word on the subject.

Casual. Not while she was at work. Not with the kids. He drew a deep breath. "Coffee. Either before you go to work, or before you pick up Hannah at the end of the day. No big interruption to your schedule, no involving the kids. Just me, getting up early or bailing on this place at happy hour, driving to you and sharing some caffeine as we chat about our lives. Come on, Rachel. What do you say?"

FRESH HAIRCUT and new lip color aside, Theo was asking a lot of her.

Or, if not quite a lot, he was asking.

She somehow, in all her careful not thinking about him, hadn't prepared for him to be asking.

Before he could finagle her work schedule and favorite latte flavor out of her, she said, "I've got an hour—seventy-eight minutes, maybe—before I pick Hannah up for bedtime. How far away is your place?"

That shut him up. Good. He cleared his throat. "Um, about two miles?"

"So it takes less time to get there than to mine?"

"Yeah." Theo nodded, a promising half-grin stealing over his face. "About five minutes."

"Great. You interested in spending a lot of minutes between now and seven twenty-five naked with me?"

She liked when he swallowed so hard his Adam's apple shifted his beard around. She liked the flush of his warm skin and the heat of his eyes and the way her body sizzled when they were close to each other.

He dug his keys out of his pocket. "Want me to drive?"

She regarded him.

"Go on and text your friend first. Tell her where you'll be."

"Where will that be, exactly?" She tried to sound challenging. Not like his reading her mind and anticipating her need for safeguards was both a comfort and a turn-on.

Theo smiled like she'd fallen into a trap. Except not a trap, since he always left her feeling like there were plenty of escape routes if she needed them. "If only I had your cell number, I could text my address to you, and then you could forward it to her." His raised brows and waggling phone and light tone squeegeed away any worries about how often he spoke to Sergei.

She'd shared the same info with Depy, after all, and heaven knew she trusted Theo three thousand times more than she did Depy. She recited her number, and swiped her screen to check the incoming message.

"Okay?"

She nodded. "You drive. I'll text Serena and Gill."

He held the car door for her. He closed it gently after she was seated. His jeans, now she got a view from the rear, seemed to have a crush on his ass.

It was possible they weren't alone in that.

CHAPTER THIRTEEN

"THIS IS ME." He shifted into park and looked over at her. She wasn't asking to be taken straight back to Elixir, so he supposed this was happening.

The about-to-get-laid part of him strutted around dancing the zembekiko. It was about boisterous enough to drown out the voice noting that she wasn't so interested in his 'let's date and start a relationship' overtures.

But she hadn't ruled it out. Also, he was about to get laid.

Entering the condo, she said the same thing as everyone else. "Wow, your kitchen is huge."

"You hungry?"

She pivoted to look at him. "Hungry for something huge?"

Gods, her every syllable was full of lascivious intent. Not enough a/c in the house to keep him cool now. He stripped off his shirt, kicked off his shoes. She dropped her bag on his sofa and wrapped her arms around his shoulders.

He hadn't spent the weeks apart overestimating the effect of her mouth on his. It was as luscious and encompassing as he'd remembered. Maybe more so. He tightened his hold on her, brought their bodies flush. Hitched her up a bit to ride on his thigh.

"Better give me the rest of the tour fast, or we'll be screwing on your island before you know it."

"Are you trying to end things early? Do you know how many pie crusts I roll out on that countertop? No naked flesh on the island, please."

She laughed, which made for some excellent undulating contact between their torsos, and he set about removing her top. "Well, aren't you precious? I'd let you fuck me on my kitchen counters."

"Sure. You say that now. Next time you're dicing carrots for dinner, you think about this conversation and get back to me." His mind was blown. She was wearing a lace bra the color of green apples, and her skin glowed, and her nipples were riveting. It was a lot to process and still speak coherently, and he was impressed with his ability to put together a logical sentence in the face of so damn much beauty.

"Carrots?"

"Potatoes? Onions? I don't know what you dice."

"Please stop talking about food and show me your bedroom."

Like he could walk straight, hard as she'd gotten him. He peeled his hands from her ass, detached his lips from her neck. "Bedroom. Tour. Right."

"Don't tell me—this is the living room, that's the dining room, and the kitchen is the huge, sterile pride of your life." Okay, so it was a self-explanatory space. She sure did relish lifting her chin to grin at him, though.

"You're terribly easy to get along with. Not a single challenging molecule to you."

"Are you judging me?"

He took her hand and led her down the short hallway, pointing as they went. "Andres's room, bathroom, and here's the master. And no, I'm not. I like your directness, and also you're really sexy. The bra is delicious."

"I didn't wear it for you."

"Never said you did." He shucked off his jeans and socks.

She stopped unzipping her shorts and ran her palm over his bulge. He throbbed at her touch. "Okay. I lied. I thought you might like it."

He pushed down her shorts, lifted her to wrap her legs around his hips as she kicked free of them. It brought his cock to her center, her breasts within reach of his mouth. Rachel reached back to unhook the bra, which thrust her that much closer. He stumbled towards the bed, too caught up sucking at the tight whorls of her nipple to be aware of things strewn in his path. The bed wasn't far, and they bounced onto it, landing with momentum that slid him along her body.

She yanked the bra off and tossed it aside, and he sat up, straddling her waist, loving the view of her flushed and open and eager between his legs. Loving even more the way she went straight for his erection, peeling down his boxers so she could wrap her fingers around his girth. Licking her lips as she stroked him.

Damn, he was a lucky man.

"How much time do I have?"

She squeezed. He moaned. She bit her lip, acting like she was considering the question. "Oh, I guess you have time to get through with me."

He reversed them, propping her up and tugging her hips forward so he could nuzzle at her core.

After that, it was all limbs sliding and plenty of panting and all his nakedness touching all of hers. She ended up straddling him again, gripping his headboard, as he licked and explored and massaged and sucked her clit until she came. Crying out his praises, her pleasure, his name. The way she vibrated above him had his hips bucking in the air, ready to sink into her.

She grabbed a condom from the side table and pressed his shoulders down, kissing his jaw and neck and taking a bite at his chest that served to ensure his cock was rigid with need. All he wanted was to pump into this amazing, ferocious woman and find his release. He held it together while she smoothed the sheath over his length, but as soon as she set him free, he rolled them onto their sides and lifted her thigh over his hip so he could thrust in deep. Her eyes widened and he had no choice but to bracket her cheeks with his palms and kiss her, tender and triumphant at the same time.

Her arms roved his back and his ass as he pulsed into her, each thrust driving them each a little higher, winding them a little tighter. He slid a hand to her pelvis, fingers gripping to anchor them together, thumb straying back to her clit to pick up the circular rhythm that made her moans high and desperate and keen with need.

His own need was overpowering. It took staring into her eyes, stroking back her sweat-damp hair, forcing himself to realize she was on the edge of another orgasm to give him the strength to hold off until he earned the high of her shattering around him. And she was close. He could wait, because she was close, and her breasts pressed close against his chest, and her clit was wet and wide, and she threw her head back and panted out his name, and she came.

And she came, and his cock was buried deep and intimate inside her. And she came, and her muscles pulsed tight around him. And she came, and his balls pulled up tighter as she gripped him. And she came, and he came, their pleasure sounding around them.

His head crash-landed on his pillow, his arms tangled slack with hers. They both panted for so long, drifting on the bliss, and every time she opened her eyes, she laughed to find him watching her, and when he opened his, the bright joy of her sprawled flushed and sated beside him sent shivers up his spine.

"Hi," she almost-whispered.

"Hey."

"Hey."

He aimed to form a full sentence. "How're you?"

"Mmm."

"Not a bad answer," he said, smoothing her hair off her forehead. Every deity help him but she was beguiling.

"Not a bad fuck," she said, and seemed to crack herself up. The laughter jarred their legs into a bigger tangle. He pulled her up tight against him, unwilling to lose the connection just yet. She played with his hair, sobering a little, and he took his chance.

"So can I take you for that coffee tomorrow?"

"Theo."

"Rachel," he said right back, but teasing instead of scolding. "It's coffee. I'm not saying we should go announce our relationship to Sergei and the world."

"Jesus, I hope not."

Ouch. Her words, the way she jerked away from him. The wild look in her eyes. "Okay, okay. I said I wasn't about to announce it."

"Well, hell, Theo. I know Depy suspects something, but this isn't—you're not—I'm not looking for a boyfriend, okay? I've had a ton of fun."

"That much I noticed."

"Don't be a smart-ass while you're still half-hard inside me."

He squeezed his eyes shut. Faced her again. "Okay. Fair point."

Sighing, she pat at his chest in a way more patronizing than erotic. "You have clean towels? I should shower before we head back."

He nodded and together they disentangled.

It wasn't until they scooted to the edge of the bed that he noticed the broken condom.

THEY WERE OVERLAPPING ECHOES. Carbon copied racing pulses and wild looks and swiping at messes as if their hands could undo what their bodies had done.

"What the ever loving fuck?" she asked.

He asked, "How the hell?"

"This is so wrong," she said.

He said, "I can't believe this."

By the time they'd showered and dried and dressed, they were moving almost in slow motion, though she at least felt like her brain was on double-speed. She joined him on his sofa. He had a little fenced yard, all landscape paths and containers and a patio set and a little pool. They stared out at it.

"I need to get back."

He nodded. She saw the motion in her peripheral, and it somehow helped restore her balance.

She swallowed, and he leapt up to fetch her a glass of water, as well as one for himself. "Thanks."

"Sure."

He dropped his head to the back of the sofa, and it triggered her slump. She let the cushions encompass her.

"Okay, so first off, I'm clean. I know I told you that before, but in case you need. I don't know. Reminding. Reassurance. I can go get a screening, though."

His words removed another barrier to her drawing a deep breath. "Okay. That's fine. I—me, too."

When she looked at him, the furrows in his brow smoothed and he exhaled slow, almost smiling. "Right. Yeah, thanks, that's good. We're good there."

She nodded. Ran her fingers up and down the cool ridges of the water glass.

"So I'll drop you back to get Hannah, and swing by a drug store. Let me know when you've got her to bed, and I'll bring over emergency contraception."

She nodded some more. It was a sensible plan. It made sense. It was the fix they needed.

"Have you taken it before?"

"No. Have you?"

He chuffed out a laugh.

"I meant have you bought it before? Been with someone who needed it?"

"Oh. No. I have seen it on the shelf. I know what to get. I'm sorry, I should have asked. You don't already have a pill at home or anything, right?"

She shook her head. "Nope. Never needed it. I'd knock on wood, but it's too late for that now."

Theo leaned her way, wrapped an arm around her. "No making jokes about wood now. Too soon."

"That wasn't what I meant."

"I know. I'm off-kilter. So, listen. From what I know, the over the counter is fine, since we're getting it right away. But if you'd rather get the prescription, I can go the pharmacy for you once you talk to your doctor."

"I work at a hospital." She forced the wry note into her voice, but only so she wouldn't burrow into his shoulder. "We have pharmacies on site."

"Right. Sure. Of course." His head shook once, swift. "Off-kilter. Is that better for you?"

"No." She stood away from his dangerous comfort and warmth. "I'd rather take it tonight."

He snagged his keys from the table by the door. She put their glasses on his precious kitchen countertop. It wasn't until they were pulling back into Elixir's parking lot that he disrupted her trance with a curse. "Fucking Sergei."

His eyes were narrowed, and she got suspicious. "What does he have to do with it?"

He put the car in park, gripped the steering wheel. Let out a long sigh. "It's not him. I'm throwing blame away from myself and that's the first place it stuck."

All the hard-earned chill that came with having a plan fizzled out. "Because without him you'd not have met me?"

Whip-fast, he shook his head. "Fuck no. That's worth thanking him for, except it would be questionable at best and sexist as hell at worst. It's the condoms."

"Sergei gave you condoms?"

"No. Well, yes, but not just me. He keeps a stash of them for employees to grab. Or whoever." Even in the near-darkness he must have seen her reaction. "It's not as sketchy as it sounds. We're not condoning whatever. Sex at work. He says it's better to have them around, in case people make. You know. Hasty decisions."

"Like we did."

Theo thumped his head on the steering wheel. "It wasn't. Well, yes, it was. I wanted it, but if I'd planned better...."

"Better?"

"Planned more carefully," he amended. "If I'd gone about asking you out a little more gracefully, maybe I'd have remembered to buy some condoms of my own."

"And instead you took from my ex-husband's clearly dodgy supply."

He closed his eyes.

Damn and hellfire. She hadn't questioned their origin beforehand. It was on them both. She reached across the console to pat his shoulder. Breathed herself towards calm, ordered thinking. "Okay, look. It'll take me an hour maybe to get her down. See you after that?"

When he leaned in to kiss her, she leaned in return. Kissed him back. And then she hustled out of his car, because she was only sure about one thing: her need to grab her daughter and retreat to the safe, familiar territory of home.

CHAPTER FOURTEEN

WHAT TRICKSTER GODS SENT him on a quest for emergency contraception when it was not yet sunset?

Theo wasn't ashamed. Frenetic, full of adrenaline kites swooping up and down his limbs. Still hanging on to his orgasm bliss. Sure he should rein it all in and settle down to the serious business of fixing the problem. After-dark feelings, all. Yet the horizon was barely orange, the clouds as white as they were pink, as he walked into the pharmacy.

It wasn't his usual store, and he wasted ridiculous minutes pacing the aisles near the dispensary before he figured out that the family planning—*ha*—section was over by cosmetics instead. The sealed plastic boxes of levonorgestrel perched on the top metal shelf, up where they normally kept overstock. Only visible because he'd done an image search before going inside, and knew what he was looking for. He retrieved one. Name brand, because it would embarrass him to show up at her door looking like he was willing to risk conception by buying generic. Another item going into his basket: unexpired condoms. And because he was looking out for Rachel, not because it put him on edge to head to the checkout with nothing but items from the personal hygiene aisle, he grabbed some pain relief, some anti-nausea pills, a couple of cool bottled drinks. His phone search told him she might throw up and get headaches and dizziness and bleeding and tender breasts. Damn.

As if he could make up for his lack of preparation by getting all she might need after the fact. Well, all except for whatever she'd need for the tender breasts. His phone had no advice about treating those.

It was dusk, and the mosquitos sprang out of the shadows as he mounted the stairs to her apartment. He texted instead of knocking, hesitant to disturb Hannah's bedtime. She wrote back "5 ok," which he took to mean the bugs would get their fill of him before she unlocked the door. A pound of flesh taken out in milligrams of blood.

Her steps, approaching the door he leaned against. He knew they were hers, which added a layer of pathos to everything else. It wasn't that he heard an adult tread and deduced it was hers; he recognized the firm and fast way she walked. He'd cataloged it, unaware of the data going into his brain's 'Rachel' file. It ate at him that he didn't know if the broken condom was the straw that would collapse the bridge they'd been building towards each other.

"Come on in."

He toed off his shoes in her entryway. "She down?"

"Yeah. It's okay; she's good about staying in bed. I'm going to turn this on, though." She clicked on the news, the volume high enough to disguise that the anchors weren't the only ones speaking.

He looked towards the sofa, then the kitchen, and back at her. She tilted her head at the breakfast bar, so he set the bags there and began unpacking.

She took over one of them, and snorted as soon as she opened it. "Really?"

Of course the tricksters fixed it so the condoms were the first thing she touched. "I didn't mean, you know, right now. I didn't know if the other expired or wore out from heat or what. It seemed like a good idea to have some fresh. I left mine in the car."

"You know if you leave yours in the car they'll have the same problem with degrading."

"I know."

Her look was all kinds of skeptical.

"I did lots of googling while I was in line. I left my box in the car for now, but I'll store it in my bedroom as soon as I get home."

She held up the package of plain crackers. "Hungry?"

"It said you might get sick."

She snorted. "Lovely."

"Or headaches." He gave her the boxes of meds. "You should take nausea meds now, then the contraception pill after your body has time to absorb it."

"This gets better and better."

"I can't tell how mad you are."

"I—" She closed her mouth and drew a long breath through her nose. "I'm not assigning blame. It's just not how I expected to spend my evening."

Theo glanced out the window above the sink. Finally, nightfall. "I know. It's weird."

She opened the crackers. "Want some?"

He shook his head, then changed his mind. "I forgot. Dinner."

Her smile was more of a relief than he'd expected. "Don't expect me to make you anything."

"I won't. I don't." He pointed towards her living area. "But, can we sit for a minute?"

She nodded. Nodded again. He stopped himself from gnawing his cheek as he followed her to the couch.

A breath to organize himself, then he plunged in. "I don't want to—okay, I was about to say I don't want to intrude, which seems weird given the situation. I'm trying to ask, can I stay with you tonight? On the sofa, or whatever you want. I got pretty anxious when I read up on the side effects and all, and I don't think you'll have any problems, but, in case."

"Theo, that's—"

"I know, you were already trying to brush off my attempts to get romantic before we went to my place. I'm not oblivious. And I'm not trying to be a creep. It's got to be clear I want more than just a physical relationship with you. And if it's not, I'll be explicit —bad word choice. I'll be plain about it." He should stop rushing his words forward like they would dissolve if he couldn't say them all at once. But it was impossible. "I like you, Rachel. I like you in a maybe too-intense way. I know you are trying to keep me at arm's length. Emotionally, anyway. And maybe that's not going to change for you, and maybe that means I have no chance for this to turn into something more."

He stopped long enough to trace back to the start of this soul-baring speech. He'd had a point, and was grateful she didn't interrupt while he located it. "So all of that aside, is what I'm saying. I hope we can talk about it later on. But for tonight, knowing I'm not looking to push it towards anything else, can I stick around and make sure you're okay? It would—I would really appreciate it."

HE MADE it hard for her to harden her heart, she'd give him that. Rachel ate a couple of crackers, downed them with a sip of sports drink. The snack, banal as it was, settled her nerves along with her stomach. "I called my friend Gillian on the way home. She'll be here in half an hour or so."

He straightened in a way she read as displeasure. "Oh."

"She'll stay tonight."

He was nodding, though looking only at the television. Too glazed to be reading the news crawl or hearing the panel discussion.

Nothing about this situation meant she should rush to defend herself, or her friend. Still. He'd voiced all manner of feelings she didn't want to address, and logistics talk was a good way to bury all of that under details.

"She's bringing me some soup. She said soup was a good thing for me to have. Goes well with the crackers, huh? And she can take

Hannah to daycare in the morning if I'm not feeling up to it. I was worried about that, you know? My neighbor, my friend, Mary Lynn. She lived next door. Once when I got real sick, a few times Hannah wasn't well enough for daycare, she's always the one I call to pitch in for a few hours. Called. Right next door, and Hannah loves her. But she moved, lives out of town now, and it's okay." What a pile of nerve-fueled rambling. "Gillian will come over. Her summer class doesn't meet Thursdays. Or Tuesdays, either one. So we're covered."

"Do you think you won't be? Okay in the morning, I mean? I can...."

"I'm sure I'll be fine. But if there's a problem, Depy won't ask questions. She'll pick her up after school and take the bonus night as if my being sick was the answer to her prayers. That's what she usually does, anyway. Trust me, it doesn't take much for her to jump in and take over."

And now she was oversharing as if he was some kind of confidant or friend or anything but a one-night stand that went too long and was ending too late.

He took another cracker. They crunched along, and she was awkward, but then his tongue swiped at a crumb on his lips, and she was beyond awkward and actively adding more images to the sexy video reel she kept pretending wasn't on autoplay in her mind. She mentally muted that tab, tried to close it, but it was like one of those pop-up ads that followed her around from site to site when she made the mistake of browsing without an incognito window. The Theo tapes were way hotter than that one ad for child life insurance embedded in every site she visited, but just as treacherous.

She needed him gone.

"What do I owe you? For the meds and stuff?"

Effective words. He drew himself taut, the very picture of restrained offense. "Nothing."

"I don't mind splitting the cost."

Tone and sentence calculated to send him scrambling for his

shoes. It only got him to shift to the edge of the sofa, on the brink of standing. Either she'd lost her touch, or he was more secure in himself than she was used to.

"I take it you want me to clear out before your friend gets here."

Busted. Last thing she needed was more time with this man who understood her motives way too well. Second to last thing. Last thing was a new baby in her life, complicating all the progress she'd built towards independence from Sergei for Hannah and herself. And the last thing would come with a side effect of the second to last thing. All told, she was glad the clutter on her breakfast bar contained all she needed to put this behind her.

No new baby brother or sister for Hannah. No second child to snuggle up against her at story time. No reason to hang on to the bins of outgrown toys and clothes.

Theo took her silence as confirmation, at last moving to the door. "Will you text me when she gets here? And also if you have any problems? I can get back over here fast. Any hour."

His relentless, tender care of her curdled Rachel's stomach. Good job she'd already taken the anti-nausea pills. She couldn't deal with the kindness and thoughtfulness and general air of focused, competent emotional intelligence. Her life plans were waiting for her.

She opted for the easiest way to stop his words getting under her skin. Bonus: kissing him meant she wouldn't say anything she'd later regret. Nothing to reveal her vulnerabilities or her unfilled needs or her secret dreams.

Breaking away, she patted at his solid, warm chest and said, "I'll text you."

And remembered to shut her mouth. To hold in the lingering heat of his lips on hers. The funny taste combo of electrolytes and honey. Her words.

His pause stretched between them. Mouth—those firm, sweet lips—half-closing, stopping, sealing closed. So he was withholding his words, too.

Good.

He'd said enough. All those words about going places and relationships and if she would be okay overnight. It was enough.

"Night, Rachel."

"Bye."

She almost managed to close the door on him without hearing him get in the last words. "I'll see you soon."

Any contradiction would be a lie, so she settled for locking the deadbolt and collapsing on the sofa until Gillian arrived.

CHAPTER FIFTEEN

'STILL FINE.' She blinked at the text, decided it worked, hit send. Nothing alarming had happened overnight, nothing dreadful, no pain. Gill had plied her with soup while accusing her of letting a pharmacy explode in her kitchen. Rachel skirted around all Theo'd said, his reasons for each purchase, and refused to comment on the box of condoms or the origin of the broken one. Gill snickered anyway, then read aloud from Planned Parenthood's site about IUDs until Rachel promised to get around to making her appointment.

She finished packing lunches and assembled a breakfast burrito for Hannah. Her girl got cranky if she didn't eat as soon as she woke up, which meant it was growth spurt time again. Rachel scrawled a note on the pad by the fridge to check Hannah's shoe size.

"I found a little wriggle-monster in my bed," Gillian said, emerging from the hall with Hannah riding piggyback.

"Morning, Hannah Banana. Were your dreams sweet like strawberries?"

"Why Aunt Gill?"

"We had a sleepover."

"How you feeling, Rach?"

She smiled as she plopped Hannah into her chair. "Good and grand. Nothing to report."

"And did you provide himself with the same update?"

"She's not going to understand what we're talking about if you use plain speech, Gill."

Her friend blinked. "That's how I talk."

Rachel laughed. "I know, love. I'm teasing. Want coffee? And yes, I texted him. As instructed."

She wasn't, in fact, rolling her eyes. But she felt like it. Gillian's attitude was more sympathetic to Theo's fretting than she'd expected. Not the worst thing. But it made it hard to forget all that genuine concern of Theo's.

Fortunate, then, that her world came pre-supplied with plenty to knock away any distractions. Who knew being a single working mom with a crappy short-term memory would be such a bonus? She tucked a note for Hannah's teacher in the ladybug lunch box, the bottles of pain and nausea pills in her backpack, and her hair into a ponytail. "Watch her while I brush my teeth?" she asked her friend.

Gill rolled her eyes and nabbed a berry out of Hannah's bowl. "Thanks."

An hour later, having brushed off Gillian's offers to take Hannah to school, gotten through drop off, and snagged herself a closer-than-usual space in the hospital parking garage, she was swiping herself into the office and taking the schedule of the day's clients from her manager. Not one spare second to think about fretting friends or nervous lovers or that brief, foolish time in her life when she fantasized about raising children with the kind of loving, bonded sibling relationship she and her own sister would never share.

CURSES PLAGUED his entire drive up to Fort Worth. Road works, a messy spat of a thunderstorm, three separate stalled cars in the main lanes everyone had to edge past. He texted Annalisa when he stopped for gas, got back a thumbs up, and made efforts to relax his tensed brow in the remaining miles before pulling up to her house.

"Bad news," she said as soon as she answered his knock. "Hi."

"Hi? What's wrong?" She looked okay, and he heard Jamie chatting away from another room.

"Come in. He's running a fever. Low, but…"

He set his umbrella in the corner and peeked into the living room. Andres wasn't ensconced on the sofa, which spiked his anxiety. "What else? Is he congested?"

She gave him the look that meant 'stop acting like I don't know how to care for my own child' and waved him up the stairs ahead of her. On the way to the bedroom, she ran down his symptoms and the meds she's already administered. "I don't think it's more than a cold, but he's not up for going out to dinner."

"No, of course." He knocked twice on Andres's door and let himself in. "Hey, darling. Mom says you're feeling punky?"

God, the dark rings under his beautiful big eyes. Theo kept the smile in place as he brushed a wisp of hair back from his son's too-warm forehead. Andres didn't even sit up to hug him, just curled his body so it pressed up against Theo's side where he sat on the bed.

"Ugh," he said. Both parents laughed a little at the disgust in their son's tone.

"Ugh, indeed," Theo agreed. "Guess we're not going out to the dance clubs tonight, huh?"

Andres shook his head. Theo kept stroking his hair, letting the rhythm do its work until Andres's eyes shut and he relaxed into a doze.

He retreated to the hallway, where Annalisa awaited him. "Sorry, I'd have suggested you put the visit off, but he was fine after camp. Then a couple of hours ago he took himself off to bed."

"I'd have come up anyway, you know that."

"Right. I know." She rolled her eyes, which Theo refused to take on board as criticism. Her opinions of his character were no longer his problem. "So, you want to head to your hotel and come back in the morning to see how he's doing?"

Sure. Because she was the only one who could watch Andres fight germs. "No. Give me an hour if you've got it to spare, and I'll swing by the store for soup and stuff, drop it at the room, then come back for him."

"He'll be more comfortable in his own bed."

"It's either put me in the guest room or let me take him, Annalisa. I'd appreciate the loan of a thermometer and a few extra toys, but he'll be as well off with me as he would be with you."

She screwed her mouth up in that displeased way which was also no longer his problem. "I don't like it."

"I don't like it, either. I want him to feel okay." She narrowed her eyes, so he got conciliatory. "I didn't like not being with him when he had the flu last Christmas, or when he needed stitches after he tripped at recess in March. I know what you're feeling, A. But like you said, it's just a cold, and he can recover with me as well as he could with you."

She didn't quite act like she agreed, but she did sigh and check her watch. "Jamie will be happy anyway. We can still make the gala."

"There you go. Good for everyone."

"Okay, but make sure you get the low sodium soup. And I'll pack up the meds so you don't need to get any of that stuff."

"And his Pokémon cards; when he feels better he can tell me six thousand facts about them all."

She laughed. "Most persuasive argument you've made. Fine. Go. We can drop him off on our way out. I'll text you when we get to the lobby. And you text me if his temp spikes or—well, if anything changes."

So an hour later he was streaming a Miyazaki film and encouraging Andres to eat a little before sinking back into the many pillows of his hotel bed. The weekend ran out of curses to hurl at him at that point; his son slept well and bounced up in the morning primed to negotiate for a race downstairs to the lobby. Which he won. Almost fair and square. They scrambled off to play soccer and visit the library and all the other planned and spontaneous things that filled their weekend together.

He dropped him back with Annalisa in time for Sunday dinner. Before Andres went inside, he smothered Theo in hugs and kisses. It was ritual: one each for all the goodnights until they saw each other again, and an extra hug for luck. It wasn't enough to sustain him, not really, but it did make the four-hour drive south slightly more bearable.

AUNT JOHNSTON CALLED, even though it was a Tuesday. She clicked on the phone soon as she saw the name. "What's wrong?"

"Lord, cricket, just you stop jumping to conclusions. Everything's fine."

The hand she'd clapped to her heart relaxed, and she gave her tight chest a couple of pats. "Okay, right. Sorry. Hi, Aunt. How are you?"

"I'm fine, like I told you. It's nice to hear your sweet voice. How's my girl?"

Rachel perched on the stool at her kitchen counter, watching the girl in question add blocks and a shoe box to her elaborate action figure-sized cityscape. "She's grander than grand. Thanks for the gift card. She picked out a troll and a Wonder Woman and they haven't left her side since."

Aunt Johnston tsked. "And what did you pick out for yourself?"

Her gaze skittered across the room, as if it would land on some feasible object she could claim as an indulgence. "Coffee." A hitched breath to slow her tone. "I got myself some very fancy beans, they're coconut flavor if you can believe it, and so delicious your tongue would kiss you, if it could. I'm going to send you a bag."

"You'll do no such thing. As if my old coffeepot would know what to do with beans like that."

So she wasn't going to get called out for the near-truth. It amounted to a grand proclamation that her aunt had some weighty tale. "Your old coffeepot is perfectly capable of pouring boiling water over flavored grounds. You're so set in your ways."

"Neither here nor there. Now listen up, ladybird."

Two nicknames in as many minutes. "Ma'am?"

"That Brent Berg came out here looking to find you this afternoon."

"Brent?" She settled her palm over her stomach. "I don't have anything to say to him."

"Well he seems to think different. He heard you're certified now, and he wants you to apply as Director of Recreation over to Brookside Care."

"What happened to Mr. Steichen?" She'd interned for four summers at Brookside, under Gary Steichen's direction. He'd been an affable boss, if not as creative and energetic as she'd thought he should be. Looking back, she'd been a pushy youngster, convinced everything she fought so hard to learn in college would transform their less-active residents into vibrant, engaged community members. Plenty of her ideas had been good ones, but she understood now why Mr. Steichen shot most of them down. Budget, resources, staffing, space: the same list of blockades at most any nursing home.

"He's gone and taken a room there himself, Brent said. It was his idea Brent look for you."

And being Brent, he thought to help his case by buttering up Aunt Johnston with some tale about how much everyone'd thought of Rachel back then. Had to be the personal touch, with Brent. Inveigle himself, praise her straightforward black coffee, drop knowing comments about how nice it would be for Rachel to move back home.

Except much as she loved Aunt Johnston—much as those five years living with her catapulted her towards a life she could be proud to call her own—Plainview wasn't home anymore. "I'm not looking for a new job."

"They still do that wheelchair obstacle course you set up, you know that?"

"I'm glad. But I'm happy at the hospital. And I could never work with Brent."

"Well, doodlebug, I can't understand you. It ain't like he's still prom king and you're the gal hanging streamers in the gym. You're a mama now. That old crush can't crush you anymore."

Hannah was stacking her dolls and action figures into a log pile against the long edge of the shoebox. The ogre and the alien weren't cooperating with her tidy pyramid. The third time they rolled away, she tucked them inside the bright yellow slipcover from her boxed set of Seuss books. Rachel tilted her head to see beyond the sofa; the books themselves spilled in an arc under the side table, but weren't splayed or crushed. How like Aunt Johnston her daughter was, in her reverence for books. And disregard for the sense of order and progress Rachel tried to build in her life. Someday she would love someone who wasn't constantly telling her what to do.

"Aunt Johnston, my crush on Brent ended when I was fifteen." Forcibly. In humiliation and headache and gravel gouges in her knees and an all-too-literal bad taste in her mouth.

"Which is my point. You neither one need to be awkward about it. His running Brookside Care now is no reason for you not to apply."

"I'm not applying because I don't want to leave Houston. I like the hospital, I like Hannah's daycare, I have my friends here."

"And Sergei, I suppose you'll say next."

She sighed. As if remembering what happened with Brent in the back parking lot wasn't enough to remind her she was a terrible judge of men. "He's her d-a-d. One of these days that'll matter to her."

"One of these days that'll matter to him, you mean."

"I can't talk about this right now." Something—Rachel's

sharper tone, or saying her name, or both—had Hannah approaching, action figures in hand. Rachel mimed a 'what have you got there?' face at the girl, uncurled the spine she'd not noticed hunching as she talked about Brent.

"I gave him your email address."

"Aunt!" She slid off the stool and moved to crouch by the makeshift city walls. Hannah passed over Wonder Woman and Rachel tucked the phone on her shoulder so she could stand the superhero atop the battlements.

"Well, I never figured you would flat-out refuse." She sounded offended on behalf of all thirty-six thousand residents of Hale County. "He said as how he remembered your energy and enthusiasm, and you'd be a great fit."

Wonder Woman's akimbo arms dared the line of ponies and unicorns she faced to approach. Hannah added a snowman and a lioness to her flanks. Rachel scooted away until her back was to the wall, and Hannah continued the game as if she'd never been a part of it.

"I've got to put dinner on."

"But you'll look at the job opening?"

"Aunt."

"Okay, June bug, you'll set your own path, never mind about me."

"We're going to go up to Colorado in August, did I tell you? Can we spend the night on the way?"

"You need to ask?"

No, of course she didn't. Aunt Johnston's bossiness and open door policy were flip sides of the same coin. But it diverted her. "Thanks. You can be in charge of running Hannah's legs off while I collapse from driving all day."

"Send me the dates when you have them. Now go feed up my girl."

"Love you, Aunt Johnston."

"Love you, too."

The solid wall had never felt more like a quiet cradle for her skull. Three Sunday calls, four at the most, until her aunt dropped the subject. She could handle it. She could write a distant but polite refusal to whatever message Brent sent. And if that didn't stop him, she'd tell Gillian about the parking lot, his oil-slick words, his grip on her head. His exaggerated tales to his friends, then theirs to their friends; within days, whispers from everyone on campus. Brent thought he could turn 'such a starved puppy she'll open wide if you call her special' into 'energy and enthusiasm'? Well, Gillian would turn 'you are a toad and will leave me and my family the hell alone' into words that would shrivel his musty balls. Gillian's stinging words made for armor stronger than even Wonder Woman's Amazon-crafted gauntlets.

She opened her eyes at Hannah's gleeful screech and the crashing collapse of several blocks. She glanced at the clock. Dinnertime, clean up time, bath time, teeth time, story time, song time, bed. Pushing herself up, she left Wonder Woman supervising the growing pile of rubble Hannah heaped on the other characters. She flipped the calendar to August and made a note to buy coffee for Aunt Johnston, set the oven, set the table, settled into the routine that kept them going, night after night after night.

CHAPTER SIXTEEN

IT WASN'T LIKE he'd never been ghosted before. Three texts the day after the literally fucked-up fuck-up. No answer to his voice mail the next day. A returned text the day after. And then radio silence for the rest of the week.

Theo knew to stop calling, stop texting. He wasn't maybe the greatest man in the universe, but he wasn't a creep.

Until this situation with Rachel, though, he'd never had to spend quite so much time telling himself to back the hell off. His mind respected her decision, but his damn soul or heart or body or all of it was having trouble grasping the concept. Not her fault, not her problem, but it would be awful damn convenient if he could at least blame her for something.

Alas, no. She was blameless, and maybe even he was blameless, but that didn't change the fact that their relationship was not happening. He kept telling himself it might be a pause instead of the end, but he'd put himself out there. Not only with the texts and voice mails he'd absolutely stopped sending, but also with his excruciating, soul-baring speech over crackers and Gatorade. She had all the information she needed to extend a hand in his direction. Unless she did, he was done.

His cousin Tomás stopped by Elixir to keep him distracted next time Rachel was due to drop Hannah off.

"Maybe your manager was onto something, breaking up with her," Tomás said.

"They divorced during the pregnancy. She had to move in with his mom or she'd have had no help with the baby for months afterward."

Tomás winced. A little late, Theo realized Rachel's situation might remind him a bit of his own childhood. Not that Uncle Enrique wasn't the best—he was. But Tomás's birth mom was deported when he was three, and ended up settling into a life in Mexico that didn't have much space for her American-born son. Whatever the extenuating circumstances, the fact remained that he was sensitive about adults opting against parenting their kids.

He gestured to the bartender to pull them each a second beer. "Sorry."

"No problem. But out of curiosity, what does Sergei say about the divorce?"

Theo shot him a look, then glanced around to confirm no employees were wandering in earshot. He ignored his cousin's grin, because to acknowledge it would be to give him the opening to ask why Theo'd brought all this Rachel stuff up at work to begin with. And they both knew the answer to that: Theo was too far gone for actual discretion.

Drawing patterns in the condensation on his mug, he said, "It's not like I've told the guy Rachel and I went out."

"Well, glad to hear you still possess common sense. But I meant, what'd he say in the months and months you worked together before you went and hooked up with his wife."

"Ex-wife."

"Right, yes, important distinction."

"It's not like Sergei doesn't hook up all the time." Even the new milk stout couldn't wash away the ick of thinking of Rachel as a hookup. "He barely shuts up about it."

Tomás pulled a face. "Professional."

He hitched a shoulder. "Just when it's him and Ron and me. He's not boasting about it at employee meetings."

"Such a prince."

Theo stifled his laugh at his cousin's dry tone. "Okay, no one claimed that. There's plenty of ways his, charm or whatever you call it, works out for the brewery. It's not like I wanted to do all the front of house jovial crap; that's why we brought him on board to start with."

"I sure as hell hope he's good at it."

Good enough to take pressure off Theo, which was significant. "He's a clam about the marriage. Divorce. Even about Hannah most of the time."

"Well then? What have you pieced together?"

"Why do you think I've pieced anything together?"

Tomás creased his lips together, maybe to keep from some kind of sarcastic spit-take. He hit Theo with yet another disbelieving look. "Maybe I'm wrong, and this is the one thing in your life you don't have data on. Your spreadsheets are empty. There are no pie charts. Not a single file folder full of research."

"Shut up."

"Prove me wrong."

He didn't answer. He did, however, learn that his cousin was capable of being smug and eating a handful of seasoned pecans at the same time.

"Fine. You're a genius. I happen to have picked up a couple of details."

Tomás raised his eyebrows, like he wasn't bursting to make more fun of him.

"It's not enough to fill out a Wikipedia entry about them. They got together when she was right out of college, and married a couple years later, and all in all they were together maybe five or six years. He put up some fuss about paternity, but it's obvious the girl is theirs. She's a total mix of them. Except in personality—she's more of the shy until you know her type, like her mom. None of that outgoing thing Sergei does all the time, you know? He treats her like she can be put away in a trophy case when he's done displaying her, but she seems pretty chill about it."

A sidelong glance showed him he'd best to close his mouth or be ready to put up with a hell of a lot more ribbing.

"So he's not winning Elixir's Dad of the Year award." Tomás cut through all Theo's too-encyclopedic reportage. "Did they split because he didn't want the baby?"

The theory felt wrong. Maybe he was overlaying too much of his own history; a few years into their marriage, one of the limited list of things he and Annalisa agreed about was the desire to be parents. His cousin once said since that was the case, they should have split up sooner and gone off to find other people to make babies with. If he'd known someone like Rachel could be part of his future, maybe he would have followed that path. But as it was, there wasn't a single step of his life he'd have changed, because those steps brought Andres into the world.

He hoped he didn't sigh quite this much every time he and Tomás hung out. "I think he's happy to be a dad. When they split —I didn't know either of them, so this is conjecture...."

"Right, yes, all caveats received. Speculate away."

"I'm basing this on a couple of comments, and Depy said a thing about independent women, it was clear she meant Rachel."

"You're driving this bus through every one of Houston's million suburbs. Are you saying he wanted a nice little homebody of a wife to worship him and wash his socks every night, and Rachel didn't conform to the ideal of Greek femininity his mom spent his whole life setting as the gold standard?"

If he was the kind of man to clap people on the back and give them jovial slugs in the arm and all that fake-fight bonhomie Sergio exhibited every day, Theo might have let loose with a slap upside the head or an overloud chuckle at that point. Something to indicate that Serg had been owned and Theo appreciated the summation.

Instead he sighed. Again. "I don't know. I mean, yes. Between the comments and the expectations he seems to have of people he dates now, it's clear Sergei has that—you remember me telling you about my Uncle Chris?"

"This is your dad's big brother?"

"Yeah." Most of the Greek-American side of Theo's family lived in Florida, so his Texan relatives didn't know them well. "My dad ran hard to get away from Yia Yia's, as he called it, smothering. The whole 'treat your husband like a god, and your sons like kings' displays she does. Did. Uncle Greg got away from it, too, but he managed to keep Yia Yia at bay without hitting the road. Uncle Chris, though, he is all about it. Even three or four years after he got married, Dad says, Yia Yia would come over a few mornings a week with a packed lunch for him to take to work. And when my aunt complained about it, Chris told her she could take over as long as she bought the bread his mom said was best for his sensitive stomach."

Tomás openly laughed.

"Right, so it's stereotypical as hell, the way she treated them all and the way Uncle Chris ate it up. But I get a similar vibe off the way Depy is with Sergei, and the way she in particular talks about Rachel, and I'm not going to be surprised if she tells me...."

When he trailed off, Tomás tracked where his attention had gone. "Is that her?"

Like there were so many women carrying toddlers entering the place. He nodded.

"Wait," Tomás tapped a toe on his shin to get his attention. "Your Rachel is Rachel Groff?"

Something tight and sharp at the same time filled his lungs, but he aimed to sound casual. "You know her?"

"No. I mean, yeah, but not really. She's done some consultation for us, for one of the group homes." Tomás worked in the licensing division of Department of Family and Children Services.

"Shit, really?"

"Yeah. She's great." He went eyebrows-up. "As you clearly know. Aren't I supposed to be distracting you from gaping at her like that?"

Theo swiveled, quick, to face the bar again. "Shut up."

Instead, Tomás got louder, standing and lifting an arm. "Hey, Rachel."

"For the love of Aphrodite, will you please not do this?"

Tomás acted like he couldn't hear him. His hale-fellow grin was almost as irritating as Sergei's could get. "Is that your little one? Look at her! What a judge of character she is. Come here and let me see if I can win her over."

If he slunk away or hid his face or knocked his cousin off his barstool, it would be all too obvious that he was somewhere on the murky plain between upset and furious. So he downed the rest of his beer and channeled all the cool moves he'd ever witnessed. "Hi, there."

Hannah plunged her upper body his way, and in the rush to step forward and catch her up in his arms, he missed whatever expression Rachel wore. Settling the girl on the crook of his arm, he greeted her and looked over to see Rachel backing up from the polite hug she'd shared with Tomás.

"I'll say right off my cousin here didn't know we knew each other, and he's going to make some big speech once I go. He asked me to come in to keep him from lurking at the door hoping you'd show up, and I went and blew it by calling you over, and see that fake smile he's giving your daughter right now? She's way cute by the way, but you know that. Yeah, it's a good thing my dad and his mom are like snow peas smushed into a pod together, cause it gives me a nice buffer of love to stop Theo from doing anything permanent in my general direction."

Theo narrowed his eyes in a way calculated to inform his cousin that he was making some very dangerous assumptions.

Rachel, though. Rachel hitched half a smile his way, and the landscape around him brightened a significant amount. "Hey, Theo."

"Hi." He'd already said it, but he'd filled his soul with post-it notes reminding himself that his feelings didn't mean she owed him a damn thing.

"You got a minute? I don't want to interrupt family time, but...."

"Oh, hey, I was on my way out."

"You were not." She laughed at Tomás's blatant lie.

"As of one second ago I was. Great to see you again. By the by, I'm giving your name to Francesca, our new inspector, so expect a call from her."

She nodded. "Good stuff, will do. Thanks, Tomás."

"Thanks for being the best of the best. And for giving me cover while I escape from Theo. Call you soon, man. Bye now, little Hannah and your even littler elephant."

"Effie," Theo told him.

"Bye, Effie," his cousin said with due solemnity to the stuffed animal, which earned him a nod from the child.

He kept his voice chill, trusting the blunt message would escape the child but be clear to the man. "Go."

Tomás kissed his cheek before following orders. To his surprise, Hannah leaned in and kissed his other one. Calmed for real by the gestures of affection, he squared up the Rachel. First thing, apologies. After, he would follow her lead.

HANNAH'S HEAD on Theo's shoulder distracted her. He was saying sorry, for his cousin, and for the ambush, and for not making himself scarce before she showed up. As if she was holding him to account.

"Hey, it's fine."

"I—if you're sure. Okay, thank you. Look, you take her and I'll go back to my office."

"Theo." Her hand slipped so naturally from brushing back her daughter's curls to sliding down the man's arm. Where was Tomás when she needed his nonsense distraction?

"Yeah?"

"Do you have a couple of minutes?"

His eyes flared and she refused to remember how wide and intent they got when face-to-post-coital-face. "Sure. Absolutely. Can I—do you want a lager or anything?"

She halted his gesture at the barman with a hand on his forearm. "No, but maybe we can go to your office? Or the parking lot. I don't mean to be intrusive. Let me drop off Miss Banana here."

With that, she filled her arms with her most-beloved burden and slipped back to the table where Sergei acted like he hadn't noticed them enter Elixir at all, much less the detour to talk to Theo and Tomás. And maybe he hadn't. Wouldn't be the first time the man paid more attention to anything in the universe besides his daughter.

She held up the list of potty training instructions until he rolled his eyes and took it. It was color-coded, with cartoon stock art. Not because it needed to be, but because it would irritate Sergei. And if something irritated his perfect little world, there was a smidge of a chance that he'd bother to pay attention to it. She dropped the bag packed with spares of everything, blew five fast kisses at Hannah, and headed to where Theo was leaning against a door marked 'Employees Only.'

If there was a politer man in the great state of Texas, Rachel had yet to meet him. She thought—then made herself not think—about Aunt Johnston's reaction if they were to meet. They'd outdo each other with smiles and accommodations and please don't bothers. It was sweet enough of him, but set her teeth on edge.

She followed him into his office. "I planned on finding you tonight."

Her bluntness seemed to catch him off-guard. "Okay?" he asked, lowering himself at last into his desk chair.

"Not because of anything to report. Just because. You were nice, last week. And ..." searching for the right word made her esophagus crawl, as always, "considerate. And a lot more up-front than I was ready to think about at the time."

"Rachel, I'm sorry, honestly. I put a ton out there. Too much, I think." His gaze flicked down to his desk, then past her shoulder.

"I can't switch all my weekends out, but I'll stop being here on Wednesday nights, so you don't have to deal with me then anyway."

"Did I ask that of you?"

That got him looking straight at her again. She didn't try to stop her face softening at the pleasure of being with him. "It turns out I may like you feeling maybe too intense about me."

He didn't quite stand to embrace her, but he leaned in, alert and careful. "You sound pretty conditional about it."

She breathed out a noncommittal answer, excavating for words again. "Theo, the thing is, I haven't started a real relationship since, well, Sergei. I was twenty-two. And not a mom. That's worlds away from who I am now. Not one part of me, the current me, thought I'd get serious with anyone until Hannah is, I don't know. Not so far out as college-age, but at least into Kindergarten? I've got a thousand things a day to focus on, big things, little things. Really big things."

"I know—"

"Well, maybe you do, a bit. But my point it, all I ever knew about that far-off dating life of mine is, I'm never falling for someone like Sergei again. I've gotten real good at picking apart anything that might match my personal collection of red flags. When I first met you, it looked like there'd be no shortage of those."

"I—"

She shook her head at his crestfallen attempt to protest. "My issues. Not saying I was right. I'm saying I was cautious. Am cautious. But also? So attracted to you. And I had to figure if that was a red flag waving me right down a path I'd tripped on before, or if it was ... separate. Just our chemistry. Just us."

He cleared his throat. It was her turn to look around the walls to avoid eye contact. When he shifted his jaw but kept silent, she filled her lungs for the rest of her speechifying. "So. We found out the chemistry is real. And I had to think about it all. And you—I guess you didn't think as slow as me. Or didn't have as much to think about. Or maybe it's all part of some quick-start charisma red flag I don't recognize the stitching on yet, but I don't think that's it."

"It's not."

"Well, probably. Just cause you don't think it's red enough to attract flocks of hummingbirds doesn't mean you're right. You could be color-blind about your own flags, you know."

She could feel her blush as he grinned about her figurative language. Talk about charm. The man's charm shimmered like heat waves on summer asphalt.

"Point taken. I might have a pile of flags I can't see. Can I ask what that means now? For us? If there is an us?"

He was light-hearted in a way that showed he had no real gauge of the vital nature of her warning system. Which was good. Better for most people in the world not to have so many ways they could fall into something devastating for them. Odds were his marriage had broken up because of an everyday kind of shattering. Infidelity or pawning her great-grandmother's ring or fights about how to load the dishwasher. Nothing that required anything like an exit strategy and backup and nerves taut like rebar.

"I think there can be an us," she told him. "Or something approaching that. I want us to find out. To ... date. Get to know each other. Share some confidences now that we've shared bodily fluids."

Theo grimaced. "You're sure you feel okay now? The pill didn't leave you with side effects?"

"Nothing much. Some queasiness, some bloat. I'm good as new now."

He mimed wiping his forehead. She laughed.

Coming around the desk, he reached for her hand. His was warm and firm and compatible as he held hers. "I like this plan of yours. Maybe we take it a little slower? Do some of that couple stuff, dinner and movies or so on?"

She leaned in. "And good-night kisses at the door?"

The playful wolf side of him came out to strut. "Oh, hell yeah. Some good morning kisses in your bed, too, if I can manage it."

"Don't push your luck." But instead of pushing him away, she linked her arms over his shoulders.

He slid his palms to the small of her back, a ripple of warmth that spread all through her. "I wouldn't dare."

"Just so we understand each other."

"Absolutely."

Their bodies were flush and their grins almost too wide to allow their lips to whisper into a kiss. Almost. And when the kiss ended, and he asked if she was free that weekend, she didn't feel the need to check for any waving flags before she said yes.

CHAPTER SEVENTEEN

NEITHER OF THEM cared about superhero movies. Both had kids, so both were aware, on the periphery of their lives, of the latest franchises and comic-based movers and shakers. It wasn't enough to get them to a screening of any of the summer blockbusters.

She claimed to like horror, but nixed the one he texted her a trailer for. "Also nothing with subtitles, and don't get me started on the dramatic lives of teenagers."

He replied with a rolling-eyes emoji and went back to searching the movie listings. It felt like he would be messing up the mandate if they watched something on the small screen. Like he was ignoring her need to be deliberate about getting to know each other, in favor of a comfy couch and streaming services and a locked door between them and the world. He came up with a choice of three Saturday-night showings of new releases that weren't immediate strikes for either one of them, and sent them Rachel's way. Just in time, too, since Sergei sauntered in and leaned on the filing cabinet.

"Got a sec?"

"Sure." Theo silenced his phone and slipped it into his pocket.

"I think I pissed off Ron, and I don't know if it's a problem or not."

The three of them hadn't met as a group for almost a week. Maybe Theo was hyper-focused on his personal life, but nothing around Elixir felt off to him. "How's that, then?"

"Not real sure. He was talking to his nephew out front, and it looked to be heating up. There were a couple of tables looking round at them, so I approached and sort of herded both of them outside. Stuck around a couple of minutes to see if they'd calm down."

"And did they?"

"Yeah, after a bit. The nephew headed out, and Ron took off towards the back entrance. But the look he gave me, it wasn't friendly. So I gave him a few, checked everything was smooth out front, and popped back out there a minute ago. He told me to mind my own fucking business." Sergei shrugged, hands in his pockets, faking casual for all he was worth.

Theo considered. He and Ron had worked together a good long time, which meant an equally long time for them to rub each other the wrong way. Theo was a peacemaker, and a planner. He preferred to avoid conflict by setting things up so it wasn't necessary. Ron was impulsive. And never one to compartmentalize—work problems went home, home problems came to work. Obsessions about the current season of the Houston Astros stayed with him everywhere he went. So if his nephew Lonnie came around giving him problems, anyone in Ron's line of sight would come under fire.

"He might be pissed, but if you stay out of his way, it'll blow over."

Sergei tensed up to shoulders, the final proof that his casual pose was a façade. "I was doing what's right for Elixir. We can't have one of our owners screaming at somebody in front of the hostess stand."

"Never said we could. You handled it smooth as always, and I appreciate that."

"*Re*, I'm not looking for a pat on the head."

"I'm not clear what you are looking for. You came in acting concerned about you and Ron getting along."

And out came Sergei's pacing. Not a lot of room in their office, but he managed to fill it with his volatile energy. So now Theo knew what his employee's conflict style was: cool and collected as he gathered his ammo, then explosions everywhere.

Soothing things over as always, Theo got Sergei to take the pat on the head and an increased tolerance for Ron's moods and head back to work. Sinking back into his own desk chair, Theo glanced at the movie listings on his monitor, and wondered how someone could live with Sergei's temper for all those years and still like horror flicks.

And there went his ability to compartmentalize. Because to him, it was clear: he and Rachel would be going public with their relationship at some point, and that meant informing Sergei. And that, in turn, meant that soon Ron wouldn't be the only one who carted all his problems to work.

<hr>

"THAT WAS TERRIBLE," he said before they'd even tossed the dregs of their popcorn and sodas.

"It wasn't that bad." She was totally lying. It was.

He side-eyed her and she tried her damndest to look innocent and honest. Must not have worked, cause he caught her around the waist and pinned her between his body and the wall. She squeaked an inarticulate protest about the rest of the moviegoers streaming for the exits, and he swiveled his head left, then right, slow and deliberate. Then shrugged. Then kissed her.

"I know when something is good or not, Rachel."

Ah, hell. She kissed him some more. "Fine. I do, too."

The man was going to grow too big an ego by the time the night was over. They'd gabbed all through supper at a Cantonese cuisine spot owned by a woman he met at some kind of restaurant chamber of commerce. She hadn't quite figured out the connection, but she'd devoured the soup dumplings and steel pot beef. He preened while she admired a video of Andres kicking a neon orange full-size soccer ball into the net.

"They make smaller ones, you know," she'd said. She used them herself, for some of her patients with grip or balance issues.

"He's all kitted out for when the fall season starts," Theo assured her. "But that's the one I gave him when he was learning to walk, 'cause it always cracked us up to see him square up to it with his stubby little legs."

She eyed him. "You have a lot of happy memories of those days?" She knew his divorce wasn't a hotbed of acrimony like hers, but it seemed unique and enviable, the way he talked so casually about his ex. From the way he told it, their switch to co-parenting and even her move to the Dallas area proceeded smooth as water sliding over river rocks.

"Of Andres as a baby? Sure. Well, we moved into my condo three weeks after he was born, that wasn't the wisest, but he was always an easy kid." He stopped and tilted his head. "You don't mean about his brief stint of colic, do you?"

She bit her cheek to not laugh at his self-depreciation. "It wasn't the precise intent of my question, no,"

"Are we having the exes talk?"

He was so matter of fact, as if her ex wasn't Sergei. Who on top of being a tough discussion topic for her, was also his employee. "If it's a bad idea, say so,"

Theo shrugged. "Not on my end. But maybe we should avoid your divorce history until date five or six,"

"If we make it that far," she quipped. Tried to quip. Somewhere between thinking of her marriage and nerves about making dating official, she'd lost the light in her banter.

He offered her a bite of curry and waited until she was chewing to cover her hand and say, "Rachel. In my mind, we're making it well past date six."

Foolish eyes burning. His curry wasn't even that spicy.

Nonsense. So she sipped her wine and got composed as can be before prompting him for the tale of his broken marriage.

"Okay, but listen. Two things to start. The worst thing I think I did, and the worst thing I think she did. The rest is almost by the book. Not communicating, keeping score, presuming the worst motives." His finger squiggled in the condensation of his water glass. Added quietly, "Presuming a baby could fix us."

After a beat, she asked, "Was he the worst thing for you, or for her?"

"No! No, not worst." He took a breath and sat back, modulated to a calmer key. "I mean, it didn't work, I doubt it would for most people, but God, no. Andres is the best thing we did. For me, and for Annalisa. He's a miracle. You know?"

She nodded, and squeezed his hand. She knew. Every cell of her knew.

After a pause for table clearing, he smiled. "I just now realized how long it's been since I dated another parent. Not that I date tons of people, for the record. I like this. The shorthand of understanding."

"I've never dated a dad."

"Never?"

"Well, if I have, it hasn't come up. Not that I've dated a ton since Sergei. Little hard while living with your former mother-in-law. Or single parenting a toddler."

"Hence your preference for one-time encounters."

She drained her wine glass and let him squirm a little longer than was polite. "You can call them something plainer if you want. I'm not ashamed."

"No reason for you to be, not that you need me to tell you so."

"Not needed but noted. So, yeah. That's been easiest, because when I've gotten to dating anyone in some kind of official way, all the schedule nonsense trips them up. As if it's so hard to gather I have every other weekend free."

"Annalisa said something about that before she and Jamie—that's the new husband—got together. Something or another came up and we switched around the schedule, and her then-boyfriend was put out that his plans had to change."

"Right. 'Can't you get a sitter or something?' As if that's not a whole other kind of planning. Not to mention, my usual sitter now lives in Brenham, so downgrade the whining about reservations and think about what actual real life complications look like."

Theo handed a credit card to their waiter, nodding. "Exactly. But you're sidetracking me, and I'm not falling for your clever tricks."

He was joking, but it lodged in her chest anyway. No one besides Aunt Johnston had called her clever in all her life. "You're the one taking the bait so you get out of telling me the worst things."

Funny how when Theo narrowed his eyes, it didn't come across a threat, like it did in Sergei's still-too-similar face. "Challenge accepted. Now you'll hear my secrets, and after if you want to skip the movie and block my number, let me thank you now for having given me this much of a chance."

"Quit being charming and get on with it."

Leaning back to accept the receipt, Theo picked up the pen and began rolling it between his palms. "Any preference of whose I say first?"

It was more nerves than his usual. Only the night of the bust condom had she seen him more agitated. "Yours."

If it sucked, she could walk out before he spoke ill of his ex. Plenty of that out in the world; no need to let him add to it.

Theo closed a fist over the pen. Nodded. Nodded again.

She was a complete and utter sucker. "Okay, wait. Tell me hers."

Lines bracketed his face when he grimaced. She'd not noted them in any of his smiles before. "Rachel, you don't need to take pity on me. I'm not fragile."

She raised her brows. "Maybe I want to know what your tone is when you trash talk someone."

Nope. No brackets when he grinned. His cheeks lifted into

arcs around his eyes. "You are ruthless. I like that so much about you."

Was she? Well then. That was acceptable. "Flattery won't save you now."

He sent a smile towards his friend who owned the restaurant. Then dropped the pen onto the bill presenter. "She bought me high-end golf clubs."

CHAPTER EIGHTEEN

Her expression was five-eighths confusion, a quarter annoyance, and just that last eighth amusement. "Talk."

He checked the time. "Want to sit outside for a bit?"

She agreed, so he guided her onto Mary's back patio. It wasn't open for dining, but she had a couple of tables for employee breaks out among her herbs and vegetables. Both stood empty, and he guided her to a seat.

"I have to tell my friend Serena about this. Of course, she'll want to trade cuttings with Mary if I do, so maybe not."

"No, she'd love that. I'll send you her number."

She nudged his knee with hers. "Only if we're still talking later, remember? Tell me about these fancy-ass golf clubs."

It seemed from her teasing she'd adjusted her ratio of how irritating she found him. Encouraged, he launched in. "Annalisa and I met in grad school. I had a job right after undergrad; they supplemented my MBA after I worked there a year or so, it was a great deal. Or, that's what I thought. The whole corporate culture of the place was pretty rancid, but of course once they started paying for my degree I didn't feel like I could leave. Anyway, it came with this, like, expectation about networking, social stuff that you think is optional until your boss pulls you aside to let you know his boss noticed that you never go to the clubs or bars, and is wondering if you're cut out for the environment. And some of the behavior, it's stuff you'd like say something about. Except it's obvious there's a gross 'boys will be boys' rowdiness all those boss's bosses are okay with, so who would you even say something to?"

"Your MBA is worth putting up with all that?"

He glanced away, not wanting to see any more of the way she closed in on herself a bit as he talked. "No. I mean, I'm glad I have it. But ultimately, the means weren't sustainable. I took the path of getting out of night outings by claiming schoolwork, and, well, curried favor by falling in with the golf crowd instead. A couple drinks at the clubhouse after nine or eighteen holes wasn't always going to lead to some kind of encounter with lightly-clad women."

She made a throat-clearing noise that didn't speak well of his past. Not that he disagreed. Some kinds of neon-and-spot-lit spaces still made his stomach tighten and set a thrumming tension up the back of his neck. Little too much time in Sunday school, his cousin always said, like the man didn't spend what spare time he had working against sex trafficking. More power to anyone who chose the lifestyle of their own accord; his wrath was for those who used coercion, blackmail, and addiction to trap the vulnerable.

He shook off his glum. "Right. Yeah, so. Somewhere in there, I met Annalisa. She was also getting her MBA. Worked for a different company. Study groups turned into study dates turned into dates, and a relationship. So. She and I golfed together, and it was almost an in-joke at first, this hobby that is not, I'll have you know, well suited to Houston for much of the year. At least, to me it wasn't. It was all about the corporate ladder, the golfing, and I treated it like a more palatable resume-builder than, you know. The other."

"I'm not going to faint if you mention strip clubs. I know they exist."

The dim porch lighting acted as a damn welcome disguise for whatever embarrassment he was sure to be showing for going along with the corporate culture. He hoped. "Okay, yes. Point is, Annalisa and I got married, and finished our degrees, and after I felt I'd done enough repayment work for the MBA, I left that place and got a job with a company that did most of its networking in a way lower key. I sold the golf clubs, and got on with my quiet desk job. Give me a cup of coffee and some spreadsheets and I'm a happy man."

"Sexy."

"Everyone says so." Theo's chest filled with nice clean herb-scented air, and he savored the fact that he wasn't surrounded by smoke and sweat and spirits. The fug of the strip clubs had lowered on him as he talked, and he blessed Rachel's snark for helping him escape it.

"I believe it. But I gather Annalisa wasn't on board?"

"If this were a golf game, you'd have a hole in one. She kept up the golfing, except for a few months of pregnancy, and didn't care to hear I didn't like it."

"You didn't like her going?"

Her words put his back up, but her tone showed her own ire was brimming over its banks. Theo reminded himself of his dad's relatives back East, and the way Depy enshrined every facet of Sergei, and did not ask what hobbies Rachel's husband had set constraints on during their marriage. "Her golfing is not a problem for me. Never was. She's good, she enjoys it, and it serves a professional purpose for her. And before you ask, I never played with her. We never formed the habit, and if I was in her foursome it made her impatient all game, knowing there was someone else, some coworker or boss or connection, who wasn't on the fairway to bond with her."

"She sounds a little cut-throat. I like it."

He laughed. He could imagine them bonding over not letting some man hold them back, which amused him even if the man in question was him. "Right, well. Point is, our styles were so different. For work, for networking, for planning our futures. And she never would hear that her way wasn't my way."

He was sure he came off as whining in a not-at-all-sexy way. Poor Theo, forced to endure a slightly unpleasant thing in order to progress in his job. Like everyone else in every workforce.

Rachel didn't look horrified. So he explained a little more—the country club, the pressure to apply at another company, the day Annalisa said, "It's like I don't even know you." Matter of fact and condemning all at once. Then coldness and comments about this and that person who fit her expectations of success. She never needed to be snide, his ex-wife. She got her point across with calm but cutting words. And actions. Case in point: the birthday gift of Callaways in a sleek silver-accented bag.

"And you were hit over the head with the realization that she was always going to ask you to be her idealized version of yourself, instead of who you really are." Rachel didn't sound like she was asking; she understood.

"Yeah." His voice was wry; his throat was dry. He cleared it. "Pretty much."

She wrapped a hand around his forearm. "Okay, I get it. And I'm sorry. Sounds tough, even if she had some reason to think you had that version in you somewhere."

Either the breeze shifted, or he was breathing more deeply and could savor the woody tang of rosemary in the air. "Thanks. I mean, it's not a horror story, I get that. I'm not trying to make it out to be...." He trailed off.

"Like my marriage?" Now she was the wry one. He closed his eyes.

"Sorry."

"No need. You're right, it was a horror story. But I don't want to talk about it. Or anything, maybe. How about let's skip the worst thing you did, and go to the movie?"

"Still willing to sit beside me for a whole two hours?"

"Well. You'll have to take a gamble on that, won't you?" But she slipped her hand down past his wrist until their fingers intertwined. Rachel would never go for cold and condemning if they disagreed. Her nature was too warm. She might cry or get snarky or even shut him out, but whatever she did, she would do it with passion.

He hoped she would stick with him long enough to find out for sure.

———————

SHE WAS LETTING him off the hook left, right, and plumb up the center. Utter nonsense. But something in the fidgeting about golf, in the joking about the movie, in the warmth of his shoulder against hers in the darkness melted away her spine.

"You don't have to tell me," she said.

"About how bad that movie was?"

"No, that's an established fact. I mean about your worst thing."

He sighed long and hung his head. "Okay. So I'm not hard to read when I'm avoiding something. That's good info for you to have, anyway. Right?"

"Stop playing. Let's go back to mine and you talk on the way and I'll determine if you earn an invite up."

"No pressure."

She thought about the intimate particulars of how he used pressure, and smiled. "Don't knock it yet."

He slid an arm around her back, resting his hand on her hip. "You are a savvy negotiator, Rachel. I capitulate to every one of your demands."

They'd cleared the parking lot before he blurted, "I told her if she took a job offer in Dallas, we were through."

She took time to play over his words, making sure she understood each and every one. "Y'all lived in Houston?"

He nodded, eyes fixed on a red light. After a beat he started in again. They'd been drifting, with Theo digging in deeper to his resistance every time she attempted another makeover of his personality. Their mutual admiration society of Andres wasn't enough to gloss over the cracks.

"And you and Ron already owned Elixir?" She'd done the math, one of those times she was thinking about him. Reconstructing his history based on a few of his comments and the 'About Us' section of his company's website. Not admitting that her actions proved she was invested.

He shrugged, and looked away maybe like he was checking the intersection was clear, maybe like he was intent on not meeting her eye.

"Was she headhunted or something?"

Shaking his head as if he was clearing cobwebs. "No. Not really. I don't know, the story changed some. And it wasn't like we'd opened the pub, we only had partnership papers and a few meetings underway. Hadn't secured the location. She was right we could have opened up there instead."

She snorted. His grip on the steering wheel relaxed, and she caught the twitch of a curve to his cheek. "Okay, I'll grant that it wasn't impossible for you to move. But if that's the worst thing, I think it's not as one-sided as you're trying to make out. Sounds like you got assigned, or maybe you took, the job of follower. Instead of leading or walking in step. Not that leading is better than following, mind you. I can tell you in my experience it's no good to be either way. Being the leader can twist a person in ugly ways."

He whipped the car into a fast food parking lot. "Shit."

"Theo?"

"Sorry. Sorry, sorry. Shit. Give me a sec."

His breathing hinted at an elevated pulse, and he'd tilted his head against the headrest. She touched his shoulder and he rolled his neck so they were eye to eye. "Theo, hey. Something I said?"

In truth, she was a tad shaken, too. Hadn't meant to mention a word about her marriage, about the power Sergei'd held over her, about the crap he did, the crap she put up with. That was stuff she discussed in therapy, and a bit with Aunt Johnston, and over the years, through one or two allusions to her friends. What kind of nonsense impulse set her to revealing her knotted, twitchy inner core, she couldn't name. With luck, given the way his eyes stared in thought, he was trapped in contemplations about his life and ignoring the way she signaled her own vulnerability.

"Shit."

"You said that."

He laughed, shortest breath of sound that could still be called a laugh. "Bears repeating, I guess. Also: sorry. That bears repeating, too. Guess I wasn't really expecting…"

"To be hit upside the head by my armchair psychology?"

"Yeah. That. You could set yourself up with a side gig if you get tired of your job."

"Nah, too much paperwork."

He relaxed enough to almost tease. "Not a fan?"

She shook her head. "I'm dyslexic. I avoid it much as I can." Clearly she wasn't avoiding the baring of her entire soul. Theo took her revelation in stride, not that she was ashamed. Not anymore. Not since Aunt Johnston taught her to accept and adapt. A little too late on the self-esteem building train from a few perspectives, but then again, Aunt Johnston hadn't gotten her hands on Rachel until her parents had washed her off theirs.

Theo drew a diaphragm-expanding breath and straightened up. "Well, I can't claim to be upset you're not about to write a bunch of notes about me. What you said—the leading and following bit —it's … not a way I've put it to myself before. Lots of times, I wondered how I missed that side of Annalisa until too late, how I let her turn me into someone I disliked. Therapy, fights, talks with my family. Never once did I consider that she and I changed each other over the course of our marriage."

"Well, people do tend to do that. "

Raking his fingers through his hair, he released another of those wry smiles. "No, you're right. But somehow I thought of her as unchanging. I knew stuff about me underwent a shift, but somehow failed to realize the same of her. And it hit me, you know? How all these years I've had this bitterness about her fooling me, or hiding her true self, or something nebulous and distasteful along those lines. I can't think of one time I even considered that I changed her the same way she changed me. Our marriage worked on both of us, turned us into extremes of ourselves, locked in some kind of duality. Shit. You don't need to hear all of this. Let me take you home."

His breathing and his color were back to normal, and smoothing her hand over his shoulder showed her that his body was no longer overpowered by what was going on in his mind. And his heart. "I've got the time, if you want to sit a bit longer."

"No. Let's blow this taco stand."

"No tacos here. Just fried chicken, it looks like. But, Theo? Thanks, actually, for pulling over. Not everyone would."

She ought to give her tongue a sharp bite to remind it to slow down instead of blurting out all these confessional thoughts of hers. Dismal to hope he was distracted enough by his own shit to not notice every damn thing she was revealing.

CHAPTER NINETEEN

FUCK if he didn't feel like an ass, and an idiot. Everything it seemed like she'd been through with Sergei, and Rachel was comforting him? He was older, and had been divorced longer, and every one of his issues boiled down to self-pity compared to what he suspected she'd recovered from.

He cranked over the engine, forgetting it was already running. She didn't point out his futile moves, settling into her seat while he pulled back into traffic. "You spend much time in therapy yourself?"

The peripheral jerk of her recoil made him realize how gruff he sounded.

"Sorry. I don't mean it in a bad way. Opposite, in fact. I'm impressed." He risked a glance her way; the streetlights glowed through her curls and highlighted the angle of her head. "You don't want to talk about him, I know, but it's not like I can't draw conclusions from the fact you divorced while pregnant, and the thing about not letting him know where you live."

"I—"

"No, it's not my business." If his words were footsteps, they'd be tripping down too-steep stairs. "I'm not prying, I swear. My point, what I meant by saying that, is you're so smart about every-thing. Insightful, you know? And I've had enough therapy of my own to know insight like yours is hard earned and takes work. Reflection and, I don't know, all that crawling through dark tunnels of uncertainty towards the light of a new understanding. So you say what you said about me, about my marriage, and my brain is blown into a shifting kaleidoscope of reframing every-thing. It wasn't what I expected to happen tonight. I'm trying to convince you to give me a real chance, let me persuade you to date, think about making this a relationship. Instead you show me how I don't even know my own past, and now...."

He fell flat, his words stopped by the rough concrete wall of inescapable conclusions.

They were both silent, rolling past blocks of quiet dark streets.

"Turn here," she said, and it was so far from where his thoughts dwelled that it didn't even make immediate sense as driving instructions. He'd eased off the gas when she spoke, though, and managed to make the right she'd requested.

He cleared his throat. "What's this way?"

"My place. It's a shortcut. Take the first left after that stop sign."

Made sense, for her to get herself away from his brain-dump ASAP. He spent a mile mulling the wisdom of asking her out again before she said goodnight. Hoping her 'get to know each other as people' plan was still an option. She was looking for red flags, and impossible to think he hadn't planted plenty of crimson banners over the course of the purportedly low-key dinner-and-a-movie date.

"That gate there. Key code's two-nine-nine-five," she reminded him.

He followed her directions around the complex until he was near her unit. Didn't say more than a couple of acknowledgments until she told him he could park in the space two down from hers. "Rachel?"

"Theo."

He put the car in park. "You want me to walk you up to your door?"

IT WAS her turn to pull the move of wrapping a hand at the back of his neck and drawing him in close. Right front and center of her personal space, so all she saw was his face. Eyes deep, lips parted with maybe surprise and maybe anticipation, nostrils flared, jaw shifting under his beard. Mouth working, silent. Eyes, soft now as she moistened her own lips. A hint of raised brow. And then she dropped her lids and they were kissing.

She unclicked his seat belt, giving them more access to each other's mouths. Theo's hands roved up her arms, back to her nape. Around to cradle her face. "Making a leap here, but is this an invitation upstairs?"

Everything snapped into an easy acceptance, as if all those times he called her clever and insightful and good knit into some kind of blindfold hiding her reservations from view. "You happen to bring a change of clothes or anything?"

Hard to kiss a man whose mouth was a wide grin. She pecked at his jawline instead. "Plausible deniability: it's my gym bag anyway. So if you saw it, you might think it didn't hold a toothbrush."

"Well, you keep telling yourself that. So long as you bring it up with you."

He met her around back of the car. True to form, he asked again. "I don't mind heading back home. I mean, once you're safely in your place. You said all those wise things about us taking it slow and getting to know each other."

"And look how that went." She laughed. Damn but her ego loved all the praiseful adjectives. "I guess we're on a bit of fast-forward at the moment, but it's not like we haven't been here before."

He slid back to give her room to open the apartment. "I am

officially going to stop arguing now. So long as you know you can point me towards the door at any time."

Instead, she pressed him up against it, so he dropped his gym duffle right there next to the shoe cubbies and wrapped his arms around her instead. She toed off her sandals and aimed her purse at the sofa without checking to see if she made the shot or not. "How'd you like to go straight to bed?"

"Yes. Fuck, yes." Theo fumbled over his buttons, not in a way everyone might notice, but she was trained to observe hand tremors. She'd never made a man's hands shake before. It sent her headlong towards the bedroom, discarding clothes as she went. Theo kept right up with her.

She giggled when he ran his fingers down her spine. Fuck if she could remember giggling since maybe when she and her sister were little and shared what they thought of as big private codes to keep their childish secrets from their parents.

Filing away the desire to ask Blythe if she remembered that code, Rachel settled her mind—and body, and overflowing emotions—in the very much right now.

On Theo.

Shirtless, crisp jeans sunk to a disreputable rumple as he unzipped and let them hang open. Olive-hued boxers that were like a shady summer day against the burnished brown of his skin. A full smile, widening as he watched her kick free of her skirt.

"You're the fucking sexiest, Rachel."

"Not a slouch your own self."

They met in a rush, his hands skimming up her sides. She burrowed into his neck, to taste, to smell, to revel in his warm and solid body. All those intentions—maintaining emotional distance, approaching intimacy with care—dissolved under the sweet touch of his tongue and the heat of his embrace. She salved her conscience with a fable about sex being different from intimacy, and allowed herself to combust.

Thing was, sex with a good partner, a partner attentive and intent and kind of engineered to look like a literal Greek god naked—that qualified as very much the kind of thing she knew she deserved in life. The kind of thing she'd attended all that therapy to welcome into her life. The kind of thing any kind of cosmic justice scale-balancing would throw right into her lap.

Her extraordinarily well-satisfied lap. The general area of said lap still pulsed with pleased echoes as they flopped, side-by-side, fingers tracing each other's wrists and palms. "If I were a cat I'd be purring."

His laugh was gruff and shallow. A very different kind of off-kilter breathing than she'd seen him experience earlier in the night.

"You okay?" she asked, and probably she sounded too concerned about the wrong parts of him. His troubled emotions instead of his tremendous body.

"Never been better."

She sat and scrutinized him. "Glib is not a good look on you."

He put palms to eye sockets, scrubbing off whatever emotion had welled up to sink him down. "Sorry. I ... it's been a while, and three quarters of me is reveling in the now, but there's a part leaping ahead to borrow trouble, and a bigger part wanting to erase all that embarrassing car confessional shit from earlier."

"A while since what, exactly?" It wasn't the only question free-wheeling in her brain, but it was the one she opted to voice.

He shifted up on one elbow so they were more eye level with each other. "Since I got this deep into relationship emotions. Since I settled into the fact that all the intense attraction and laughs and so forth is a side of the learning to communicate part. The knowing all sides, not just the light and sexy and talking for hours side."

It took her several insensible moments to realize why she was holding herself still. Not to prevent backing away from him, but to stop from edging closer. Damn and blast but she kept surprising herself. Or Theo kept surprising her. He really needed to stop saying appealing things or she'd get back to worrying it was all a calculated veneer designed to suck her in to cycles of manipulation and mistreatment. She forced out a long, slow breath. "Theo, I wouldn't be here—well, to be correct, you wouldn't be here—if not for the car confessional. I don't mean it's a pity fuck, if that's what that face was for. I mean the experiment, if we're calling it that, of us dating? We set it up so we can get past the light and sexy part. Right?"

His hand crept forward and traced her upper arm. It gave her goose bumps, and she slid down to intertwine their legs under the sheet. He tucked it higher around them both. "Right. I know. It's that small fraction of me, is all. Three-sixteenths, if that."

"You and numbers."

He grinned back at her. "Don't go getting all light and sexy on me again."

Ridiculous man. "Fine. Point is, I'm no stranger to endorphins, but yeah. I get what you mean. This is ... more than the usual. And it's scary."

"Goddamn frightening," he agreed. Somehow his mouth still tasted of movie theatre popcorn.

"I'm not at my best when I'm scared."

"Duly noted."

"And you're always looking for the trigger that will make me run."

When he squeezed her hand, it felt like acceptance and an intention and a sheltering space. "See how well you know me already?"

"So if we're doing this—"

"We are doing this, Rachel. I'm not frightened off. I don't think you are, either, no matter how paranoid I get searching for proof of that. I think we both want more."

"Be that as it may. I've got a point to make. It's that I may be on the reluctant side to talk about some of my past, and not just because you know Hannah's father. Some of it I packed up all careful and stored off-site, you know? Not cause I am suppressing it, but cause I've done the work to put it there. But I think you knew that. And I know it's not on the equitable end of the spectrum to get you to talk about things I won't talk about for myself.

But I really, really want you to know that when you do, it builds bridges for me. And I appreciate it."

He kissed the hand he held, and she went all aglow with a combination of pleasure and stammering vulnerability. His heated gaze served to send the flush to her core instead. "Damn if I'm not impressed with you again. Always. That's one of the things I appreciate about you, you know? The hell of a way you make your points."

Heart-stopping man. She swung herself over him and didn't need the caressing hand at her nape to guide her mouth to his. "Thanks."

"Mmm?"

"For hearing me. While I labored out how to make my point."

"It's never a problem to listen to you, Rachel."

"Ditto. If you have any points of your own to make." She accompanied her words with a teasing twist of her pelvis. Next she knew, he's flipped them and caged her within strong limbs while his mouth roamed her torso.

Wicked, wicked man.

CHAPTER TWENTY

HE WOKE IN A DOZY MOOD, stretching half his limbs to the edges of the bed while the other half remained buried under Rachel. Damn but she made his heart thud. And damn if he hadn't guessed right about the bedhead curls as she snuggled into her pillow.

"Morning." It was more a mumble than a word.

"Thought you were the early-bird type."

"Not the two days a month I don't have a toddler to chase."

He extracted his arm and smoothed back her hair. Her eyelids were fluttering but never quite open. "Okay if I make coffee?"

She shrugged the shoulder not pressed into the mattress. He tucked the blanket around her before slipping out.

He was a morning person himself, which Annalisa made sure to mention often back when he and Ron were elbow-deep in Elixir's business plans. She'd dismissed his assurances that the managers would handle closing, and he'd do his side of things during daylight hours. She'd moved to Dallas before his chance to say, "I told you so." Good thing he never found it satisfying to rub people's noses in things.

He'd just found his wallet in the lust-trail of possessions down Rachel's hall when she emerged from the bathroom and went straight into his arms. "What's up? You ordering me a box of chocolates? I like coconut very much, for the record."

He tucked his credit card back into place and nudged aside her hand enough to pocket his wallet. "Noted. But, no. I got an email about paying the balance for the soccer camp while Andres is down here."

They retreated to her little table, and she poured herself a black coffee before joining him. "How long do you have him?"

"Our forty-two days start in two weeks."

Something silent and displeased crossed her face, which she hid behind the mug as she drank.

"What's up?"

She shook her head. "Nothing. Not you, anyway. I'm picturing Hannah going with Sergei for that long. He's taking two weeks at the end of the month; I'm being all valiant here not whining about it."

"It's because he lives in Dallas. If y'all keep living in the same city it'll be shorter, even once she's old enough for the standard order to kick in. I drive up there every second and fourth weekend, but that and every other school break aren't much time." He looked into his own half-empty mug. "Aren't enough time. So this gives me and him a chance at everyday life together, you know?"

Rachel took his hand. "I get it. And I wasn't criticizing. I just had a moment."

He squeezed back. "Makes sense. You and Hannah, it's different. Andres was older than she is now when we divorced. I'm not saying Sergei's a bad parent, but you're the center of her life."

Electric blue eyes, flashing codes. What was her message? He watched her body cycle through something: shoulders tensing, breath hitching, jaw clenching. Then releasing it all. He pursed his lips, opted against biting his tongue, spoke up. "We need to talk about him."

She shook her head, but said, "Yeah, I know."

"I'm not going to do anything to fuck things up with him and you, not on purpose, but—Rachel. I think at some point it's going to be obvious we're dating. I mean, if I'm honest, I'd be shouting from the rooftops given half a chance. You...." He bit his lower lip to hold in his feelings. Like that would work. "You're sort of my ideal woman, okay?"

She examined the depths of her coffee. He lashed out at the brain-imps who'd prodded him into making grandiose statements and then taken off to run gleeful circles round his roiling gut. Why couldn't he go more than two days in her presence without declaring his undying devotion? Some part of him was determined to sabotage everything before she even knew him well enough to choose him.

He scooted the chair back, ready for a fast exit. "Sorry. Want me to go?"

"No."

"No?"

"You're right."

"I am?" About what? About how desperate he sounded?

"Yeah, I think so. Unless I switch something about custody, I'm going to keep going to Elixir a bunch, and I know Depy's already clocked how much you and I are talking there."

He restrained his snort. Depy made a point of watching the door when Rachel and Hannah were due to arrive. "She's pretty intense."

"Tell me a surprising thing next time."

"Ha."

They both fell silent, and he strove to be patient about it. He'd said more than enough unprompted for one morning.

"So." Rachel stood abruptly. "Want breakfast? Eggs, cereal, smoothie?"

HERE SHE THOUGHT she'd be orgasming her way through her morning, with little breaks for caffeine and snacks. Instead The Talk loomed, and she was so not in the mood.

She'd age and die before locating that particular mood.

Theo slumped some and said cereal suited him and offered to help in a careful voice which he might have thought hid his frustration, but did not. She slid behind him and looped her arms over his shoulders. He released a sigh and captured her hands against his kind and earnest heart. His hair, when she kissed his crown, brushed soft against her lips.

Point: Theo. She'd been pricked by Sergei's coarse hair too many times.

"You remember when we met?"

He nodded, his head rucking up her shirt a bit as he moved.

"I don't see it anymore."

"See what?" Theo sounded casual, but she refused to be fooled by him or by any man.

"My ex. In you. That day at the gas station, I was steaming over him being late, and then you showed up and I didn't have one clue who you were, and you were holding my daughter. And you looked like him, like the worst man I can never get away from."

His hands tightened on hers. She pressed closer in so he couldn't swivel to face her. If they made eye contact, her runaway words would halt, and it was well past time for her to set them free.

"When I was younger, back in high school and once again in college, there were some guys who were forceful with me, insistent. Not quite—not." This conversation always tripped her tongue. Not even from the memories of the guys, but from the futile effort to leap into her own past to shake caution into her reckless younger self. "Coercion. Hard to say no. Using words and peers and the idea that I'd be proving myself worthy if I did ... whatever. Taking off my top. Rubbing against him in public. Sex.

"When I moved down to live with Aunt Johnston, so much changed for the better for me. She understood my dyslexia, knew how to teach me through it, how to deal with schools and catching me up where I was behind and proving to me college was an option. My parents and sister still treat me like it was some big trick I pulled off, got away with, but Aunt Johnston never once from the day I moved in with her treated me as less than."

He cleared his throat. "How old were you then?"

"Just gone fourteen. She kept me back a year so I could catch up a bit before high school. It worked, you know? Not that I ever made honor roll, but compared to home? Where every grade some teacher would say, 'Are you Blythe's sister?' which was code for, 'I expect you to ruin the grading curve for this class.' My parents would put awards nights on the family calendar as soon as the schools announced the dates, and every time Blythe was invited to the stage, and every time for my class they'd cross it off without a word. Like, okay, I couldn't read for shit, but some things don't need decoding to understand."

"Jesus, Rachel."

"It's fine. I mean, I love Blythe, and Mom and Dad, too. I wasn't a kid they could figure out. Too different from her, and from them. They couldn't wrap their heads around the idea that it took more than me being willing to try harder, no matter what Aunt Johnston or any of the specialists told them. So when Blythe was off to college and they needed more money for that, they sold the house and I went to live with Aunt Johnston and like I said, those five years with her made all the difference."

"Except for the boys." His flat voice was hiding emotions again.

She shrugged, and interlaced their fingers. "Small town, kids who knew each other forever. I was the oddball. And I hadn't packed any great social skills with me when I moved from Colorado. Never quite fit in there, either. Of all the options I had for acting out, being too eager to please the pushy boys who might tell me I was special wasn't the worst."

Despite the wall she'd made of her body, he managed to turn towards her and slide one arm around her waist. He stroked up and down her spine like she was some half-broken thing he needed to smooth into place. Which she was not.

"I'm sorry you were used like that. And lonely. I'm sorry you were lonely."

Damn man found a crack she'd sworn was plastered over. "It's fine."

He kissed her belly, between her breasts. "You're fine. It's unfair and rotten, but you're fine."

Fuck a duck. All she meant to do was tell him three or four things about her marriage, and instead she cut straight through her own defenses. She gave up and sat down. "Okay, it's rotten, and I'm fine. I don't know why I told you all that anyway, I only meant to say I knew better by the time I met Sergei, and wasn't letting myself fall for the physically controlling types anymore. No more of the half-promises and insinuations and leaping after acceptance. I had my friends—Gillian and the others we roomed with—and I knew how to do okay at college and everything seemed lined up."

God, she'd been arrogant back then. Maybe no more arrogant than everyone else at twenty-two, but she'd been almost smug with it. Always talking about the challenges she overcame, the things she'd beaten. Like the litany of hurts and abuses and travails were some kind of scorecard proving that she deserved to be as prideful as she wanted. Like she was being modest, all things considered. Such a young fool.

"He wasn't like the others, Sergei. He told me I could be important to him. He told me I completed him. And that he completed me. That he made up for all my ... my lack of common sense, my getting things wrong." She cleared her throat. "My bad ideas. And when my friends suggested I take a look at some of his behavior, I dug in. I already knew what abuse was. They hadn't been through that like I had. And Sergei wasn't Brent or those others. So that was my pride kicking me down the wrong path, because I wouldn't let go of my arrogance long enough to consider he was a different kind of wrong for me."

Somehow she found herself leaning up against Theo, and his stroking had moved to her arm. He rested his temple on her head, and listened, quiet.

She managed a shrug. "You know his smiling face. The whole

'everyone's best friend' act, except it only lasts as long as he profits by it."

"Jesus."

"Oh, you're fine. He's big on appearances; he'll never turn off the charm for Elixir."

"That's not what I'm stressing about."

She laid a palm on his thigh. "No. I know. Thanks."

For a peaceful moment, she focused only on the warmth of Theo beside her, his morning scruff pulling at her curls, her breathing synching up with his.

"So. He set me on a pedestal made of sugar, all sweet and light and refined as could be. And I felt like the queen of the world, and anything he asked of me was easy enough to do, to please him, and didn't he deserve to be pleased after how well he treated me? So what if he changed his mind from one day to the next, it wasn't that big a deal. What did it matter if he forgot to tell me about some event; he would go alone if I didn't have time to spare for his obligation. I was the one who said he was insatiable, so fucking other people was his way of sparing me, even though none of them pleased him like I did."

He twitched. She squeezed his thigh and he coiled himself back in. Kept listening.

"And there I was, a royal on her sugar tower, reminded and reminded about every sacrifice he made for me, every dinner he paid for and every ride to class and every outing with my friends he went to even though I knew he didn't get along with them. But he did it for me, because he wanted me to be happy, he wanted me to understand how I was his treasure. How even if I wasn't quite smart enough to get it, he was the only one who could make my life better."

CHAPTER TWENTY-ONE

FUCKING HELL.

He pictured it all too well, and it snapped so much into place. The consistent way she analyzed their interactions. The laying bare of every perceived flaw in herself and her world. The guardian friends.

And who enters her orbit and refuses to be set aside? A man who hired her ex, who looks a bit like her ex, who's a non-custodial parent like her ex. It almost was enough to make him laugh, or hang his head in defeat. Or slip away.

Except Rachel opted to tell him everything, and the only reason to do that was because she'd stopped seeing him as a version of her ex. That was a gift worth sticking around to receive. He brought her hand to his lips and kissed the knuckles. "You're no princess, Rachel."

It made her shoulders shake, and he lifted his head enough to check she wasn't crying. "You say the most romantic things."

"Believe me, you want romance, I'll go big. But not because I..." How to categorize the difference between him and Sergei? "Not because I am keeping a tally to throw in your face later. Or so you have to come up to any kind of standard. You're great already. I'm not trying to change you or keep score."

Whatever incoherent nonsense it sounded to him, she relaxed more into the crook of his arm. So maybe he wasn't messing up.

"I know you're not." She sounded more calm than sad.

"Thanks. I mean, good. That's great. I don't mind if you question me, if you get worried about anything. About my reactions or whatever. I'll try to stay open with you. But tell me if I'm messing up."

She nudged an elbow to his ribs. "Free rein, huh?"

"Ha. Don't make too much of it; I'm as apt to screw up as the next man."

And that statement sure loaded the atmosphere with grim fog. Like he couldn't wait one single morning to prove his point about screwing up. May as well plunge them back to the topic that kicked off the whole talk.

He cleared his throat again. "Not apt to take after Sergei, though."

She nodded.

"But..."

With that, she straightened away from him, letting the cool creep between them. "But you're working with him every day, and we're not hiding that we're dating, and it's like to be wiser to mention it up front to him than for him to speculate and feel upper-handed about it."

"Yeah."

She retrieved the coffee pot. Gave them both refills. Accepted his light kiss. "I don't want to talk to him."

"Easy enough," he said. "I'll do it. Tell me what you want me to say, and when."

"Just like that?"

"Well. Probably not." He and Sergei got along, at least so far. Most of the time, Ron liked him, and Ron could be testy. The division of labor worked, give or take Sergei's aversion to sitting at the desk. Were they friends? Not in the same way he and Ron were friends, but friendly, sure. Hard to imagine them getting closer, now he knew more about Rachel's marriage.

"What are all those thoughts tumbling around your skull?"

He tried for lightness. "Oh, nothing big."

"Wow. Here I thought we were still new to each other, but already I can tell when you're lying to me. I don't know if I'm pleased or pissed."

Her eyes twinkled. He wanted her to tease him forever, so he could keep seeing those sparks. Instead he figured he was about to extinguish them. "Fine. It's something I have to figure out on my own. Or with Ron, I mean. About the future of Elixir, and how we feel about someone who'd do all that being in such a key position. Whether we need to act to protect employees or customers. Sorry."

"Sorry, for...?"

"You look like you want to glue my lips closed."

The half-smile she gave him kept her own teeth out of sight. "Can't really tell you what to do about that. Selfishly, I'm hoping he keeps his job, cause I'm still waiting on arrears." She gestured to a drawing on her fridge.

"What's that?"

Cute blush. "It's silly. I mean, it's utterly vital, but it's also silly. I keep track of the amount he owes by coloring in parts of that garden."

He went to examine it. She had a dozen or more pictures held by colorful magnets—thumbprint ladybirds, a series of traced triangles, something that could have been an exploding sun—but only one with flowers that stayed inside the lines. Some of the petals were shaded with crayons, some with marker, some with pen. But close to forty percent still needed some kind of color. "Each one represents an amount?"

"Hundred bucks per petal. Another six months and I'll be able to trade in my car for one with proper air conditioning."

"How is he so far behind?" Why did he buy that flashy SUV instead of paying up?

She read all the questions behind the one he asked. "When he was freelance before he started with you, he managed to jump from place to place faster than the Attorney General could serve the papers. Mostly. So the arrears built up. I know it's a bigger decision for you than what he owes, but it's been nice having him in one place so I don't have the wait while the system figures out where to garnish."

"That only explains the arrears if he was job-hopping on purpose and not remitting support on his own." He turned at her dry laugh, and grimaced.

"You're a smart one, Theo."

He lifted a box of cereal off the top of the fridge and carried it to the table. Smart? Maybe. But obtuse, too. He was reassessing every time he'd given Sergei the benefit of the doubt.

Well. Whatever else, if he kept Sergei on while he paid Rachel off, or if he and Ron looked for a replacement, he knew now to keep doubt in place. It didn't resolve much, but it might stop him from making more mistakes.

ONCE SHE AND Hannah were unpacked and settled down, they called her parents. Dad answered, all smiles and wearing an Uncle Sam hat.

"Getting ready for the fourth?"

"There was a festival this afternoon, we went with Blythe and Jason."

Of course they did. Nothing against people who got on with their extended families, but it seemed sometimes like these monthly video calls were nothing but a chance for her parents to mention all the varied and fulfilling hours they spent with her sister and brother-in-law. "How's Blythe doing? Everything with the pregnancy good?"

"You should see her," Mom said. She was in a star-spangled shirt and a red-and-white striped scarf. "That baby does nothing but squirm around inside her. Jason's already talking about padding out the basement and building a toddler-sized gym."

"Cute. Can't wait to see it." At her pettiest, she hoped that Blythe and Jason had a wonderful, healthy, happy baby who set about destroying every single one of their preconceived notions about parenting. It wasn't such a mean wish. She'd yet to meet a parent whose offspring hadn't spun every controlled thing about their life out of alignment. The parents had to adjust, but tended to not mind all that much.

Hannah leaned into the screen to poke at Dad's image, and they all spent a few minutes focused on her. Mom and Dad asked the right questions, remembered the names of her school friends, spoke with age-appropriate words.

Not for the first time, she wondered if they updated a cheat sheet after each month's call.

"So your sister is trying to get me to move back home," she told Dad, once Hannah wandered off.

Mom looked around her own living room, like Aunt Johnston might be lurking. "Here?"

"No. I mean, Plainview."

"Be nice, having you closer," Dad said.

"Plainview is not your home." Mom's narrowed gaze moved between Dad and the screen.

"I know. I told her I wasn't interested. This jerk guy from high school is running Brookside; remember where I used to work in summers? He wants me to take over as Director of Recreation." She didn't know why she was telling them. She'd turned down the job within seconds of getting Brent's email, giving him no room for ambiguity.

Okay, she did know. She wanted a damn gold star. She wanted them to hear how people from across the state were recruiting her. She wanted them to see she wasn't some pitiful less-than, never as accomplished or valued as her brilliant doctor sister.

Thin a veil as she'd draped over her request for praise, her parents didn't see it. "I don't know why you call her place 'home,' Rachel. You only lived there for high school."

"Mom, I don't. I call Houston home." Eighth grade through graduation, and she'd only been an hour away during community college. And lived with Aunt every summer even once she started at University of Texas. But Mom never wanted those reminders.

"This hat is making my scalp itch," Dad announced. "I'm going to go shower. Talk to you next month, love?"

"Talk to you and see you," she reminded him. "We'll be there the twelfth or thirteenth, depending on how the drive goes."

Mom didn't even watch her husband's retreat. "I suppose you're staying with her on the way?"

"For a night or two, of course. And we'll stay a bit longer on the way back. I haven't taken Hannah on this long a road trip since before she was walking. I can only guess what our schedule will be like."

"You went to stay with her last summer."

It wasn't like it had been some teen rebellion, her running off to live with Aunt Johnston. Her parents organized it all, then told her the day before the 'For Sale' sign went up in her childhood home's front yard. Well, mostly Mom told her. Dad managed to stay in the room, but didn't contribute much.

Despite all that, Rachel couldn't remember her mother saying Aunt Johnston's actual name once since then. It was always 'her' or 'your aunt.' As if Aunt was a pariah for taking her in when no one else would make room for her. As if she'd done something egregious by guiding Rachel to high school graduation. As if her success required Aunt's head on a chopping block.

She sighed. "I had my friend with me then, remember? It's different, being the only adult in the car. Anyway, we're excited about seeing you all in person. And I get to take in the reality of Blythe, pregnant. I don't think the photos do it justice. I want to watch her abdomen ripple. And see her stand up from a too-deep chair."

Mom let herself laugh and be diverted, talking about the

nitrates in the hot dogs at the Fourth of July festival and Jason's paternity leave negotiation until everything else had sunk down and the surface of their chat was nothing but calm.

"Sergei, step in here if you're free."

"What's up?" He started to lean as usual against the doorframe, but whatever was on Theo's face spurred him to his desk chair instead. He swiveled to close the door, and then rotated back to face Theo. "I didn't want to bring up the Ron and Lonnie thing again, but I guess he came complaining to you? I get that he's also the boss, but everything I do to keep the front of house staff happy, I can't ignore the rules because it's him."

Theo pinched the bridge of his nose, in no mood to switch gears and deal with the tension between Sergei and Ron. "No, he didn't come complaining to me. I didn't know Lonnie came by again."

Sergei shrugged. "Twice more since we talked about it before. I don't know what his fight with his uncle is about, but this last time I intercepted him in the foyer and told him to take it round to the dock."

Theo eased into the back of his chair. "Okay, that's fine. If he gives you a problem let me know."

"Good stuff." Sergei slapped his hands to his thighs, and then halted his forward momentum. "Hey, okay, so what did you want to talk over, then?"

"Rachel."

He hoped they weren't true mirrors of each other, or if so, that he'd never worn such a sneer on his own face. Sergei slicked his hair back and asked, "What'd she do now? Is she going after my paycheck again?"

"That money's for your *kid*, Sergei. You know what it costs to dress and feed a child, much less send her to a decent daycare? Your business is your business, but that brand-new SUV in your parking space retails for like seven times your arrears, man. How'd you tell yourself it's okay to buy that and not make sure your daughter's taken care of?"

He cut himself off. They'd both stood, stances tense across Theo's desk.

"You're saying a lot of words about something that's not your business."

It took effort, but he nodded twice. "Yeah. I shouldn't have." He could concede, but he couldn't quite apologize.

"So that's what she's done? Recruited you to her side, in all those little chats you two've been having when she drops my child off? I didn't figure you to be a sucker for those faux-innocent baby blues of hers."

"Jesus, Sergei, listen to yourself. No one's taking sides. There aren't sides here, just court ordered support and being adult enough to take responsibility."

Sergei snorted, and Theo couldn't even blame him for it. His denial of side-taking was as transparent as his phyllo dough.

He sat again. Sergei didn't, but Theo opted out of the body language wars. He said straight out what he needed to say. "Rachel and I are dating."

Sergei left the office, which was, all in all, an eloquent response.

CHAPTER TWENTY-TWO

SHE PULLED IN ALONGSIDE THEO, and caught the gleam of her pink top reflected in the dark gloss of his car door. While she unlatched Hannah, he emerged and opened her passenger door to retrieve the diaper bag.

"Can you grab Effie?" she asked. An exuberant toss during the bouncing song resulted in the toy sliding into the front foot well. Her girl's aim needed finesse, but she had a strong arm.

Before they headed inside, Theo kissed both Hannah and her. Right there in front of the pub windows, no looking first for lurkers. Funny the way her chest warmed to his affection while her stomach curled against confrontation.

If she pitched it right, her question wouldn't at all sound like her nerves had a hold of every finger and toe, leaving her unsure about basics like walking head-on into the brewery. "You're feeling sure about this?"

He smiled, and the lift of his cheekbones helped ground her. "Oh, yeah. But it's up to you. Plenty of options if you change your mind."

Tempting as retreating to his place for naked time was, she held fast to the reasons for their plan.

The whole point of this dating experiment was to see if they had more to them than chemistry, which meant lower key nights less likely to land them in intense talks or bed. Or both. Also, Elixir was Theo's place and he wanted to show it off to her. And Sergei and Depy needed to see all their scorn and derision and snide comments—they'd both received plenty in the two days since Theo told Sergei about their relationship—had no impact on Rachel's dating life.

She deserved freedom from all that.

Leaning into the arm Theo wrapped across her shoulder, she smiled. "Let's do this."

DEPY MOCK-SPAT THRICE at the floor when they walked in together. He almost lost all composure. Nearly straight-faced, he turned to Adela at the host stand. "Can you set us up at table fourteen, maybe? Is that Marti's section tonight?"

"It is. You got it, boss."

"Thanks, mastermind."

Rachel raised eyebrows at him. "It's what she calls herself; don't blame me. Besides, Sergei hates it."

"Okay then." She kissed Hannah's curls. "Let's get you over to Dad and Depy, eh?"

"Want me—"

"Nah." She took the diaper bag and he placed Effie in Hannah's hands. "Meet you at table fourteen, wherever that is."

He did laugh at that. "It's the one by the window over there. Far side of the bar."

"Got it."

He could head that way himself any time. No need at all to watch Depy snatch up Hannah, to smirk at the ostentatious way Sergei put a hand each on his mother and daughter, to share a grin with Rachel behind their backs.

She didn't want him acting the dragon, so instead of walking towards her, he leaned over the reservation book and scanned the parties for the rest of the night. Not that anyone needed his input; Adela had everything under control as usual. He pulled out his phone and made a note to offer her hours if she wanted to stick around once the school year got underway.

"Ready?"

There, he'd filled his head with enough Elixir business to pretend he wasn't lurking within earshot of the Matsouka family. "For you? Absolutely." He guided her to fourteen and held her chair, positioning them both with a view to the kegs. And out of Sergei's sight. Not for his sake, but so Hannah wouldn't be confused.

He swallowed the nervous awkwardness and jumped in with the boilerplate details about brewing and cuisine. How he and Ron became friends online, back during their home brewing days, and partnered up when he dropped the hobby and Ron was ready to elevate it to a career. Market research and flavor profiles and remodeling the former service station to make it their own. She didn't quite glaze over but he knew wandering interest when he saw it. "Right. You don't need the sales pitch. Sorry. I'm pretending neither of us are listening for Hannah or wondering how powerful Depy's curses are."

She took the oil from the cruet set and coaxed a drop into her water glass. It floated. "We're safe."

He laughed. "How did you know to do that?" He'd never encountered a non-Greek who knew the trick to ensuring no evil eye cursed you.

"It's not like I ruined every moment of Depy's life by taking her one and only grandchild away the moment we met. I had a good few years of being her daughter-in-law first. That woman spat three times as I walked up the aisle at my wedding. She taught me to be as Greek as possible, despite my inferior DNA."

Three seconds with the woman and he strained to leash his

effusive feelings. She was such a danger to his equanimity. "I can totally imagine the stare-down you'd have with my own grandmother."

With a deft move, she spooned the oil out of her water glass before it had a chance to sink. "Does she live in Houston?"

He launched into his family tree—the Greek-American and the Mexican-American and the few outliers in between. And included the reassurance that Tomás was the only one she risked running into in Houston.

"But didn't you grow up here?"

He nodded. "My parents moved to Georgetown for Mom's job last year. And my sisters and their families are all in Austin, which explains why Mom was looking for a job out that way to start with."

"Is that hard?"

He sensed a deeper meaning in her question. "Which part? Having everyone out of town?"

She shook her head once. "Your parents choosing your sisters."

Ah. She'd mentioned this with her own family a bit. "I don't think of it like that."

And damn if his throat wasn't wrapped in thorns all the sudden. He'd caught himself in a lie, and couldn't scrape up the presence of mind to move past it. He licked his lips. "Or maybe I do. Some. Not ... not that I'd realized before just now. It helps that Mom's so into her job. And they were here when Andres was a baby, which helped us out a lot. I know my sisters both groused about how easy I had it with the babysitting, especially Helen when her twins were new. Anyway, since I travel to Andres most of the time, they only were seeing him during the longer visits, and that was hard on them."

She nodded, but left him with the strong impression his revelations had skittered right past her. Which was fine. He was the one who needed to process a truth about himself.

She, though. She'd asked about his parents choosing his sisters like physical proximity determined emotional connection. "Do you and your sister get along?"

She blinked a quick code, and he second-thought bringing it up in the middle of his pub. She answered, though. "When we were little, we did. She's four years older, and she liked to play good cop for me. Looking out for me, telling me what to do. But helping, too, you know? Reading me all the rules when we played a game, picking what I'd like off restaurant menus, that kind of thing."

"Because of your dyslexia?"

She stilled, and he wondered if he'd broken a rule by mentioning it. But she'd brought it up earlier like no big deal.

She blew out a breath and sipped her water. "No, I think because she was that much older and a little bossy. But telling you about it, I see how many of my examples are her reading for me, and how it became the norm for us. For all of us. I wonder ... it's nothing. A question Aunt Johnston asked once, about how I went undiagnosed until I was eleven. Mom and Dad went poker-spined at that, and it infuriated me, you know? But now...."

"Hey." He took her hand. "It's fine. Maybe your sister picking menu items was part of your coping mechanisms, but it wasn't anything she or you did deliberately to.... To whatever. Trick anyone. Delay your diagnosis. Whatever else you're thinking."

Her knuckles tensed under his palm. He circled his index finger on her wrist. Smiled up at Marti dropping off their beer. Waited.

"Way to take my mind off Hannah."

He drummed the fingers of his free hand on the table. "Not my precise intention, but I'm glad to help?"

Rotating her hand, she intertwined their fingers. Squeezed. "Okay, stop being cute. Tonight's supposed to be chill hanging out, not more heavy shit. I showed up all ready to enjoy a meal and be low key flirted with. You keep making those eyes at me and I start wondering if anyone notices us disappearing into your office."

Yeah, he wasn't standing up from the table anytime soon. She laughed at his expression. He shook his head in resignation. "Way to derail me from all the deep talk about families of origin."

She raised her drink for a toast. "We're quite a pair."

They sure were. And he devoted the rest of dinner to keeping himself from getting intense about the increasing perfection of their pairing.

His home turf date ended with Hannah's visitation hours. Serg brought her to the table where they lingered over his peach-rose pie. "She says she wants to go potty."

Rachel glanced at her phone, not that her ex stuck around for feedback about cutting short his time with his child.

"Sorry." She gathered everything for the trip to the restroom. "Half the time she just wants the experience of going bottomless, but I have to check."

"Of course." He meant it, too. He'd kept his expectations for the night low, anticipating interference from Serg or Depy. So he savored the miracle of eating in peace, skirting past family issues and diving deep into her passion for knitting.

"What a couple of old fogies we are, with your baking and my needles," she'd said, and hadn't pulled away—emotionally or physically—at his offhand comment about them taking up roller derby and hang-gliding when they reached their sixties. Just laughed and added traveling to music festivals to the list. Like they were in accord about sharing decades of adventure.

So Sergei's interruption didn't derail him at all.

"I'll hold her while you finish your pie," he offered when she returned.

"Oh, I don't...."

"It's fine. Besides, I asked Marti to bring me a dish of I-C-E C-R-E-A-M in case you need a reward. You can wave her off; I warned her you might."

"You're uncanny."

"Promised a treat, did you?"

"I meant a couple bites of this," she pointed her fork at the pie. "But your idea is better. She'll make a mess grabbing at your shirt, though."

He shrugged. "Must be an inherited trait."

Her wide eyes and hasty bite told him all he'd wondered about her thoughts on them missing out on intimate contact that night. But soon ... one more week and they'd be at his place, and he'd make her moan without a single slice of his pie in sight.

CHAPTER TWENTY-THREE

"Seriously?" Rachel laughed. "You promised to stop calling my dates that over a decade ago."

Gillian smirked at her, no surprise. She'd kept the gals all in the loop, of course, once she and Theo decided to be all official about dating. They were up to date on the texting and late-night chats and the morning he met her at that cute brunch place near the daycare that she'd never figured she would take the time to try. Lots of contact, nothing intimate. It was ... odd.

Odd, but nice, getting to know him, and not just in a carnal way. Feeling a little sneaky about squeezing in all these moments of connection while they went about their lives. His muffled but echoing laughter when he phoned from the bathroom of the hotel in Fort Worth, once his son was asleep. His entirely wrong opinion about the best season of the *Great British Baking Show*. The ridiculous triumph when he admitted his weakness for Jell-O salad.

She summed it up in a way calculated to poke at Gillian's smirk. "Everything's fine."

"Oh, he's inoffensive, is he?"

One of these days she'd learn that Gill was the queen of poking back at people. "Shush."

"Nope. New rule. I'm buying you loaded nachos, and in return you give me legitimate answers to three questions."

"Wow. Lunch has gone transactional. Didn't you once tell me relationships shouldn't be like that? That keeping score was a bad idea?" Look at her, parroting back the good advice like she'd internalized it. She sipped her iced tea.

Gillian mirrored her, eyes bright with good emotions. "I love you, Rach. And I'm so proud to know you."

"Stop trying to make me cry when you haven't even provided one single nacho yet."

She closed the menu and signaled the waiter. But she was Gill, so Rachel knew she'd be unable to let it go. No matter how many diverting topics she dangled. The aggravations of the summer online courses, shopping plans for Serena's wedding dress, even the heartrending terrors of the national news. Before they'd finished the nachos, Gillian pointed a fork at her and asked, "Is this Theo individual some kind of embodiment of 'lack of red flags' for you?"

Thing about nachos was, they didn't provide much of a distraction to hide behind. Didn't take all that long to chew and swallow even the most loaded chip. She wiped each finger clean. Smoothed the napkin back over her lap. Gave in and looked up. "I mean, yeah. He is. You know how hard I've worked to be sure I'm not vulnerable to the same old BS, right? He's not rushing me into something I'm not ready for, he's not isolating me—he said he wants to meet y'all. Hell, he wants to introduce our kids, which is nonsense but whatever. He backed off when I told him to, after the condom thing. He took responsibility for his part in it all. So. You know. There might be other things wrong with him; I'm not an expert in his inner self. But it's been a month or more since we met and we've spent a bunch of time communicating and I haven't found any red flags. Yet."

Gillian said ... nothing. Kept her face all still and unreadable like she was considering how best to contain an explosive situation.

"Why is it bad that I've checked him for bad news and haven't found anything?"

Her friend stopped circling her straw through her drink. "Okay. I'm agreeing with you, it's all positive. And you can introduce us any time. Let me know."

"But?"

"Rach, I know you rolled the dice for all those superficial things. Hair and eyes, as if those are the key components of a partner. And I know you have your checklist of ways to avoid anyone like that pox of an ex. That's useful, of course. You're listening to your gut, alert to warning signs, and I'm, to be honest, in awe of you for how you've created that safety for yourself."

She shrugged. "I have to, for Hannah."

"I know, I know. But you did it for you, too. I hope you did it for you, too."

She shrugged again.

Gill's smile was full of love, and Rachel let it fill her, too. Then, of course, came part two of the big nacho-fueled speech. "So it's good you have safety. And you know I'm up for being step one in any escape plan you need in life. You and Hannah both, forever. But. Rachel. Have you got a checklist of the things you want, or only of things you want to avoid?"

"What do you ... what does that mean?"

"What I said. Every time you talk about Theo, it's about what he's not. How he's different from the slimy crust on month-old fried okra you call an ex-husband."

Predictably, she laughed. Gillian's insults for Sergei always made her laugh. Even when the sound had to battle up through a few layers of swallowed-down emotion. "Well, he is different. I told you how I confused them when I first met him. So of course I notice all the ways he's not even week-old fried okra."

"Sure. I'm not suggesting it's a negative, protecting yourself like that. Of course that's important. It's vital. And other than my lingering fury that you ever had to come up with a protective checklist to start with, I don't have a thing to say about it."

"Then I don't see the problem." Lies. Lies she was pretending to not understand uttering.

Instead of calling her on it, Gill asked, "What do you want from dating? Is a relationship, commitment, something you're open to right now? What does it take to elevate someone from 'not a danger' to 'enriching your life'?"

"Hell's bells, Gillian." She rubbed at her midriff. Too many jalapeños, too many questions. Something.

"No, listen. You all get on me—don't pretend you don't, it's fine —about all the people I date. But I have lists, too. And not about external markers, height and hair and dimples. I can pick all that off an app, which works for hooking up, but when I get myself into a relationship? Dimples aren't what I'm going to evaluate. It'll be how they treat my work commitments. If they jump to their own defense if I question them, instead of taking a second to consider my position. How they value family, or how they let me value mine, anyway."

"Theo values his family. And Hannah."

"As he should. She's the best little person in the cosmos. And I'm sure valuing her will be key on your list, if you compile one. Hell, it's key on my list, has been since she was born. The question is, are you taking steps to ensure you're not settling for someone good enough? Have you thought about who your best possible partner would be? Not to hold everyone you meet to an impossible ideal, but because knowing who suits you best helps you look past 'good enough.' Helps you know you deserve 'fucking amazing.' Because, Rach?" Gillian leaned in like she was telling the most precious secret in the whole state of Texas. "You absolutely do."

FATE WAS FEELING sprightly and full of vicious nonsense, maybe. Or everyone on Wednesday night's shift succumbed to an attack of sunstroke. Or his ex-wife's predictions were overdue to come true.

Whatever it was, the bus boy called in sick, the dish washer didn't bother showing up, and one of the bartenders turned several wrong shades before dashing from the prep area twenty minutes after she clocked in. Sergei, big surprise, commandeered the bar, claiming it was so he could be available if Depy needed him. Which left Theo holding the tote bin when Rachel walked in. He hadn't had six spare seconds to figure out who could cover Thursday's shifts, much less call her to explain his hasty text canceling their dinner. The rope tethering him to any sense of calm had frayed during Sergei's snit over not being able to locate the citrus slicer. Watching Rachel smirk at his apron-clad self left him that much more unraveled, but a second later he discovered he was wrong. She hadn't unraveled him: she'd unwound him. Gossiping line cooks, ass-pinching customers, whatever was happening with Ron—the stranglehold of it all loosened. His back and neck and head all lifted.

He propped the bin of dirty dishes on his hip, and smirked right back at her. She finished up with Depy and Hannah, then that firm stride of hers carried her towards him. Each solid step grounded him, and he took the brief length of her journey to remind himself that they were taking it slow. That he couldn't be in leap mode while she was still in look mode.

"Aren't you cute."

"Aren't you cute your own self?" he replied. "Sorry about tonight."

She shrugged. "I get it. Owner's burden."

"Yeah, well. I mean, you're right of course. I'm—it is what it is. Part of the job." He blew out a breath. "Not explaining myself well. Doesn't matter, anyway. I appreciate you being flexible about it."

One half step further into his space, as deliberate as always. "You making an insinuation there, Theo?"

Damn. He took a sec to be grateful for the apron around his waist. "Maybe."

"Well. Good. I'm looking forward to finding out more about you and ... flexibility this weekend."

The rim of the bin cut into his fingers. He loosened his grip, leaned in for a kiss hot enough, any of his employees would've been busted for interrupting their shifts. Owner's privilege to counterbalance owner's burden. "Siren."

"I'll say this for you." She did that hip-jutting thing as she studied him.

Something thoughtful about her expression notched up his curiosity. "Oh?"

"I think I really like that you're so calm and up-front about the change in plans."

"You're the one who was promised dinner and insinuations. I'm the one not following through on our plans. It's on me to thank you for being calm and accepting."

"I know. I get that, I appreciate it. But you could be a lot more of a jerk about it. You could be acting like I have no right to whatever emotions a broken date brings up in me. You could be.... Ugh." She shook her head. "The point isn't all the things you're not. I'm the one not explaining myself well now."

Something about her flustering left him fizzing. "You're saying you like me."

Her curved lips. Those electric eyes. "I'm saying that. Yes. I like you."

"Best news I've heard all day. I like you, too, Rachel. I very intensely like you."

"Get back to work, you flirt. But text me tonight." She kissed him again, thanked him for the to-go order he'd set aside for her, and left him grinning as she exited. He didn't mind at all when she was the one pinching his ass.

GOOD WITH KIDS. Good to kids.
   Calm about plans changing.
   Takes responsibility for his part in—whatever.
   Nurturing.

Really, really honest and thoughtful about his feelings, even if they're not sunshine and kittens.

Doesn't put himself first all the time.

Whatever superpower makes it so I keep smiling all the time, even when we're not together.

Rachel scrolled through her list, muttering and feeling full of nonsense for muttering. It wasn't like anyone could overhear her, in this stolen moment in the parking garage. Hannah was at school; she had seven minutes before she needed to clock in at work. And Gillian had cajoled her into promising she'd name the qualities of this mythical ideal partner she somehow was looking to add to her life.

She couldn't remember quite how she'd come to agree that she was looking to add him—not Theo specifically, but the invented ideal—to her life. It sure as hopping toads wasn't anything she'd admitted to herself before her latest lunch with Gill. Putting aside the always-possibility that Gill possessed witchy abilities to see inside her soul, she supposed it was a lurking desire she'd forgotten to hide from herself. Paired nicely with the lurking desire for more children, and a tighter relationship with her sister. Did not go so well with her bank balance or the logistical truths of her work-life juggling or, it turned out, her ability to name a few things that would build a net of security about the guy she chose to fulfill that desire.

She gave her list of qualities one last read-through and hit send.

She got hearts back from Serena, and a gif of a dancing llama from Natalie, but it was Gill's reaction she wanted. At last: 'Phenomenal work, reframing the bad shit of ex-hole as positive things you want instead. Way to go. Can you push further? Can you name a trait you want that doesn't reflect him at all?'

She dropped the phone to her lap and pinched the bridge of her nose. Lucky for her, it was time to head in to work, so no. No. She couldn't push further. She tucked away her phone and resolved —*ha*—to not give her friend's probing questions a bit of thought as she went about her day.

CHAPTER TWENTY-FOUR

UNINTERRUPTED HOURS STRETCHED, sensual and expectant, ahead of him. When Annalisa offered to fly down with Andres on Sunday instead of his driving up on Saturday, he'd outright lied to everyone at Elixir about the change. As soon as he put the accounts to rights, he was out of there. His detailed plan involved cooking, then cleaning, then fulfilling Rachel's every desire until his son's plane glided across the tarmac in Houston.

He checked the time. Again. Banished the image of half-asleep pre-dawn sex. Of waking beside her. Of cajoling her into naked pool time. Clearly his brain needed focus.

Finish checking the payroll. Follow up with the Houston Greek Festival committee. Spot-check the POS. Engage with social media. Text Rachel. Anticipate holding Rachel. Input the inventory numbers. Add coconut chocolates to his shopping list. And a candle. Were candles cliché, or romantic? Not too many, not one of those movie scene spreads of candles on every windowsill and countertop. Only one, with a nice scent. Nothing too floral. A spice, maybe.

Damn, he was a disaster. Two weeks since they'd last slept

together, and no work task had a hope of claiming his attention. He prioritized everything with a hard deadline, wrote up a longer-than-it-should-be list for himself for Monday, then shut down his computer. Time to go bury his nose in various jars of wax.

Almost out the door, his cell rang. "Boss?"

"Yeah?"

"Stop right there."

He turned, and spotted Marti wedged between the bar and a party of twelve. She tilted her head at the man at the end of the table: slick suit, thinning hair, flashy watch. Mr. Low Tips was back. Theo heaved a sigh, pasting on his 'good to see you' smile as he approached. The guy was in the process of making himself a regular, showing up with a few different groups over the last month. Sergei was off charming a table of well-liked regulars, which left Theo to navigate the man who demanded lunch menu quickness during his weekend dinner party lifestyle.

And, as it turned out, who combined racism with sexism while harassing his favorite front of house employee. He sent Marti away before playing the 'Sir, I'm afraid we can't serve you anymore, yes, I'm the owner, no, please enjoy your meals, I'm sorry to hear that, I'm afraid if you consume the alcohol already at the table we will have to clear everyone's drinks, that's certainly your right, no, it's a final decision, we will not be serving you in future, I understand, and who's responsible for tonight's check?' rodeo.

He staggered home, nerves too tight to deal with laundry or dusting. Some days were more of a waste than others, but with any luck, the hours ahead with Rachel and the weeks ahead with his son would help him track down the reasons he put up with it all.

GIDDY. What a thing to be. She shoved the gearstick into park and flipped the visor for a quick check. Quick and embarrassing. Flushed cheeks, bright eyes, grin not at all contained.

Well, and so what if he saw her eagerness for their weekend on her face? His expression when he suggested it hadn't put her off, for all that it glowed with lustful anticipation. They had time to be adults with each other, before their focuses both split for their children. Nothing wrong with a little bounce in her step as she landed herself at his front door. Nothing wrong with her playful rap and the little hitch in her breathing when she heard his approach.

She dropped her duffle next to his mop bucket and wrapped herself around Theo. His cleaning glove-clad hands squeezed her once, then he backed away. He disentangled and shut the door, apologizing.

"For what?"

"Wet floor. Sweaty self. Not finishing up all this before you got here."

She grinned wider. "Oh, no, a sweaty man. I guess I have to lure you into the water to cool you down." She kicked off her sandals and pulled the sundress over her head, revealing a green checked bikini she'd last worn before she started spending her pool time with a kid all too ready to yank at the various straps and ties preserving her modesty.

"Fuck."

"Well, that, too, if you like. But not underwater. I looked it up, condoms won't work in pools."

He brought a hand to his neck, jerked it away, and yanked off the gloves. "Give me two minutes to put all this away."

As he moved to pick up the bucket, she pivoted and, deliberate as could be, bent from the waist to collect her bag and dress. She glanced over her shoulder at the mess he'd made sloshing water across the floor. "Two minutes and counting, Theo."

She deposited her stuff on the sofa, and left the sliding door open, the better to relish his laughing curse when she tossed the bikini top over her shoulder before diving into the pool.

SHE FLIPPED over underwater and popped up like a naiad, sun glinting in the wet curls she scooped back over her head. She began lazy backstroke away from him, thighs flashing open and closed, water lapping against the peaks of her bare breasts. Singing an off-key pop song.

He shook off his frozen-statue state, stripped, and strode towards the far end of the pool, his cock the only part of him still marble-hard. He reached the far deck just as she did, and was about to plunge in beside her when she stopped him.

"Stand there a minute."

He met her gaze. Her eyes, a brighter blue than the water, were wide with hunger. She pulled herself to the edge, then grasped his ankles.

"Kneel down."

His toes curled over the edge. His squat trapped her hands under his thighs, which seemed to be all the anchor she needed to pull herself up. The slide of her wet thumbs along his shins made him shiver, but not as much as the vision of her dripping torso rising out of the water.

"Did you bring out a condom?"

He sucked in a breath at her question, at the way she whispered it into his inner thigh, at the biting kiss she planted near his knee before sinking back down. At the playful, sexy, lusty aggression of her.

When he tipped his chin to the opposite deck in answer, she tugged to release her hands. "Come make me come, then," she said, and kicked off the side of the pool.

He launched himself towards her.

As soon as they were within his depth, he caught hold of her calf and reeled her in, wrapping hand over hand up her leg until he'd stroked every inch. Tucking that leg behind his back, he pressed her crotch into his belly and drew her body up into his arms. His erection stiffened, straining up towards her ass, but all his urgency was focused further up. He needed to tongue her nipples, to swirl the tight peaks and suck and nibble and taste until she moaned his name.

Rachel bucked her pelvis against him. Her arms clasped his head tight to her chest. He feasted on the sweet, slick mounds. Buried his nose in the valley between them, nipped the undersides and then, as she cried out yes, groaned out his name, rubbed her increasingly frantic crotch against his body, he left her to hold herself up and trapped each nipple under his thrumming thumbs.

Such a goddamn goddess, half-submerged and all wet, breasts thrust high and tight into his hands, mouth wide on a demand for more.

He would give her more. He would give her everything she ever wanted.

Banish the thought. It opened the door to the problems. Not the right time to resurrect pledges he'd promised to stop making, the emotions she wasn't sure about accepting. Not the right time to daydream about the future.

That was the past.

In the now, he held Rachel Groff's every wet, luscious curve, and only a scrap of fabric separated him from the wettest part of her.

He tugged the knot at her hip, working his hand under the fabric. Her palms cupped his jaw, and the kiss made it clear she was pleased with the ways his fingers explored. Her tongue thrust into his mouth, and he returned the favor. With tongue and with fingers. She writhed. Her slick breasts slid and pressed against his chest. His thumb circled her clit, and it was all he could do to keep his feet planted so she could anchor to his body while the water and her undulations sent her flashing, swirling around him.

"Jesus, Theo, I need more."

In the now, in the future. It didn't matter when. He'd give her everything.

Pushing off, he drew her to the edge of the pool and eased her up so her ass perched there, cushioned by a towel he'd dropped on his way outside. He ducked long enough to slide his shoulders beneath her thighs. She laughed when he shook his head and water flew from his hair to land on her belly, but gasped when he dug his fingers into her hips and plunged his tongue into her pussy.

She tasted like chlorine and salt and a tang that was all her, all Rachel, all sex. He took his time, as much as he possibly could, considering the way she used her heels and thighs to lock his lips at her entrance. It was the only place he wanted to be.

Her clit swelled in his mouth. Each flick of his tongue, each little suck and graze of his teeth, drove her higher. She'd given up on words, nothing so coherent as a full syllable echoed around them as he focused, intent, on the quivering message of her every movement.

As soon as she shook her way through orgasm, he moved. The buoyancy of the water, the propulsive need of his throbbing dick, the way the dappled sunshine painted patterns he needed to touch all over her body: something or everything made him urgent. Hard and fast and urgent.

The condom was on the lounger and he swiped a towel across his face and hands and cock so he could roll it on with maybe a tenth of the urgency he felt. She'd followed him, pressed him into the cushion, and straddled him. "Fuck. Rachel."

"That's the general idea." Laconic words, but she fitted them together and slid down with all the heat and haste he needed. One thrust, his body and hers working together, and he was in, deep, planted inside her warmth. He braced his feet on the ground and pushed and pulsed and pulled her hips to match their rhythms.

"Too much?"

"Hell no. Faster is good. Faster, harder."

"Rachel." He couldn't get enough of the way she leaned over him, the way she palmed her breasts, the way she panted.

"More."

"Serious?"

She toyed with her nipples, groaned. He pressed a thumb to her clit, and she moved faster, wilder. Louder.

"Serious, then." And then his hands gripped her ass and she

braced against his chest and he drove and dove and plunged and thrust and his cock felt so right inside her, and somewhere in there he noticed the tight pulses of her orgasm but he was so lost in the wonder and primal joy of his own he could only moan, and come, and shudder alongside her.

So, the sex was great.

It wasn't on her list, but odds were everyone took that as given. And she'd long since confirmed to the gals that Theo matched several of her rolls from Serena's romance prediction game. So no one would be surprised by how he met every promise of the 'sexy-times' column's lightning bolt icon.

But it was her list, and she could put anything she craved on it. And 'great sex' didn't beat out 'good with kids' or even 'honest about emotions' but it was up there. Because she craved it, and because she deserved it. Deserved a partner who cared about her desires. Who was passionate about their physical connection, and who responded to her overtures, and who was damn adept at it. She deserved all that.

Deserved ... him. Theo. And sure, she was supposed to make a general list, not just name good things about him. She had an idea there were one or two things about him she would never have searched out in a partner. But no dwelling on potential faults when they were collapsed together in the warmth of summer sun and post-orgasmic endorphins.

The day flew forward in delightful ways. He'd put together a spread of hummus and salads and his homemade pitas for lunch, which they followed up with a movie cuddled together on the couch. Making out, talking about life, bragging about their children, a little complaining about their children, making out some more. Narrowly avoiding a permanent rift over pizza toppings before going out for tacos and dancing instead. Rumpling up his cool crisp sheets, and drifting off to sleep as his fingers drifted up and down her spine.

And waking him up later, to find him all too ready to indulge her desires.

So. Yes. Great sex was staying on her list.

CHAPTER TWENTY-FIVE

SHE DROVE from Theo's place to the boutique. Serena and Natalie were there, but no Gillian.

"Are we surprised?" Serena asked, trailing a hand along the long row of plastic-encased bridal gowns. Other than for lip color, Gill was not much of a shopper.

"More surprised that you picked this place. I thought we'd be tailoring something from a thrift shop and we would all think you were way off-base but you'd turn up looking like a goddess in some transformed orange polyester jumpsuit."

At the look Natalie shot her, Rachel said, "What? You know it's true."

Serena's shoulders shook. "Okay, not polyester, if I can help it. But, yeah. All this is much more your kind of thing, Nat."

They caught Natalie admiring her engagement ring. Again. And she blushed. Again.

"Oh, you're too easy to bait." Rachel turned to Serena. "So, is this a stealth mission to find Nat's dress instead of yours? Or did Dillon talk you into a big elegant formal affair?"

She snort-laughed. It was not elegant. "Hardly. I promised my mom I would look at traditional dresses before going my own way."

Rachel's forehead creased. "Your mom expects you to get all poufed out in white?" Caricatures of aging hippies were based on Serena's mother.

She shook her head, rueful. "I know, right? It's because of Ridley and Neera's wedding." Serena's stepbrother had married not long before, and Serena claimed she'd heard every story about the event at least five times. "She wasn't allowed to do anything to help, so now she's devouring bridal magazines and coming up with all these tradition-bound schemes we have to keep shooting down."

The shop assistant showed them to a seating area when Serena refused to make any preliminary decisions. "I'm trying on two dresses, so I can show her the pictures, and I'm making Gillian help because that's her punishment for showing up late."

"Okay then, someone distract me from all the pretty lace," Natalie said. "I promised *my* mom I'd dress shop with her, and this place is seriously tempting to me to break my word."

"Go for it. You can tell her how Serena is thwarting Becky's mother-of-the-bride fantasies, and she'll forgive you anything."

"I would, but I also promised Evan's mom—remember Marisa?—she could join in the dress hunt. I have to have someone there who won't tell me a princess dress is magnifying my hips. Mom already agreed to that, and I don't want to push her too far."

Rachel nodded, then shook her head.

"What?"

"No, your reasons make sense. But talking about Marisa reminded me of my mother-in-law problems. Ex-mother-in-law problems."

Serena extended a water bottle across the gilt mirrored table. "This sounds distracting. What did Depy do now?"

She tucked the bottle against her leg and pulled out her phone. "Okay, you know about name days, right?"

Natalie glanced towards Serena, then back at her. "Um, maybe?"

"Basically, if you're named after a saint, that saint's name day is a big damn deal. Party time, everyone gathers round. No cake, but for Depy, anyway, it's bigger than her birthday."

"I'm sensing this is where the problem comes in," Natalie said.

"You're a regular Phryne Fisher. Of course that's the problem. Despoina's name day is August fifteenth, and that's the week I'm taking Hannah to visit my family. And I'm already on her shit list because Hannah's name day is Thursday and I won't let Sergei take her."

"Did he put it on the schedule?"

She rolled her eyes at Serena. "Ha. Anyway, he's doing some nonsense at Elixir on Wednesday instead, but that hasn't stopped Depy moaning about it. Or about August."

"So, she wants you to cancel your trip?" Serena asked.

"Her first suggestion was that I leave Hannah with her all week, and visit Blythe and my folks on my own. She tried to make out like I would have all this great freedom to stay up all night gabbing with my sister. As if she doesn't know that perfect Blythe only breaks her early to bed routine if she's on an overnight rotation."

"One of these days that woman will have a problem she can't solve with seven solid hours of sleep at night." Serena rolled her eyes.

She scraped her hair back from her forehead. "Mom and Dad will be there to help stop whatever tries to bring her down."

"Never mind Blythe. What did Depy do?" Natalie asked. She nabbed Rachel's phone. "Can I?"

She nodded. "Read the two newest emails."

Nat tapped in Rachel's passcode and began scrolling. After a bit, she passed the phone to Serena, asking, "What's it called when you combine blackmail with emotional blackmail? There should be a special term for that. Remind me to ask Gillian when she gets here."

Serena snorted again, more elegantly now that she was expressing disdain instead of humor. She must have gotten to the part about Rachel's job. When she'd refused to switch her vacation dates, Depy had phoned her boss to check Rachel's story. Rachel's boss had refused to confirm or deny her ability to change her schedule, which offended Depy but didn't stop her campaign.

Her current offer was to pay to fly Hannah to Colorado after the party. Alone. 'She takes her dose of cold medicine before take-off, she will sleep the whole flight, she'll never notice a thing.'

Rachel had paced the perimeter of her apartment fourteen times upon reading that, working up the calm with which to ask Hannah questions about her bedtime routine at Daddy's house. Two-year-olds were not reliable witnesses. Even leading up to the topic—'what color is your Daddy house toothbrush?' 'do you want to pick another animal friend to sleep at the Daddy house with you?' 'does Yia Yia read you bedtime books sometimes?'—she didn't expect an easy yes or no to 'do your father and grand-mother make you drink cough syrup so you're easier to get to sleep?'

In the end, she only learned the toothbrush color. Though Hannah might have been thinking of her purple toothbrush in their own bathroom. She might never have noticed toothbrushes came in any other color, since Rachel tended to buy purple ones for them both.

"This is ridiculous." Serena handed back the phone. "I get she cares a lot about her party, but if she wanted to be sure Hannah was at it, she should have checked the custody schedule."

"If we can, she can," Natalie agreed.

Rachel stashed the phone and locked together her fidgeting fingers. "I know it's ridiculous. But how should I respond?"

Natalie was scrolling through her own calendar. "If you want, I could fly up with Hannah, so she isn't taking the trip on her own. I can even hang out a while and drive back with y'all. Depy would have to pay for my flight, though."

"That's also ridiculous," Serena said. "If anything, Depy can pay to fly them both round trip, then Rach can save herself the long drive and still have almost as much time with her family."

Natalie had opened her browser and was checking flight schedules. "Tell her she'll also have to rent you a car."

"And a car seat," added Serena, waving off the boutique assistant who was trying to lure her to a rolling rack of dresses she'd selected.

"Right, and a car seat. Tell her it will be a thousand dollars. Then she can decide if it's worth a grand to her to have Hannah fall asleep at the table halfway through her party."

Rachel was circling the heel of her hand against her heart when Gillian plopped down beside her. "What are we talking about?"

"Oh, hey, you made it. What's the word for blackmail on top of emotional blackmail?" Natalie asked.

"What's the context?"

"Depy wants to change the schedule for Rachel's vacation."

Gillian's snort was more eloquent than anything Serena could manage. "In that case ... blacklighting."

Natalie leaned across to grab Gill's knee. "You're the best."

"Right back at you." She turned to Serena. "What dress did you choose?"

"Nope. Nice try. Haven't even looked at them. I waited until you got here."

"You're the worst."

"Maybe, but it gave us a chance to brainstorm ways to get Depy off Rachel's back."

Pivoting towards Rachel, Gill arched her brows. "And what prompted us to brainstorm that?"

She explained about name days and the options that would let Hannah attend the party.

"Three questions," Gillian said, once her narrowed eyes silenced Rachel's justification of their thinking.

"Okay?"

"Did Sergei ever make up his child support?"

Across from them, both Serena and Natalie hitched themselves forward on the chaise cushions. Rachel applied the heel of her hand to her stomach. "The ombudsman should be giving me a case update next week. It's clear-cut, so I expect the order will go through to increase his withholding by twenty percent until he's caught up."

"And never mind that while he wasn't paying you because he wasn't working somewhere they could send a court order, he bought that obnoxious vehicle?" Gillian held up a hand. "That's not my next question, it was rhetorical. Next question: is Despoina Matsouka the pattern of motherhood you want to copy and model for your daughter?"

"God, of course not. I mean, at least she loves Hannah. And Sergei. But she helped turn him into the narcissistic ass to begin with."

"Okay, then. Why the hell are you considering any change to a plan you made with the full forces of the law, morality, and common courtesy behind you?"

The bridal salon likely wouldn't approve of her hugging her legs to her chest, since it meant pressing her tennis shoes into the brocade couch.

Gillian slipped a palm onto her back and rubbed gently. "That wasn't a rhetorical question, Rach. Why are you defaulting to accommodating them? They don't get to change your plans. If Sergei wanted Hannah that weekend, he had the option of requesting it as part of his summer custody. Maybe he'll remember to do so for next year, and maybe he never will, and so what? So what if Depy is mad about it? So what if Sergei blusters? It's not your problem, Rach. It certainly doesn't matter one way or another to Hannah. You don't change your plans. Even if she charters a plane for you. He can learn how to follow the rules, and they can both back off instead of asking you to bend over backwards."

Rachel wasn't having any success putting her words together to answer, so she hugged her knees tighter and let Gillian's touch soothe down her breathing.

Across from them, Natalie peered at Rachel through a cage of fingers over her face. "I did it again. Oh, crap. I'm sorry, Rachel. I always try to make his crap make sense. I treat him like he has the right to anything he wants, no matter what."

She shrugged. Gillian's palm shifted over her shoulder blade. She was still not used to being touched by hands so much larger than Hannah's. Not that she would trade her girl's cling-strong grasp for any amount of adult contact, from her friends or from Theo or from anyone. Good for Natalie and for Serena that they'd found men to spend forever with; good for Gillian that she filled her spare time with anyone who attracted her. She had Hannah, which made even dealing with Sergei and Depy for the rest of her life tolerable. "You're not the only one, Natalie. Don't kick at your heart over it. You were carefully taught, and I was caught up in a gaslighting net so secure it will take me years to remember that Gillian is right."

"Or you could BCC me on every email exchange with Sergei and Depy," Gill said. She knocked the water bottle against the back of Rachel's hand, so she accepted it and took a swig.

"That wouldn't annoy either one of you," Serena said, snorting in derision again.

"Judgmental much? You want me to leave?" Gill asked, a little too eagerly.

"Try it. I was going to model two dresses then take you all out for tacos, but if I have to, I'll make Rach and Natalie hold you down while we take pictures of me in every single gown on that rack." Serena nodded at the sales associate, who was floating their way with a champagne-ivory gown draped in her arms.

Rachel scooted over, bumping her hip into Gill's. Together they made room for Natalie to sit on the sofa with them as Serena pulled the changing room curtain closed. Despite the bride-to-be's threats, Gillian and Natalie were the bulwarks on either side of her, keeping her grounded in the moment and fortifying her for the next—the final—email to Depy and Sergei about her refusal to change anything.

CHAPTER TWENTY-SIX

IT BORDERED ON OBNOXIOUS, the cheerful mood he'd slipped into over the weekend. Rachel in that bikini ... Rachel out of that bikini. Everything after, and then the pivot to settling Andres in at his place. Sweaty soccer gear everywhere and a constant stack of dishes that didn't add up, given his son's small size. He'd woken up smiling five mornings in a row, and maybe he should examine if that meant something about the rest of his life. But he refused. The everyday joy felt too precious to ruin with scrutiny.

Or even by Sergei rapping on the frame of their office door.

"You'll stop by tonight, yeah?"

Most upbeat Sergei had been with him since he dropped the news about dating Rachel. Maybe his happiness was contagious. "Tonight? You're not on the schedule, are you?"

"No, I put Marti on duty like you're always suggesting. But we're having a name day dinner for my Hannah Iliana. Six o'clock." Serg tipped his head towards the back tables, where there was enough room to shove tables together for groups and still navigate to serve everyone.

He glanced at his phone, like that mattered. "Got to pick up Andres from camp by five." And they'd planned to kayak before dinner, if his son wasn't too wiped out. And if the afternoon's rain hadn't brewed up a bayou full of bugs.

Sergei leaned down to kiss Depy, who'd barreled her way into the employees-only area with a couple of bags that looked to be full of nothing but pink glitter. "Hey, Mom. I'm telling Theo to bring his son tonight. Nice to have more kids around for it."

Ah, of course. It wasn't a child's name day party if the only guests were her father and grandmother. He could imagine the lengths his uncles would go to in Sergei's place, searching for anyone under ten to fill out the ranks.

Well, fine. The guy wanted to look like super-dad? Let him earn his faux-heroic pose. "Nice of you to have the party. Building tradition for Hannah and all."

"Her real day's tomorrow, but I do what I can." The false modesty in his words intertwined with the false aggrieved tone.

Theo ignored all he knew about their custody schedule and played along. "Andres and I will be happy to stop in. Can't think of the last time we went to someone's name day outside the family. You want the truth? I take pride in being a parent who meets his obligations, child support and all the driving up to Fort Worth. It's important, you know? Couldn't call myself a real man if I didn't care about it all. But I'm glad you're reminding me about the intangible influences I have on my son. Culture, guidance, shared experiences. I'm going to think a lot about it over the next few weeks with him."

Sergei narrowed his eyes all shifty while he talked about responsibility, but he also puffed out at the compliment. Theo clapped the other man on the shoulder, raised a hand to farewell Depy, and headed out. If he wasn't mistaken, he'd couched his barb in terms Sergei could relate to. If it did Rachel and Hannah any good at all, he'd count it as a win.

THEY'D HUNG AN ACTUAL BANNER. At least it read 'congratulations' instead of anything custom, but the table was overloaded with bling. A neon pink tablecloth over the normally bare wood, party hats with metallic foil fringe, a cake covered in giant frosting flowers.

It was clear her daughter would be too keyed up to go to sleep well that night.

She couldn't even exchange wry looks with Theo, because he was off picking up his son from soccer camp. So she waded right into the fray, letting Hannah's short steps lead the way. Depy swept her up, full of kisses and repeats of 'Hronia Polla!' and carrying her around the whole table to show her the various decorations. Her ex, of course, was nowhere in sight. Well, whatever. Rachel set the diaper bag on the table between the cake and a small—thank goodness—pile of presents. Maybe they'd take everything back to Sergei's and she wouldn't be the one checking for choking hazards or finding space to store yet another ugly outfit.

Hannah and Depy, absorbed in each other, didn't glance her way. Fine. She was learning to make drop-off smoother, and if that meant walking away to relish her hours of running childfree errands, so be it.

When she returned, the party was still in full swing. Hannah's frosting-smeared fingers gripped a stuffed slice of pizza with pepperoni eyes. She waved it at a boy who animated a plush hamburger in her direction. Its eyes were pickles, which struck Rachel as a bad idea for anyone who didn't like soggy buns. Before she got over there, Sergei drew her aside.

"Your receipt."

"Sor—" She cut herself off. No apologizing to the rotten ex. "What?"

He handed her a piece of paper. "Your precious arrears. It'll take a few days to show up through the system, so I printed a confirmation."

She didn't—couldn't—say anything. Kept reading and rereading the details, in case her eyes were lying to her about the contents.

"You can tell the ombudsman to back off now, and all your

other bulldogs, too. No need to keep begging people to fight your battles for you, Rachel. You've got what you wanted. And look at you. Can't even say thank you."

Bulldogs? She couldn't figure out his nonsense, but one thing was clear as the sky after a spring rain: he'd paid something like seven months worth of back child support, in one click of a button. Astounding. Also, he was speaking like an ass to her again, which tracked, in her experience, to his guilty conscience. Maybe Depy found out about the arrears? Would Theo have told her? Would Theo have spoken to him? Because really, who was Sergei more likely to call a bulldog, his boss or his mom?

And if Theo interfered in her business ... if he stuck his nose in, and the result was Sergei sneering at her.... *Ugh*. At least directing her anger at her ex made sense. She wasn't letting him speak to her that way, not when she's have to turn around and tell the gals about it and explain why she wasn't capable in the moment of hearing their virtual cheerleading of her retorts. So she looked straight into his smug-ass face and said, "Thank you? No. I'm not thanking you for saving yourself some months of interest on a debt you made a game of incurring over the whole course of Hannah's life. Say goodbye to her if you intend to; your time tonight is over."

She pivoted away. No giving the moldering pillowcase stuffed with fresh maggots a chance to respond. He sputtered some nonsense but she walked off, because damn it, she could. Her life, her choices. Her right to confine interactions with Sergei to a narrow, child-focused space. Her right to insist on her lawful, court-decreed arrangements. Her right to banish his snide voice when it tried to weasel through her mind.

And Theo. The apparent bulldog in this story. Sitting there, crouched on the ground with the kids, giving her such a smile. Such a look as he helped Hannah play with his son—of course the hamburger-wielding one was Andres, she could see that now they were side by side. Never mind any opinions she ever had about introducing their children to each other, never mind running this encounter past her first, never mind his attending a damn party with Sergei and Depy and everyone else the Matsoukas drummed up to turn this into a whole thing. Like Hannah had the first clue about name days.

Not to give Sergei any wriggle room, but maybe bulldog wasn't the worst name to call Theo. Leaping in anywhere he wanted, stubborn enough to stick his nose in her business and in her life and in her daughter's life, like he'd never once heard her request to slow down.

"Hey there, Rach."

She reached down for Hannah, who dropped the frosting-spackled plush pizza and started babbling about cars and pink hats.

Theo, intent as always on his own thing, stood up and lifted his son. "This is my Andres. Andres, here's Hannah's mom, Rachel. I wanted you to meet her."

And she might be irate, but it wasn't the child's fault. Rachel held out a fist for him to bump. "Hi, there. I hear you're a good midfielder. Are you liking soccer camp so far?"

He nodded but wasn't about to talk, it seemed. Fine with her. Nothing against the child, but she needed to get far away from everything to do with Elixir, and fast. She located the diaper bag, checked Hannah didn't need a potty run before they left, and tried to give a general wave to encompass everyone. Her luck wasn't quite that favorable, though. Depy swooped in for too many of her musty kisses, and by the time Rachel disentangled them, Theo and Andres were lying in wait on the path to the door.

"Night, y'all," she tried. All friendly and everything.

It didn't quite work. "Walk you out?"

She squeezed closed her eyes for the merest sliver of a breath, then nodded. "Great."

Andres still carried the hamburger, so she thanked a luck-filled star for one item she wouldn't find stuffed into Hannah's bag some day.

"Sergei asked us to stop in."

"I guessed."

"Course. Just—okay, not now." He glanced at the kids. "I'll owe you an explanation and apology, when we're clear. How was your evening?"

"Good, fine. Checked a lot off my list." She opened the car door. He stepped back to give her room to help Hannah to her car seat. His own car was across the lot, but he didn't move towards it, even when she finished with the buckling and emerged to open her own door.

"So, we're off home." The dark didn't hide that open brightness of his expression.

She sighed. "Okay. See you later. Nice meeting you, Andres."

Theo tilted his head. Leaned in a moment, but backed off when she didn't meet him for a kiss. Glanced down at his son. "I'll call you later?"

She shrugged, because really? She needed out of Elixir and he could obviously sense it. So why couldn't he let her leave? "She'll be wound up from the party. I'll end up putting her in bed with me and we'll fall asleep over story time."

His frown brought out furrows in his forehead. Such a bulldog. But at last he backed up a couple of steps.

Was she giving in to his manipulative puppy eyes, or was her fondness for him nibbling away at her pissy mood? Either way, she caught his forearm under her palm. "If I don't conk out with her, I'll text you, okay?"

He ducked forward for a quick kiss. Waving his and Andres's joined hands, he said goodnight and the two of them took off across the parking lot. As she backed out, she caught a glimpse of Sergei in the bar's doorway, arms crossed over his chest, watching her like the creep he was. Hurling all the rest of her ire his way, she tuned in to the song Hannah was chanting and imagined coloring in the rest of her flower garden next time they got out the art supplies. Thanks to the festive explosion inside Elixir, she decided to ban pink from every single leaf or petal on the page.

CHAPTER TWENTY-SEVEN

'Happy name day to Hannah. May she be healthy and bring happiness to your life!'

He reread his message, then closed the text screen without sending. Rachel never called after the party, which he admitted made sense. After he got Andres home and cleaned up, he copied her plans and drifted off to sleep while reading with him. The queen bed in his son's room had been a good investment. He'd picked it so he could have his parents stay with him when they came to Houston, but patted his earlier self on his well-aligned back for the choice. He could start awake at midnight and stagger to his own bed without the aches he used to get from falling asleep on the floor during stories, back when Andres was in a toddler bed.

The tossing and turning he did after flopping across his mattress, he didn't have anyone to thank for. He drifted in and out of sleep wondering if Rachel was irritated with him, and if so, was it for introducing the kids or something more, and also what to do about it.

Thirty-six years old and his emotional life tumbled him into a whirlpool like he was sixteen. At one point overnight he calculated the number of days since he and Rachel met. He hoped the number-work would lull him back to sleep. Instead the total—sixty —spun him into soul-searching about the intensity of his feelings. It wasn't just that he'd dated women before for a couple of months without the same sense of connection and belonging. He'd fallen deep before. He'd fallen fast before. He'd built what he thought was permanence and security before.

Combining all of that smashed everything into one big ball of jaw-tightening, stomach-lurching confusion.

Because he was all in. Had been since ... when? Since she let him in on the close-held secret of her address? Since kayaking and popsicles? Since being confronted in a rain-damp parking lot by a fury wearing three pairs of cheap sunglasses?

Whenever it was, it stuck claws into him, and that was fine. They weren't sharp claws. They anchored him in a place he was happy to be. But it wasn't the same for Rachel. Either she wasn't hooked, or it made her feel pierced in uncomfortable ways, or she resented claws in general.

Which left him sure of himself, very unsure of her, and without tons of options for bridging that divide. But he did wish wonderful things for Hannah, so before heading to wake Andres, he sent the name day text, and assurance that he hadn't said anything to either child about their relationship. She might appreciate it, or she might be irate, but he couldn't spend another night tossing and mulling over her silence.

She had tons of crap on her mind. It was her refrain, her excuse, for too many days on end. So much crap, she justified not making time for in depth texting or calls or dragging Hannah to spend some awkward hours trying to entertain her and Andres together while she and Theo acted like things weren't strained between them.

Besides, it was too hot for the zoo. And his next suggestion, the Children's Museum, was extra crowded on summer weekends.

And the water park meant a whole rigmarole with swim diapers and Hannah's newfound love of running to the toilet every thirty-five minutes in hopes of praise and rewards. So it made sense to put Theo off. More sense than his argument that it was the only full weekend they both had custody and were in town at the same time.

If they were going to be in some kind of long-term relationship —and in her mind that was still an 'if' no matter his current hold over her—they could force the kids to make friends later. Their Christmas custody arrangements aligned. If they managed to last another five months they could all decorate cookies and visit Santa together.

One more unnecessary weight on her mind was the gut-twist yanking her headlong towards the image of hanging stocking with Hannah and Theo and Andres. Of taking over the vast expanse of his kitchen island with spices and flour and sprinkles and racks of her grandmother's pfeffernüsse cookies. Of everyone snuggling up with hot cider and holiday movies.

Far as she knew, they didn't even celebrate with Santa. And if Andres was going to spoil Hannah's Christmas fun by shattering her childhood illusions, there wasn't a future for any of them anyway.

She snorted, the picture of elegance walking down the hospital corridors. Classy, on top of being full of dismal fantasies about the future. Catastrophic thinking. Turning every potential good into a disaster. A fine way to protect herself. And a grim way to proceed with a relationship.

Her gut tugged at her more, so she texted Theo suggesting they get coffee later in the week, after she sent Hannah for the two weeks with Sergei. All those nights alone groaned and stretched ahead of her. She sent a second text saying she'd be happy to join him and Andres for dinner some night, if he wanted to invite her over.

Pulling out her phone to text made it impossible to ignore the notification she'd known was burning its message at her all morning. Squeezing her eyes closed after reading it didn't make it go away, either. She'd set it up after her ridiculous gut threw a strange idea at her on Thursday evening. She'd abruptly stopped coloring in her flower garden and stared off long enough for Hannah to tug the purple crayon from her unresisting fingers. She'd shoved the thought away over and over during the weekend. Gone back to her colorful garden drawing. Given herself the deadline of Monday at work to deal with it. And she had a free quarter hour before her next appointment.

So. Fine. Dealing with it would mean one thing off her mind.

Unless it turned out wrong.

Or right.

Her gut was far too twisty for her to figure out which answer she wanted. Theo did that to her. Loused up her instincts. Made it impossible to know if she'd ever thought straight one minute of her entire life. Or if every instinct was wrong until they met, and somehow now they were all right, and she didn't know how to operate with a gut she could trust. Left her floundering to take the next step, in case the directions were reversed or her path was down uncharted, pit-filled roads.

And this next step.... She sighed. Time to get on with it.

She made her way to the pharmacy. And then the restroom. Locked herself in the stall. Peed. Waited. Waited more, ignoring her gut and the text message buzzing in her pocket and the gossip happening by the sinks. When she couldn't bear more waiting, she looked. And the grin and the trembling arms and the soft buzzing in her head all told her something she'd for sure told her gut to not go getting excited about.

It didn't fit in the plans she narrated about her life.

It disrupted the thousand and six precarious pillars keeping her world semi-stable.

It didn't make one lick of sense.

Despite all that, despite all reason, there were millions of bouncing bits of spinning whirligigs within her, each and every one of them thrilled to find out she was pregnant.

CHAPTER TWENTY-EIGHT

WHEN THEY FOUND out she was expecting Hannah, Aunt Johnston was the first person she called. She'd said, "Gracious, cricket, I didn't know you all were planning to have children." It might have sounded like surprised delight to anyone else's ears, but Rachel had no difficulty reading the censure behind it. Aunt never liked Sergei, but it took her mild comment to set Rachel's wheels spinning about all her aunt's reasons for regarding him with suspicion and caution.

She didn't end her marriage cause her aunt told her to. But her aunt's sad supportiveness somehow clicked a shit-ton of factors into focus, so by the time she announced her pregnancy to her gals, she was also announcing her separation.

Not that she was ready to announce anything, beyond making an appointment with her ob/gyn. She had all the same crap on her mind, plus a new overwhelming fact to wrestle into place in her life. Or to jettison, because abortion made more logistical sense. If she channeled Serena and drew up a pro/con list, she'd need three times the room to list all the negatives of adding another child to her life the way it was.

As if the length of a list meant it was her own right choice.

Another call to make, canceling the trip to see some couple's for-sale car. She'd stick with her old sedan, slow starts and occasional engine knocks notwithstanding. A new air filter and, fingers crossed, her car would get her and Hannah and anyone else she was carrying where they needed to go. She had other expenses now that took precedence.

There. One decision made; one piece of crap off her mind. Only a million or more other things left. Theo replied and they arranged to meet right after she dropped Hannah off for two weeks of what was looking like way too much time to consider catastrophe scenarios.

Like what kind of nonsense was it to think of having yet another child while essentially single? *Who are you trying to prove something to? You think your parents will finally be impressed with you?* snarked the Sergei voice in her mind. *Are you incapable of learning from your past? Your sister is doing it the right way—successful career, strong marriage, nice house, and then baby. No wonder they're always choosing her over you, the way you flounder and panic your way through life. And this time, you won't have Depy to take you in.* Not that she wanted Depy as her last resort, but snide Sergei was right, it wasn't an option this time. If this time was going to happen. If everything was okay from the medical front. Because who even knew if there were consequences from that morning-after pill that didn't seem to have worked.

And okay, Theo was devoted to his son, but that didn't mean he wanted more kids. If he turned truculent about the baby it was sure to cause all kinds of ructions for her little family. She worked like hell to be a good mama, but in the long term, how would her children process having two different but equally reluctant fathers? Or what if Theo was all-in on fathering his own child, and Hannah resented her mother, her father, her sibling, and her sibling's dad for the slight? Living with that every day would sour her on relationships. Maybe they should move to Plainview after all. She could stay with Aunt Johnston and take the job with loathsome Brent Berg, and cross her fingers it wouldn't wither her soul. At least that way their fathers' neglect wouldn't cause as much impact on her children. They could bond over resentment that she'd taken them away from their dads. Hadn't she always clutched deep the dream of giving Hannah a sibling to bond with the way Rachel and Blythe never had? If the only way to ensure her children loved each other was to make herself the common enemy, so be it.

The con list was a super cell tornado ripping through every coherent thought every minute she tried to ignore it and get on with her job.

But the pro list was a thrumming neon glow warming her heart with each racing beat, so bright it made the cons waver and whirl out of focus.

Maybe by the time her next Sunday call with Aunt Johnston rolled around, she'd have the slightest of clues if she wanted to break her news.

Depy waited on her stoop for them, like clockwork. "My little princess!"

Seemed like a sweet greeting but it always grated on Rachel's ears. She released Hannah's hand so she could run across the lawn and into her grandmother's arms. By the time she'd unloaded the suitcase from the trunk, they'd disappeared inside, leaving the door open the merest crack.

Fine with her. She'd let herself in all the time until Hannah was ten months old. Hadn't given back her key when they moved to the apartment, either. If any of the Matsoukas were bothered by that, they could ask for it back. Or change the locks. She let herself in, tucked Effie into the bed in Hannah's room, stacked the reward chart and stickers on the bathroom counter, and taped her updated emergency and medical contact list to the fridge. She found Depy and Hannah in the backyard, tumbling a big orange ball between them. Some angle of their smiling profiles created the kind of echo someone who loved them both would enjoy comparing. Rachel wasn't that person. Every curve of her baby's face was perfection, but in her current mood she didn't adore the reminder of all the ways Hannah wasn't only Rachel's to raise.

Fourteen nights apart. Maybe when Hannah was four or five. Or seven. Maybe then two weeks apart wouldn't be so hard on them both. Maybe then it would make sense to her bright little brain. No matter how she tried to explain it, her girl was only two. She hadn't developed a concept of time anywhere near sophisticated enough to understand not returning to Mama for two weeks.

But instead of even pretending to understand and give her space for a long goodbye, Depy placed herself between mother and child to have her say. "You're spending too much time with that Theo. Hannah will get confused."

"I'm not." Too late to bite back her words. She aimed to reframe. "I'm free to spend what time I want with who I want."

"She'll wonder why you're so nice to that high-and-mighty boss man and so mean to her father."

"She'll do no such thing. I'm always polite to Sergei." To his face. "And she knows the difference between them."

"He's got his own child. He should leave mine alone."

Oh, too far, Despoina Matsouka. "Her elephant is on the bed. She's trying to cut out a nap, so you might have some fusses late mornings. Why don't you go see if there's anything else you need before I go?"

With that, she swerved around Depy and intercepted Hannah for a series of truly epic hugs that, sweet as they were, would barely sustain her for the all the days and nights until they got to snuggle again.

HE GOT to the coffee shop first. Not because of over-eagerness. It just worked out that way because drop-off for soccer camp didn't take as long as expected. Andres was full of thrills about the mini-tournament they were running. His team was in the quarterfinals.

Of course, so were all the other teams—it was a camp full of five to seven year olds, but try telling them it wasn't a competitive environment. The coaches managed the teams so every one of them made it to a final match.

Some of his son's buzz infected him as he awaited his latte. He kept on grinning. Which he'd been doing since Rachel texted earlier in the week. Feeling favored by Eros. And Hestia, for that matter. Planning nice meals with the three of them followed by nice private moments after tucking Andres in. The daydreams distracted him; he was surprised when she fetched up beside him.

"Hey!"

"Hey, yourself." She leaned up for a kiss, but kept it appropriate to their locale, more's the pity.

"Coffee?" He linked their hands to lead her back to the line.

"Yeah. Well, no."

He laughed. And okay, no one really would find it a funny comment, but that buzz had trebled as soon as he touched her. The laugh was like steam billowing through the safety valve to keep his boiler pressurized. "Okay. You want something, though? The coffee shop was your idea."

"Don't be funny. Yes. Tea. Mint tea. I need to settle my nerves after dealing with Depy."

He hugged her tight, and never mind the appropriateness. "Sorry. It was hard to leave Hannah, I'm guessing?"

"The worst." She rubbed at her midsection once he stepped back. It was such a wrench, the long periods separated from the kids. He'd adapted over the years, but this was the longest time Sergei had ever had custody. No wonder Rachel was a pile of nerves. He listened to all the drop-off details while their drinks were prepared. At their table, her fingers clung to the hot mug like it wasn't going to be another hundred-degree summer day.

"You still up to come for dinner this weekend? How about Friday?"

His attempt at distraction did nothing to restore color to her pale face. "Um, not Friday, no. I think Saturday would be better. Anyway, Andres will be wiped out after his last day of soccer."

Yeah, he'd kind of counted on that. Seemed like Hestia was raking up more points than Eros, that slacker. Well, better to have one god favoring him than none. "Saturday works. Lasagna okay? It's one of his favorites."

"One thing we have in common already." She smiled in a way that warmed him from the inside out, so his latte was redundant.

"Excellent. I mean, I'm biased, but I think he's great company. Especially if you have even the slightest bit of interest in Pokémon."

"Can't say I've given it any thought before now. I'll come prepared to learn. And I'll bring dessert."

He palmed his heart and swayed back. "I didn't know you could be so cruel. Are my pies so abhorrent to you? You're sick of my baking already?"

"Goof. You bake all the time. I thought you might want a break."

"It's as if you don't know me at all."

She dimmed. "I don't, do I? I mean, don't look all bulldog like that. I like you. Maybe a silly amount. But there's so much.... Unknowns. For both of us. For all that seems comfortable, dating you, I know we haven't gotten much below the surface. Yet. It's a little strange to think about, is all."

His Adam's apple scraped a line down the inside of his throat. "Strange bad?"

She shook her head, quick like she meant *no* for sure. But it took her a moment of tea-contemplation before she clarified. "Not bad. I meant it, how I feel about you. Then things happen. Like seeing you playing with Hannah and Andres together, that jolt of confusion. I know you were careful to not say anything to them, but the image added all this sudden weight to my mind. Or like Sergei paying his arrears, and knowing you had something to do with that. And it's good to get the money. Obviously. But still unexpected. And strange. And I'm not sure how it fits, and if I want it to fit, and if you...."

He waited, hand still placed to contain the thrumming of his heart. His whole self leaned in to catch the meaning of her words, her body language. Any further definition of how she felt about him. Not that it had to be quantifiable. He could live without quantifiable. After too much silence, he filled the space between them with, "Sergei paid his arrears?"

Piercing blue eyes. Turned out they were a weakness of his. "I thought you forced him."

"No. Of course not. I mean, yes. I mentioned it to him. Not, in so many words, though. All I did was explain that name days were important to me, but so were other parts of fatherhood, like paying my child support."

"Hmm. Any chance Depy overheard that?"

Now he was the one contemplating his drink. He shrugged. "I know it wasn't my place to say anything. I don't mean to push your boundaries so often."

Her palm, warm against his cheek. Wrapping to the nape of his neck, tugging so their foreheads met across the table. "I know. I mean, I think I know. It's a balance. And if we have a future—"

"Wait, 'if'?" He pulled back. No containing his racing heart now. "Shit. Interrupting. But, Rachel, I'm here, I'm in this. You called us dating, just now, and that's not all it is for me. I'm thinking of you as a relationship. I know it's tough, for both of us; we have to be careful for Andres and Hannah's sakes. Protect them first. That's a given. And I know I've screwed up interfering with your child support, that's not my business. Probably screwing up now being all intense about my feelings. I'll hush now. Please go on with what you were saying."

But she didn't.

His pushiness once again worked against him. Instead of talking about the future, she gave him a wry shake of her head and suggested they table the relationship talk for a while. He complied. Of course he complied. The woman had depths he had yet to probe—not in that way, Eros the Currently Useless—and some of those depths were treacherous. The best way to plumb them was with her as his willing guide, and that, in turn, meant accepting she knew what pace was best.

So he skimmed the surface, asking about her work drama and showing off the latest pics of his sister Helen's twins and taking her suggestion for the best ice cream shop to visit when he and Andres were at the beach.

As he walked her to her car, she squeezed his hand and said, "You are definitely great, Theo."

"Serious?"

"So serious."

"Well, thanks. And you definitely are, too."

And the kiss they shared promised to explore some future depths that both Hestia and Eros would appreciate.

CHAPTER TWENTY-NINE

IT WASN'T OKAY, by some measures, to run off without spilling the pregnancy news. But the words refused to bubble up, so fine. She'd go to the doctor Friday, take the night to absorb whatever info that gave her, and try again after their dinner Saturday.

Super reasonable plan. Didn't make her twitch with regret at all. Or guilt. Not one negative feeling. Certainly not by the time she was gowned and sitting on the paper sheet of the exam table, legs dangling. Toes curling in her socks, then flexing while she pushed out a breath that did not calm her down. Proof: the way she startled when at the knock on the door.

"So, yes." Dr. Saavedra raised her eyebrows, watching for her reaction to this confirmation.

Rachel didn't know it herself. Relief? Terror? Her toes were still curled, for whatever that was worth. "So."

"Do you need a moment? Or should I launch in with calendars and blood draws and the ultrasound?"

She flexed her toes. "Okay. Sure. Let's launch. It's five weeks. From conception, I mean. My cycle ended almost nine weeks ago, it's never reliable but I looked it all up. And that night was five weeks and two days. The condom broke. I took an EC pill, but ...

well, you know better than me how that might not have worked. So."

She really liked how Dr. Saavedra never interrupted her. Maybe it explained why her words finally bubbled up. And Dr. Saavedra accepted the flood, not even using the time to make notes. Rachel confirmed she hadn't thrown up or bled or any number of other things in those five weeks.

"Okay, we'll take a look now. Sometimes people end up on the slim side of statistics. Let's take today in hand, and go from there." Then she did lots of typing and bustling and directing Rachel to lie back and such. Then: silence.

Waving a wand around inside her, clicking, staring at a screen. And silence. Machine noises, but no words. Granted she was steeped in a super emotional fog in the early weeks with her Hannah pregnancy. Dealing with that news and the urgency of needing to leave Sergei and the impossibility of supporting herself after all the money he'd taken from their joint account to invest in some friend's scheme and telling her *you've never had a head for numbers, Rachel, stop acting like this is a problem. You fucking question me at every turn when you're incapable of grasping the most basic things. All those vows to cherish and honor me, and you can't even get a decent dinner on the table on time, never mind understand the details of a business arrangement.* So maybe that first ultrasound was super silent and she didn't remember.

"Dr. Saavedra?"

"It's looking good. Uterus is good, cord doing its thing. Heartbeat great." She checked her notes, smiled at Rachel, then went about putting away her ultrasound. "Based on what you said, even with your irregular cycle, you should be a bit over seven weeks. I'm checking my measurements, but that's not right. The embryo's too big, too developed. I'm calling it nine weeks, three days. Which puts you back in line with your last menstrual. Does that fit with your experiences? If you conceived about two weeks before the night of the emergency contraceptive?"

Well, there went her toes again. She understood that the

subtext was, "Do you feel the same about the pregnancy if it's two weeks further along than you thought?" But all she could ask was, "Is it dangerous for the baby? The morning after pill?"

"No. It was a great deal of progestin, but well past the time that would have stopped pregnancy. Obviously. The timing was fine."

She nodded, sinking back enough for the paper under her butt to rustle. "Cool."

Dr. Saavedra took her relief as confirmation that the essential nature of the conversation hadn't changed. Which, it hadn't. Not that every other damn thing was clear to her yet. But confirmation that the pregnancy was real, and healthy, settled something within her. Smoothed down all her prickles, so even her toes managed to relax.

It didn't ease all those Sergei-snide fears about how Theo would react to the news. Or how she might manage the whole single parenting two preschoolers aspect of her next few years. Or what long-term fallout the decision to keep this baby would have on it, on her, and on Hannah.

But knowing she contained a fast new heartbeat and over an inch of busily multiplying cells working away within her? Even the scariest questions lifted up and away and gave her room, for now, to process one thing at a time.

Almost immediately after Theo opened the door to her, she was gaga for his son. Probably hormones or something. He was ferociously cute, and spent her first three minutes there hiding behind Theo's legs, big brown eyes sparkling like he was giggling to himself the whole time. By the time he crept out to take the box of toy cars she'd set on the coffee table, he was flirting with her. But still not saying a word. She could tell from Theo's smirk that he knew the kid was playing her.

Call her a guitar, then, cause Andres had no trouble strumming her heartstrings. By dinnertime, they were all friends. By dessert, he'd offered to give her some of his duplicate Pokémon cards so she could start her own collection. Not too many. But a few. She declined, but it didn't seem to faze him. Theo left her watching a movie while they disappeared for bedtime.

His mistake. She was more than half asleep herself when he returned. Way too fuzzy-brained to start a serious conversation. Way too lethargic to get intimate. They snuggled and stroked and spoke idly for a bit, long enough to wake her up.

"I should head out."

"Mmm." His tongue had other ideas.

"Theo. If you lure me to your room, you're not getting rid of me tonight."

He wrapped a leg over hers. "Right."

She laughed. "So that's what you want? Your son to find me here in the morning?"

He withdrew his mouth, but his hands didn't get the message. Her body kept trying to convince her to jump in on the action, too. Ridiculous body. Good thing her mind still knew how to be stern. She scooted to the other end of the sofa.

"I could wake you up early and sneak you out."

"And what's your son's track record on sleeping in?"

"It's been known to happen."

"On the morning y'all head to Galveston? When he's already got his beach toys and boogie board stacked and ready to go by the front door?"

Theo snorted. "That's my proof I've got a real influence on him."

"Excessive planning? I'd say so. Have you introduced him to spreadsheets yet?"

He rubbed his neck. "Well. I mean. Checklists are so useful."

This man. Her gut really needed to stop tugging her towards him. They were so much more bound up in each other than he even knew, and until they talked.... She stood. He deserved to enjoy his vacation without all this future hanging over his head.

Discussing it now, too tired and too cautious about being over-heard by a wakeful child and too close to days upon nights with no follow-up time. No. Bad plan.

"Thanks for dinner."

"Thanks for dessert."

"Your son's super."

"Thanks, I think so, too."

Oh, the hidden messages in all their words. She was too sleepy to read it. Dreadful to imagine how much more exhausted she'd be trying converse during the second trimester. She covered her yawn and leaned against the warm welcome of Theo's chest. "Okay, I'm off. Have a great time on your trip, drive safe. Text me."

"I will, if you'll text me tonight when you get home."

She squeezed him to her. She'd miss touching him so often, now he'd gone and gotten her used to it all the time. "Promise."

Another kiss. Damn he tasted sweet. Another. Palms on backs. Shoulders brushing. One last kiss.

"I'll miss you."

"Have too much fun to miss me."

Another kiss. "Not sure that's possible. But we'll try."

"Night, Theo."

He watched her to her car, waved as she pulled away.

Next time they saw each other, everything would change.

CHAPTER THIRTY

THE AR BALANCE didn't mesh with his receipts.

He scrubbed at his face and checked he'd run the right dates on the report. Scanned the credit card reconciliations. Went back to the start of the month and highlighted each row on his spreadsheet as he compared it to the daily sales.

Despite his haste to finish this report, get through the monthly meeting, and steal some time with Rachel before picking Andres up from his aunt's house, it wasn't his sex-starved brain. The receipts were off. The cash deposits to the bank were short almost five grand.

Fucking. Hell.

He'd spent their nights at the beach with his laptop open once Andres was crashed out, compiling everything for the monthly meeting and the reports to their lender. He did the same tasks every month. Sunburnt neck and too much fried seafood in his gut and the laughter of the people around the hotel pool had made no difference to his ability to power through the meeting prep part of his job. He'd expected his return from vacation to be just as rote: reconcile his reports with the paper receipts, email off a pile of documents, check off lists during their meeting. But then he showed up at his office, lined up his piles, and ... the balance didn't mesh.

It wasn't the tips. The ins and outs of reported tips all lined up. The missing cash came out of four day's totals, three week-nights and one hefty Saturday. Each day's deposit showed up on his general ledger correctly, but the cash never made it to the bank.

Which meant ... well, it meant one of only a few possibilities. A shift manager—two shift managers, due to who was on duty on the dates in question—recording sales but still pocketing the money without anyone noticing. Something hinky at the bank. Or straight-up malfeasance on the part of the man in charge of ferrying the deposit.

Sergei.

Unbidden, an image of that flower garden drawing on Rachel's fridge flashed in his mind. He'd gone out of his way to censure Sergei about his child support arrears, and now this. The missing cash would have gone a long way towards what the man owed Rachel. The money she needed to get a safer, more reliable car. The reserves that, he sensed, would give her a feeling of security and independence. Draw the lines she needed to be less suscep-tible to Sergei's and his mother's manipulations.

And if he didn't act, what kind of funds would go missing in three weeks, when he took Andres to visit his parents? What's to say Sergei wouldn't take the chance to pocket everything that came in. Two summer weekends of receipts, on top of the week-night happy hours and trivia night? Could he keep the man on, after this? Would Rachel blame him for firing her ex, right when she'd gained the financial security she so craved?

No, she wouldn't. Her fair-mindedness would put the guilt on Sergei's shoulders. But no matter that she had nothing to do with it, she would also censure herself for having mentioned how much Sergei owed. As if she was the one who'd pressured the man over it. Meanwhile, she'd be wondering how she would manage Hannah's expenses with Sergei unemployed again. And probably keeping her worries to herself because of his track record of over-stepping.

What a crappy impulse. Not wanting to confront Serg in order to preserve Rachel's peace of mind. And pretending it was for her benefit, as if she was incapable of separating everyone's actions. As if his lies could build a solid foundation for the future he craved with her.

Fucking, fucking hell.

Ron picked up on the fifth ring, curt and resistant when Theo asked him to join him in the office.

"No, it needs to be now." Theo closed his eyes against the color-coded sheet on his screen.

"Fine."

Two minutes later, Ron shut the door and hefted himself into the chair across from Theo.

"We've got a problem."

"Hey."

"Hey yourself." He lounged in her doorway, looking all cute and calm and not one bit like there was life-changing news hurtling towards him.

Not that he knew there was.

She stood back to let him in, managing to get the door shut before he plastered her against it. She knew he'd left the beach the day before, so it made zero sense, him still carrying salt and breeze and wild, churning undercurrents inside her apartment. Maybe he wasn't. Maybe she was projecting.

He didn't give her tons of time for analysis, though. Tugging her to the couch, kicking his shoes towards the door, yanking off his shirt.

"Got a little UV exposure, I see." See. Felt. Her palms had their own agenda, searching out the sun-kissed planes of his chest. Goddamn greedy sun, kissing him when she wasn't there to stop it.

"Yep. Let's see if you did, too."

Ah, hell. She wanted his hands on her. His hands, his eyes, his mouth. And it wasn't like she was so very different yet, so early in this pregnancy.

It wasn't like he was such a connoisseur of her particular body he would detect any differences anyway. Even if she did feel a little tight in the midsection when she wasn't in her scrubs. One of the other daycare moms had given her an interested look the other day, but didn't blurt out any questions about how occupied her uterus was, so it could have been anything.

The main problem was the life-changing news thing. Sex with Theo counted in general as a superb idea, but not when it filled up the limited time she had to break it to him.

Never mind if the news would maybe also break her heart. Silly thing was thudding up a storm, and only the knowledge that the baby's heart was beating even faster grounded her, calmed her down. "Theo. Hang on."

He moved his hands to bracket her hips. "What's up? Everything okay?"

She snorted. "Oh, that's a trick question. I think so, yes. But also, everything is complex."

Because the world was funny like that, his phone buzzed then. Twice. And then rang. The stretch of tension she thought she's spotted in him at the door returned. "That's Ron. Um. Hang on."

He glanced at his discarded shirt, but left it alone as he scooted a bit down the couch. "Hi.... Sure. I'm a few minutes away, but— no. Right. I appreciate that, but I think we should both...."

She moved into the kitchen. Not that she couldn't still overhear the tension in his voice, couldn't make out the words. But it maybe gave him a sense of privacy, because he sank into the sofa cushions, ran his hand through the hair she'd just mussed.

He was talking about Sergei.

Not that she was eavesdropping on purpose. But the name was too bound up in her life, like kudzu vining its way through every facet of her world. Ridiculous and invasive and clingy. Too hard to escape. And too ugly to bear. How she would navigate his heaps of scorn when he heard about this pregnancy, she didn't want to consider.

Whatever Theo and Ron had to say, they were done now. And so was her view of Theo's chest. He tugged his shirt's hem into place. "Sorry. I ... things are a little...."

"Something up with work?"

"Yeah. I need to see if my aunt can keep Andres a bit longer. Hang on a minute?"

She nodded, and got him a glass of iced tea while he talked to Tomás's parents. When he pulled out the stool beside her and sat, she linked their hands on top of the breakfast bar. He'd spread all those purchases out across it—the painkiller and the crackers and the new box of condoms. Such a caretaker. Such a researcher. She'd had no clue that particular combination of sweetness would melt away so many of her barriers.

He blew out a long breath. "Okay. So. This isn't something we've resolved yet. Or even decided on a plan of any kind. Except Ron suggested, and I agree, no police."

"Wait. Police? What's going on?"

"I haven't even finished all my accounting yet. And there could be some other explanation. It's weird, is all. Normally I would be doing this directly with him, and I know he's got Hannah another few nights, and that doesn't affect anything. But."

All those undercurrents in her apartment were from him after all. "Theo. I think you're trying to soften a blow somehow. But you've been talking about Sergei and cops and my *daughter* and I need you to be extremely up front with me right now."

"Shit." He scrubbed at his beard. "She's safe, I would never hide that from you. I'm not clear exactly what's happened, and it makes it hard to explain everything. At the office today, I was matching up the work I'd done in Galveston with some paperwork on site. And we're short a few grand in cash. And Sergei's the one who takes the night deposits."

She slipped her hand away so she could cradle both chilled

arms at once. "I don't know what you mean. Are you saying Sergei embezzled from you?"

Theo slumped. "I think so, yes. Sorry."

"Don't apologize to me, he didn't steal from me."

"I know, but...."

Sometimes undercurrents ripped you right off your feet and dunked you underwater. Riptides. She remembered Aunt Johnston telling her about them, so full of her knowledge as if she didn't live in a landlocked area. But Aunt went on about the tumult, the sucking of seawater into lungs, the dizziness of not knowing which direction was safe. So many details, and still Rachel hadn't grasped how all that was bound up with a slap of betrayed surprise. "Oh. I see. You think he took the cash for me. For Hannah, I mean. Her account."

"We don't know for sure it was even him. Or that I didn't make a mistake with my books."

She snorted. "Yes, out of nowhere you are a terrible accountant now."

His shrug was a small thing. Imperceptible, almost. She buried her head in her hands. "Okay, so I'll pay you guys back."

"The fuck?" His vehemence made her jump. "Rachel, no. That's ridiculous."

Oh hell oh hell oh hell. Her stomach was flipping and curling in a way she'd have blamed on the baby, a few weeks down the road. Except it was all too familiar from her marriage, well before Hannah made the scene. That 'you've made him mad so now you have to placate his anger' feeling. But screw him. She hadn't gotten clear of Sergei just to fall into the same goddamn patterns. "Do not call me ridiculous."

Whatever he heard in her voice sent him back against the sofa, speaking at her with fucking condescending exaggerated care. "I didn't mean you are ridiculous. I only meant whatever happened, your money is yours. Hannah's. It's not on you to return it."

Right. Easy to say now. Easy for him to ignore the truth of how Sergei operated in favor of some fantasy of fair play. It wasn't like he'd be the one Sergei belittled and browbeat to redirect any blame.

"And we don't know for sure it was him."

"But you don't have a better explanation."

"No. That's not proof though."

She shook her head. Her damn jaw was trembling, and she was almost proud of herself for not curling into a ball. "When you fire him, can you make sure his August child support is taken out of his final check? I know it's the start of the month, but I think the OAG allows for that."

"Sure, but. We might not fire him."

Weird, how her head was still shaking. Some sort of perpetual motion action, back and forth, back and forth. Must be hypnotic to watch, to go by Theo's expression. "Good thing I canceled that car appointment."

"You did? Why? I thought it was a great deal."

Oh. Hell. Inadequate hands, no good at making a barrier between her belly and the whole invasive terrible world. Inadequate shoulders, freezing halfway through a shrug to hunch around her neck. Inadequate lips, not curving around a convincing lie. She was, head to toe, not good enough to deal with all this. A failure throughout. "Didn't work out. Not important now."

"The money's yours," he insisted. Because of course he did. Living in his dream world, where rightful things worked out and no surprise children came along to wake him to harsh reality.

She nodded. The abrupt change from shaking sent a throb up through her skull. "Hannah's."

He nodded, too. She was not placated. "Right. Hannah's. But no matter what, not your problem. You could still get the car."

"Right."

"Rachel, listen." But he stopped talking when his phone got buzzy again. "Shit. I have to go. This isn't your problem, okay? It wouldn't have been fair to hide the truth from you, and I could be wrong anyway. I'm sorry if telling you before I know all the facts was a mistake."

That knife twist, she knew, was in her heart, not her belly. Her goddamn impulse to reassure him. To say she'd rather know now even if things changed. To not be treated with evasion or kid gloves either one, like everyone her whole life. *Rachel won't understand the menu, you pick for her. Rachel, Dad and I discussed this and decided it's best. Rachel, what's the point of trying to explain things to you? Rachel, do your little assignment and let us handle all the rest. Rachel, I'll let you know when I need something—go away until I ask. Rachel, don't you think you're at capacity already?*

She almost blurted out the pregnancy news, but he had his shoes on and was back to looking like she was a barely-contained beast. "You going to be okay?"

"Can we talk later?"

"Of course. Sorry. You wanted to tell me something complex." His tone was wry. "Guess I beat you to the punch there."

She met him at the door. It seemed like a small enough step to take, given the everythingness of this whole convoluted mess. Even if he retained a tinge of condescension in the way he looked at her. "It will keep. But I need us to talk, when you're up for it."

"I can call tonight after Andres goes to sleep."

She bit at her lip. "In person, Theo. Sometime before Hannah gets back to me would be best. Just give me a little notice. I can take some time off work. Meet you here or something."

His eyes.

She did not reach for him.

"Rachel?"

"It's okay." She wasn't sure if she was lying or not. "Complex, is all. We need some privacy, and time."

"Oh gods."

She didn't quite mean to smile, but it did seem to dial him down a notch.

"And to think yesterday I was building sandcastles."

When she laughed, he flashed a grin. It drew her in. "Text me later, okay? Let me know if your day gets any better."

Tentative, he stroked a curl along her neck. "Can I give you a kiss? That'll help."

"Oh, hell yes. Please." And she wrapped herself to him, and he was a solid pillar supporting her, and yeah. The kiss was tender, his warmth filling the cold spaces within her. She aimed to return the favor. It wasn't a hardship, this attempt to comfort him after a shock of a day. To bolster him against fraught times to come. And her deep wish to share a moment of connection with Theo told her more than she wanted to contemplate about feelings she wasn't prepared to let loose just yet.

CHAPTER THIRTY-ONE

BEFORE THE SATURDAY lunch rush started, he called Sergei in to the office.

"What's up, *re?*"

Nothing like owning a restaurant to inure a guy to personnel problems, but he'd gone and unearthed a hellish new twist to the process. "Sit down, will you? Shut the door."

Sergei complied, and damn if Theo could tell if his calm reaction was a facade or genuine.

"Take a look at these reports."

He peered for a cursory moment. "Spreadsheets aren't my thing. This is the monthly income?"

"Right."

"Is it down or something? Up?" Serg passed them back, looking like someone who'd never considered a balance sheet in his life. Theo added number sense to the qualities he'd search for in his next manager.

"The raw numbers are fine. But these days, where I highlighted, the cash never made it to our account."

Sergei leaned back. As if proximity to the spreadsheet itself was the problem. "Hang on. Hang on."

He did. He waited, like a fool trying to imitate some movie detective, letting his perp break the tension of silence.

Sergei fished out his phone and tapped between gesticulations. "I don't know if you're trying to ambush me on your own or if you and Ron cooked this up together. Trying to force me out so I don't get in the way of you banging my wife. I mean, my mother's been telling me to protect myself, and I told her, no. I said to her, come on, Theo's more interested in Elixir running well than he is in Rachel, for god's sake. So I shouldn't be paranoid. But I guess it's good I was trying to appease her, because here we are."

Theo's calves hurt. Of all the places to notice he was holding himself back, the calves were a strange choice, but there it was. The effort to not surge to his feet had them straining. His hand was clenched on his pen, and his jaw ground up into his molars, but it was the calves that he tried to relax first. "I'm not ambushing you, and Ron didn't cook up anything. I'm showing you facts. The cash is missing. I'm asking if you know anything about it."

"Of course I do."

He shifted his jaw again. "What does that mean?"

Sergei shoved his precious cell phone his way, like it contained five thousand dollars and a reasonable explanation. "Because those are the nights you had Ron take the deposit."

TEN DAYS since hugging her girl goodbye. Sergei had bothered to return her texts twice, so she didn't have any overwhelming worries about Hannah's health or safety. Just everything else. What was she eating, was she getting all the bedtime stories she wanted, had they lost Effie and not bothered to look for her? Was she happy? What did they do when she fussed or cried?

Her neighbor joked about enjoying all her free time, when she saw Rachel standing at the mailboxes with no Hannah in tow. Said it must be nice to sleep in. And okay, yes. She was as well rested as possible for someone wrestling with her conscience. Oh, and whose body was busy diverting resources to the cell-dividing factory within. She'd been through every shelf and drawer in Hannah's room, organizing toys to their proper bins and matching up socks and folding away outgrown clothes for storage. Also deep-cleaned the bathroom, restocked the medicine cabinet, flipped her mattress, filed all her paperwork, took herself out to a movie, and planned a five-dish meal for her friends.

The chicken was marinating, the onion was pickling, the potatoes and cauliflower were chopped and ready. The lentils in the crockpot smelled great. But if Theo called at any point, she would walk away from dinner and the gals. He only had texted her things were fine. "Complex," he wrote, and she didn't know how to take that. She was deciphering everything about her life from the qualities of the silences.

Serena, Natalie, and Gillian brought noise, bless them. Laughter, and chatter, and the pop of a cork from a bottle of rosé.

"None for me," she said.

Gillian slowly set the bottle down on the table, never taking her eyes from Rachel's face. Which was ridiculous. It's not like she even drank that much. She'd stuck to water plenty of other times. Sure, usually those nights were the ones when she had Hannah with her, but that didn't justify Gill's air of suspicion.

"I haven't even had a chance to tell him yet," she blurted out.

So of course everyone stared at her then. More silence surrounding her, not that it was hard to decipher.

"Rachel Elizabeth Groff, are you pregnant?"

She grimaced at Gill. It was enough of an answer. After that, silence was banished. She gave them the basics, ending with, "And I was going to tell him Friday, but something weird happened at Elixir and he had to go."

"We haven't even met this man. How can you be pregnant when we don't even know what he looks like?" Natalie asked.

"Right, where's a pic?" Serena took Rachel's phone and navigated to the photo album. "All of these are of Hannah."

Gillian appropriated the phone. "Why didn't you send me this one of her in the pool? What is wrong with you?"

"Focus. We need to see this Thad person."

"Theo," Rachel corrected.

"Until I meet him, I'm calling him Thad," Serena said. "Just in case."

"In case what?" asked Nat.

"In case." Serena followed her ominous statement with a hefty sip of wine.

"Wait. Important question." Natalie held her hand in the air like they were in grade school. "When you rolled the dice for Thad on the game board, what did he get for sexytimes?"

"Thunder bolt," Gillian said. Quick as can be. Not even pretending to think about it first.

Nat lowered her arm enough to high-five Gill. "Awesome recall. Thanks. And?"

Rachel glared at them both, though they knew she didn't mean it. "And what?"

"Are we talking floodwaters? Hurricane? Gully washer?"

Serena laughed. "What even is a gully washer?"

"You know." Natalie threw up her hands and did the same motion as 'down came the rain' from the *Itsy Bitsy Spider* song. "Quick cloudburst, lots of noise but gone before you even have time to go out and get wet."

They all cracked up.

"I have mango and coconut sorbets for dessert and I don't have to share," Rachel warned.

"Wow. That'll teach you to talk about weather patterns," Gillian told Nat.

"Can I blame my fiancé? He's a very bad influence."

"Only if you tell us one of his dirty limericks." Serena's smile glinted.

"Hmm. I'll think about it," Natalie said. "Meanwhile, look at how Rachel is sitting there hoping we'll stop asking about Thad."

"Theo."

"Nope. We're all calling him Thad now. I decided. Only way to get us to stop is to tell us all about his lightning rod."

"You people are childish."

"Answer the question, Rachel."

She shook her head. "I think you're the bad influence on Evan, not the other way round. And if you must know…. Okay, those summer storms, the ones that move in right when it gets dark outside? And suddenly everything is quiet and still, but then the skies open up and the water's everywhere, thunder and lightning hitting right on top of each other? And it's pouring all night long, so you may as well give up hope of sleeping, and let nature have its way with you? Like that."

All three of them reached for their wine glasses and drained them. She kinda wished she had one of her own, to be honest. That night they'd spent together before Andres came to town felt way longer than three weeks ago, with so much else happening since then. And probably it was all over with her and Theo, as soon as he found out about the baby.

"Okay, we really need that picture now. And why are you looking wistful?" Gillian asked. "We're the ones jealous of your nightly thundershowers."

"Speak for yourself," Serena said, and she and Natalie clinked their glasses together. Smug almost-marrieds.

Rachel passed over the wine bottle so they could refill anyway. "It's weird to think about dry spells now, is all."

"Why dry spells? Your doctor didn't give you anything to worry about, did she?"

She squeezed Gill's hand. "No, nothing like that. But I don't see how we can go about at dating if we're co-parenting."

"What is this, the last season of *Friends*? Of course you can date the hot man who fathers your baby."

"Jesus, Gill."

"I hope he looks more like Joey than Ross."

"Seconded," Serena said. "Text him to send us a selfie so we can check."

"Y'all should fuck right off."

"Aw, you know you love us." Serena's self-assurance was well founded. And that was good. Having three such friends in her life was good. They'd never yelled at her about how much she'd screwed up by letting Sergei abuse her, and staunchly seen her through the dismal, messy end of her marriage, and stuck by her when her world revolved around things like whether Hannah was ready for solid food and if her sleep schedule would ever smooth out. And here they were, ready to go through all of it with her again. Loving her, no matter what.

"Hey." Gill rubbed her shoulder. "Did we even say congratulations?"

The overfull water balloon of tension in her chest popped, and tears spilled all down her face. Arms reached her from all sides, hugging and tugging her up until the three of them surrounded her, held her together.

Who needed thunder clouds, when she had the steady strength of sheltering arms like these?

CHAPTER THIRTY-TWO

HE SIGNED Andres in for science museum day camp and headed straight to Rachel's. She'd taken a half-day off work, which was ominous.

Or encouraging?

Hard to know. Things were fraught enough at work, and it irked him beyond what he'd have believed possible, how impossible it was to get a read on Rachel. Which, okay, had more to do with his own issues than her. The painful awareness that half his summer with Andres was over, the suckiness that he couldn't chuck in all his responsibilities to spend that time hanging out with his son, the way those responsibilities chose this precise moment to ramp into high gear.

The evening before, after a video chat with Annalisa, Andres said, "I miss Mom a million times but when I'm home I miss you a million times." And then they cried a little. And then they jumped in the pool because their faces were already wet, so it made sense. Or so Andres said, and Theo couldn't think of any reason to disagree.

Later, he phoned his mom to check on arrangements for their visit. But mostly because—like father, like son—being emotional made him want to talk to her. Which she figured out, of course. And when he talked through the Ron and Sergei situation, she asked what he thought of selling out and moving to live closer to his son. It wasn't the worst solution to the whole mess.

Which slammed him full force back into his uncertainty about Rachel. Here he was taking her into consideration while making major decisions, without knowing if they were on or not. Or on, but in such a casual place, to her mind, that she'd think him weird for making plans around their relationship. He was full of concepts like commitment and love and the future. As far as he knew, she wasn't.

He was used to being low priority in his relationships. Everyone had someone else to think of first. He looked after his own self. He was a grown-ass man, so he was plenty capable. He and Annalisa never even pretended to prioritize the other once they had Andres. And of course their son would forever get top billing. Even happy as Annalisa was with Jamie, who she'd practically programmed up from a Perfect Husband Wish List, she put Andres first. Maybe when he was grown that would shift; his own parents didn't seem to have any trouble filling their empty nest with each other. His sisters were the same with their spouses. Or Phoebe and Max were. Since Helen and Tracy's twins were younger than Hannah, they were at the stage when taking care of each other meant letting the other take the occasional nap.

So Rachel would never sideline Hannah's best interests. He'd be dismayed if she did. What he needed to figure out were the chances he could make it to second place with her.

Maybe it was some latent Greek son selfishness, the kind his dad and uncles worked against while Sergei dove headlong into stereotypes. Maybe it wasn't his most shining quality. However petty, he harbored the dream of ascending the ranks with someone. Even his own son lumped Jamie up there with him. Because Jamie was around. Jamie was teaching him tennis. He and Jamie did puzzles.

They had a secret handshake. It wouldn't shock him to learn Andres also gave Jamie a '#1 Dad' mug for Father's Day.

What a fucking tangle. The looming countdown until Andres returned to Fort Worth. Ron and the future of Elixir. And whatever it was that Rachel labeled complex.

"YOU'RE ALL WET." She stood back to let him in.

"It's raining."

Hard to kiss him hello and suppress a chuckle at the same time. "Summer storms. Come in. You need a towel?"

He ran a palm down his face then wiped it dry on his t-shirt. Because it wasn't already doing a fine job of clinging to his muscled torso. "No, I'm fine."

No argument from her. Note to self: check pregnancy site for info about horniness in the first trimester. Also, send an irritated text to her friends about how they had no right to stir up all her lustful feelings towards Theo. He could well be three minutes from walking right out of her apartment and only communicating through lawyers in the future.

"Sit. Can I get you anything?"

"No. I ... you're making me nervous."

She moved from the side chair to the coffee table in front of him. Their knees knocked together and she put a hand on his wrist. "Sorry. I've got some nerves, too. And it's really good to see you. I've—" she cut herself off. No confession of emotions. He might read it as manipulative after the fact. It might even be the truth. More than a few of the long lonely hours she'd spent processing the reality of her pregnancy featured rosy-tinted fantasies of a big happy blended family. So no matter how much she missed him—missed the sex, yes, but also his company, and the way his eyes were always steady and clear, and his thoughtful questions, and how he was a shelter in the storms of life—it was not fair to jump him. Or to bare her trepidatious heart.

"Nerves because of the complex thing?"

"Oh, so much so." She wiped a presumptuous raindrop trying to sneak its way along the sharp line of his beard. "How are things with your complex situation?"

He shook his head. "Not good."

"Shit. Sorry. Do you want to keep it to yourself? Or talk about it?" Was she putting off the inevitable? Was it wrong to offer herself up as a confidant in case he needed to put some distance between them?

He didn't give her a chance to navigate the quandary. "It wasn't Sergei who embezzled. It was Ron."

"Jesus, are you serious?" Oh he looked wrecked. "You are serious. I'm so sorry. What happened? If you want to say."

His hands wrapped around hers. "He—Ron—set Sergei up. Told him I wanted Ron to take the deposits, that I was experimenting with changing the system. He figured Sergei would be paranoid it was because of, well, you. That I was treating him as suspicious because I'd learned something about him from you. Which I think means there's something more Ron knows about Serg that I didn't try to find out, but...."

"Wow. Yeah. I mean, I don't know why Sergei wouldn't be good at his job. He's for sure full enough of himself to be confident about it, which seems like half the challenge when you're managing people."

He smiled. Rueful as hell, but it was a smile. "Little more to it than that, but yeah. Anyway, Sergei bought Ron's story, and once the place emptied out for the night, Ron made duplicate deposit slips, pocketed the cash, and counted on me being distracted by Andres and, well, you again, to not notice."

"But you'd notice sometime. What did he think would happen then?"

Theo shook his head. "He meant to pay it back before then. His nephew has a gambling problem, and needed the cash to get a bookie off his back. There was some plan about selling his truck that hit a snag. So in came the backup plan: stealing from the company."

"Wow. And he just told you all this? But you were talking to him about it on Friday, right? And you thought it was Sergei then."

"He didn't count on me talking to Sergei until he paid us back. Figured if he confessed after restitution I'd shrug it off or something."

"That's kind of an asshole move. Why didn't he ask you for a loan or something instead of stealing?" She didn't know Ron. But she knew Theo. He'd have figured out a way to help his friend out.

"His nephew's been coming around a lot lately—begging Ron to bail him out, as it turns out—and it was getting disruptive. He's not the quiet sort, to understate the matter. Sergei tried to corral him a few times but it didn't work, and in the end I had to tell Ron to ban Lonnie. So he didn't think I'd be sympathetic."

"Well, that's ridiculous. You're the most giving guy I know."

Huh. Well. That ... that was nice.

Her a/c kicked on, or lingering drips of rain were sneaking under his collar. Or it was emotion giving him goose bumps.

"You are," she said, maybe because he hadn't managed an answer. She shifted over to sit alongside him.

"Thanks."

"I'm not buttering you up or anything. You're always going out of your way to be nice to people, and making things easier for everyone you know. If that weren't who you were, we wouldn't even have met. You were doing Sergei a favor bringing me Hannah that day. And don't even pretend you volunteered or he asked nicely. I bet he acted like you owed it to him somehow."

"He set up a meeting with our liquor vendor."

"Even though he had Hannah on his schedule. Whatever.

That's him all over, but I guess I'm glad he isn't a thief on top of everything else."

His laugh was as hollow as uncooked penne pasta.

"Right." She leaned into him. "I guess that's not much comfort for you. What are you going to do? Did Ron even sell his truck?"

He shook his head. "Lonnie, that's the nephew, he pawned some electronics and paid back about a quarter of it yesterday. And Ron had appointments with some buyers over the weekend, but I haven't heard if any of them bought it or not. Meanwhile, I've got to audit everything, going back at least as far as when Lonnie first started coming around. So that's going to be hell. But I'll do it next month, because at this point, I just want to spend time with my son and think about what comes next."

"I'm so sorry you're dealing with all this."

He shrugged, which rubbed together their shoulders, and the contact was nice. So he wrapped his arm around her and held her for a bit, which was even nicer. "You smell good."

She laughed. "Thanks. It's my lotion."

"It's you, too." And then he bit his tongue. Not hard, but he needed the reminder that they still had to address whatever topic had her taking off work. And despite his libido's insistence, it wasn't like she'd missed sex so much she intended to jump him at nine on a Monday morning.

Though was any time a bad time, really? His libido thought not, and who was he to wage an internal war?

And her hand was on his thigh, and when he pressed his leg into hers, she started toying with the seam on his jeans, and she did smell so good, all clean and sharp with an undertone of warm spice, and her hair was back off her neck so it was easy and delicious to bring his lips to the tender spot below her ear, and then she drew in a deep, breast-swelling breath and he almost didn't hear her whisper, "We're pregnant."

CHAPTER THIRTY-THREE

He said nothing.

It was almost fascinating, if she hadn't herself gone so still she risked fainting. She unstuck enough to take a look at his expression. It wasn't revelatory. He was looking plenty of places that were not at her. Wall, sofa, kitchen counter, hands. Kitchen counter again. She slid away and swiveled to face him, hugging her legs up against her chest. "It wasn't that night, with the broken condom. It was the first one, the one when we ended up here, you remember? A few days after we went kayaking?"

"I haven't forgotten the first time we had sex." His voice was flat, but not with that studied, too-patient calm that signaled one of Sergei's explosions of scorn. She forced out a slow breath, realizing what she'd been bracing herself for. But this was Theo, who had never waved the palest of red flags in her direction. And if she had to deliberately remind herself of that fact, fine. It was the least she could do so they could have this conversation without her deciding in advance what his reactions would be.

She let one leg drop to curl under her. "You and me both. Sorry. I'm still nervous. I know this is a lot. And I've had a few days to process it."

He still wasn't in a rage. "How long?"

"Have I known? I took the test while you were in Galveston. I ... it crossed my mind that weekend, before you left. I didn't want to think about it, and I told myself a story about you deserving a nice holiday with Andres without all this mixed up in your life."

Another thing about Theo: he made it so easy to read his emotions. A real 'eyes are the windows to the soul' kind of man. It made everything better and worse at once, because it would be so much easier to pretend she didn't know how she'd just cut him. But she hoarded all the ways he was unlike Sergei, and that made his readable eyes more precious than rubies.

"So you took the test a week ago?"

She sighed as she nodded. Because hard as it had been to process it all on her own, she knew it was a big advantage to have gotten that chance before breaking the news to him. "I went to my doctor on Friday. She confirmed the pregnancy, and told me about the real conception date. So it seems the first time condoms were bad, too, but we didn't notice. It's a big pile of small odds that got us here. The pill didn't cause any problems, though. It's healthy. Heartbeat, limb development, all of that."

More silence, and she would not cry.

"I have a sonogram picture. If you're interested."

"I.... Give me a minute."

"Oh. Sure. Yes. Sorry." She started to stand, but he reached out and took her hand.

"Can you sit with me? Please? Quiet for a sec."

Her smile felt off balance. She slid back under his arm. Nodded and thought about meditation. About intentional breathing, and defining what she'd hoped for as an outcome, and filling her heart with love. Her heart, his heart, the baby's heart. Not to force anything from him, but because the world did not always hold enough love for all the hearts, and this was a good moment to work on correcting that.

He ... they.... A baby.

He blinked himself into focus, discovered his gaze was locked on a studio portrait of Hannah as an infant. Unbelievably cute, of course. Those big blue eyes with her solemn, knowing expression. A little skeptic right from the start. Not much hair. All her curls must have come in later, but he resisted the urge to scan the room for other photos.

Andres was born with a whole mass of hair.

Rachel squirmed beside him. She felt heavy, waves of nervous energy pulling her down beside him. Like she would slip to the floor if he took his hand from hers.

He didn't take his hand from hers.

Everything he tried to voice made no sense for the moment. Reliving the night of conception, no. What happened, happened. Asking how much Hannah weighed when she was born, no. He wasn't ready to start treating this pregnancy as a fact for his future. Wondering if Rachel had been scared taking the test and going to the doctor on her own, no. He bristled that he'd been left out of those moments, but there was no traction in arguing her logic. He wasn't even sure he'd believe any points he made trying to adjudicate the past.

His lips felt too dry to shape words. "When the condom broke, we didn't give it any thought. The contraceptive pill was the immediate choice."

"I know. And I think it would've been the same if we'd known about it when this happened."

He nodded. That was true. So was it the semantics that made this feel so much more? Instead of saying they needed an abortion, she said they were pregnant. Even without the heartbeat and the sonogram and a due date. Spring, he supposed. She probably could tell him something much more precise. Give all this that much more reality.

A springtime baby. He was back to studying Hannah's infant picture. Her soft cheeks and wrinkly wrists and the way the toes of one foot curled on top of each other.

Those infant wrist wrinkles were his favorite.

"You want this." He wasn't asking.

She sank deeper into the couch. "I wasn't—it wasn't deliberate."

"I know."

"And even though I felt a pang taking those meds, I would've done the same thing if we'd known about the condom failure at the time."

"A pang?" Had he felt a pang? He remembered worrying that the whole situation would put distance between the two of them. That it would cause her to back away for whatever reason. He remembered worrying that she felt okay in the moment, that she wasn't suffering side effects from the drugs. It never occurred to him to think of it as a genuine pregnancy risk, though. Which maybe didn't make sense, but there it was. He'd approached it like an awkward moment to traverse for two people who did not know each other very well yet.

But she had felt a pang.

"Well," she said. "Okay. There has always been a deep-down part of me that wants more kids. I love raising Hannah, and if she's my one and only, I'm not arguing that fate. She's more than enough to fill my heart. But...." She trailed off, quiet.

"Siblings."

"Exactly." She smiled at him, brighter than she'd been. Lighter. "You have your sisters, your cousin. So maybe you get that. Even though it's not practical in one million ways, I did have that twinge of regret. Just for the idea that Hannah could've had a sibling."

So, it wasn't about him. Her feelings hadn't been so overwhelming that she was afraid the broken condom would get between them. And no mention that the hypothetical little brother or sister would be his child, too. He didn't factor into this top-secret dream of hers.

He wasn't sure how he factored into her reality now. All her skittishness about them getting closer; all her firm setting them on a slower path; all her stopping them from spending time with each other's children.

"Do you want me to be the father?"

"What do you mean? You *are* the father. I went through all the paternity test bullshit with Sergei. I'm not loving having to do it again. But if that's what you need."

"No." He reached for the hand she'd yanked from his when he asked his badly-phrased question. "I'm not suggesting the baby's not mine. Not at all. But I want to know, in this dream future of yours, where you and Hannah are cooing over a bassinet, am I a part of it?"

Now she was marble. So he had his answer. She was picking motherhood; she was picking Hannah and the baby. She was not picking him.

"I don't want to terminate."

He shook his head, not that she was looking at him. "That's not what I'm suggesting. I can tell you're happy, you have plans. And that's good—"

"Theo."

Hell if he wasn't crying. He blinked dry his eyes, focusing on baby Hannah's tiny pink fingernails until he was ready to say more. "I don't know if I know where my mind is going. It's overwhelming. Thoughts flying in from all sides. Feelings."

"Okay. Sure. I know you need time to process. Or, I did, anyway."

"To be clear, you've definitely decided to go forward with the pregnancy?"

She lifted her chin just enough to indicate yes. It was a tiny movement, but it shot straight down his spine, spreading throughout his nervous system like an injection of adrenaline.

"Why are you laughing?"

"I did not think this is what you meant when you said we had to talk about something complex."

"What, you thought I was going to confess to hating pie?"

He rubbed at his chest, miming agony but really he had to

contain the jet stream of giddiness until he had some clue what it meant. "Oh, unkind fate, to pair me with such a cruel woman."

"Hush. You know I'm a fan of your baking."

He sighed. "Okay. That's a solid foundation. If we're going to embark on some kind of ... okay, let's not define it yet. But it's a lifetime, isn't it? Somehow or another, this means a lifetime of knowing each other."

Her hand circled her belly, mimicking the way his still cradled his heart. "The baby's lifetime."

"Wow. Heavy. Okay. The baby's lifetime. Our baby's lifetime." He was tentative, giving her room to edge away. But she let him settle his palm over her hand. They sat quiet for a few minutes, pressing their joined hands over her womb. Where his baby grew. A sibling for Andres, too. Not just for Hannah. Someone who would call him 'my big brother' and kick a soccer ball with him and share a secret handshake and be forced to learn way too much about the various triggers for Pokémon evolution.

He stirred. He needed both hands to wipe at the tears again, and she had a few of her own to deal with. "Can I see the scan?"

She reached for her phone. As she pulled up her photo app, she told him the due date—March first—and a few more details from her doctor visit. And then she showed him the picture she'd taken of the sonogram. "It's not much to see right now."

"No, I remember. A lima bean with a heart."

"Little bit more than that, but yeah." She zoomed in on nascent limbs. Pointed out the measurements.

He took the phone. And that adrenaline rapid-fired throughout him again, bounding heart and vibrating knee and the thud of reality slamming into him. It was real. It was happening. He had a gut reaction and that scared the hell out of him, because damn if he wasn't leapfrogging past a thousand important conversations and straight into the years and years of family life with her. With them. The two of them, their two children, and their child.

And whatever her new dreams were, they didn't include that.

And whatever his dreams of being treasured were, he hadn't envisioned going straight from serious dating to family life.

He couldn't put coherent words together, he couldn't info a navigable path to discuss any of it, and her phone started buzzing with an incoming call.

And it was Sergei.

———

SHE SNAGGED the phone back before he could extend it her way. Or silence it or whatever he was going to do, she didn't care, because Sergei and Hannah were supposed to be at the zoo. Or so he'd said, when he was explaining that he shouldn't have to pay for daycare for the time he had custody.

"What happened?"

"Calm yourself, Rachel, it's not some emergency. You always leap to the worst conclusions around me. I'm her father, I know how to keep her from running into traffic."

Sure, maybe. Or maybe her daughter was inside the tiger enclosure at that moment. "Fine, I get it. You can stop with that tone. What do you need?"

Sergei's most long-suffering sigh reverberated down the line. "She's got some kind of cold. Probably germs from that place you dump her every day."

"Her daycare is a highly rated, state certified facility and is full of her friends. And germs," she conceded. "Because all daycares have germs, and unless you want to pay spousal support so I can stop working, it's going to remain a part of her life. She likes the bubblegum flavor decongestant, if you can find it."

"I think you should pick her up."

"What, now?"

"She's whining for you, and we can't do any of the things I planned if she's throwing up."

"She's throwing up? I thought you said it was a cold."

"Well, whatever, some kind of germ, don't ask me for a diagnosis."

"Does she have a fever? Have you taken her to the doctor? I gave your mom the updated contact list, but her pediatrician's the same."

"Look." He cut in with the impatience she remembered all too well. "This is your thing. She's crying for you, and, not that you care about my life, but things are screwy at work, so I can't be taking this time off to babysit right now anyway."

"You aren't babysitting. She's your child."

"Okay, feminazi, calm down. Are you coming to get her or not?"

Jesus. "I have a job too, you know. Why aren't you asking your mom?"

"She's busy."

Rachel sighed. "Where are you?"

"At the zoo, like I told you before. Keep up, if you can."

"She's crying and throwing up and you took her to the zoo." She was about to turn into a live gif of banging her head against a wall. Theo stroked her arm and she looked over at him. He mimed talking on the phone, pointing to himself, then held out his hand.

Well, her world was a strange mess already, so why not. She stopped listening to Sergei's sputtering self-justifications and handed over the cell.

"Serg, hey. Listen, do you have Effie with you? …The elephant, yeah. Okay, so head to my place, we'll meet you there."

Not what she'd expected. But interesting. She left him to it, going to pack a bag with some meds and books and a change of clothes. He came down to stand in the door to Hannah's room. "I figured since I'm closer to the zoo than Elixir is, or that gas station."

"Makes sense. And no harm in cutting short that cycle of blame we had going on. I'm sure Hannah was sitting in the back seat listening to him talk to me like that."

"Hard to avoid old patterns."

Damn he was nice. Insightful, and nice. She straightened. "I just realized it's still raining."

"Yep."

"And he took her to the zoo."

"Yep."

"I hope he paid for admission before she got sick."

"If you tell me you also hope she barfed on his shoes I may have to reconsider how I'm taking the news of our pregnancy. Want me to drive you over or would you rather follow in your car?"

She stared at him. How quick everything flew out of her mind when she was focused on Hannah. "Theo. Oh. I'm being so unfair. I'm really sorry. Do you—what should we, should I call Sergei back and tell him to deal with it? It's not like he can't figure it out. She probably just needs some crackers and downtime."

"No, let's go. I told him to be in before the lunch shift. I'll take the day off. Give myself some time to think before I pick up Andres. About Ron and everything, too."

"Going through a real when it rains it pours kind of week, aren't you?"

"You and me, honey, we can weather any storm."

He was teasing to set her at ease, and he was the one taking on all the heavy news. She leaned in to kiss him, hug some warmth into his still-damp torso. "As soon as I get Hannah cleaned up a little, we'll head out and give you some space."

He returned her warmth tenfold. "If she's okay, maybe you can stick around a little. If she'd be comfortable napping at mine. I'd like if we could spend a little more time talking."

She nodded. Not sure what the next hours would hold, much less the next weeks and months and years, but they had to start somewhere. And it seemed that 'somewhere' would take place between naps and episodes of *Peppa Pig*. Which was all too fitting. Time had a lot of telling to do.

CHAPTER THIRTY-FOUR

POOR HANNAH REALLY WAS SICK. One look at the flushed cheeks in her wan face and he knew talking was done for the day. And on top of dragging a feverish toddler through the rain to the zoo, Serg lied about having her stuffed elephant with them. He was tempted to fire the guy on the spot, just for being an abysmal father. Instead he carted Hannah inside so her parents could get through whatever conversation they needed. She refused toast and water but agreed to help him make her some strawberry juice. When Rachel came back inside, Hannah was sitting on the counter, squeezing a lime into the blender. "Grab us a cup?"

She did, and then got hands on her daughter, checking her fiery forehead and rubbing her back while he pulsed together the ingredients for an electrolyte drink. The pride that surged through him when she drank down a few ounces and held out her cup for more was way outsized for the actual service rendered.

They went into care-taking mode. He ran a bath while she phoned the doctor. He found a few age-appropriate toys while she coaxed Hannah to let go long enough to be stripped and cleaned. He took the laundry and cleaned the kitchen, and then he was out of tasks. He tidied Andres's room, took a towel to the wet footprints in the foyer, but it was busywork, not the essential stuff required for a sick child. It did nothing to distract him. When he found himself tempted to offer to run Hannah to the pediatrician so Rachel could get to work, he admitted defeat. He was grasping, and on top of that, unnecessary. She had it under control. Her boss knew she wasn't coming in, her friend was bringing them both dinner and Effie later, her point about keeping germs away from Andres was solid. All he could do was hold the umbrella on the walk to her car and kiss them goodbye.

Alone again, he called Ron to come over once he got the lunch shift underway. Which gave him around an hour to skim their partnership agreement and email their lawyer. He wasn't decided on anything, though Ron's betrayal felt more fraught in light of the baby news. Maybe it had stripped away some veneer of calm, some willingness to smooth it over for the sake of peace. Maybe Elixir's success meant more now there was another person to support.

Maybe all of it.

The only sure thing was how fucking tired he was of nothing being sure.

EAR INFECTION. Not a raging one, not one that went untreated for days and days until her eardrum burst and pus was oozing out of it. More than enough for Hannah to be cranky and make herself sick from the stress of feeling bad and being off her routines.

So, another day off work. Another day to remind herself she needed to line up emergency childcare, now that Mary Lynn was happy off in Brenham. Natalie and Gillian pushed around their schedules to cobble together a few afternoon hours so she was able to meet with clients on Tuesday, and never mind that her first trimester picked this convenient moment to throw more symptoms her way. The morning nausea opted to meander unpredictability throughout the day, and crap but her boobs hurt.

Meanwhile Hannah was a portrait of misery unless she could flop her head upon her mama's breast.

Entertaining as it was to one-handed text her friends with misspelled, gripe-filled updates, she was more than ready for the distraction when Theo stopped by Wednesday morning. "Are you infectious?"

"I think we're clear now, but maybe don't lick my dishes."

He handed over a bag of bagels and a plush rhino. "Noted. Do you want me to clean the kitchen? I don't mind."

Melting her heart when she was almost shaky from exhaustion. Rude. Unfair. Adorable.

And too much an echo of the way Sergei treated her in the early, solicitous days of their relationship. And then again whenever he'd come close to crossing an inviolable line. Because: cycles. Like her therapist explained. If he'd started strong then veered only downhill she'd have gotten out sooner. Instead he had been attuned to all the ways she responded to his escalating derision and demands, and knew just when to pull back and love bomb her with his charm again.

She needed ... something. Something surefire to show her she wasn't falling for Sergei all over again. "Are you disgusted by me right now?"

He leaned back, head tilted. "Am I what?"

"This?" She gestured to show off her flop of an unwashed ponytail, food stained tee, and yoga pants she'd been wearing since he'd last seen her on Monday. "My general unclean state and not bothering to even put away the laundry when I knew you were coming over?"

HE WANTED to parse her question, get at the hidden meaning. But he couldn't. "Hannah's sick. I mean, not like it matters if you're, I don't know, a little sloppy in your own home. It's not a national emergency. But you're pregnant and Hannah's sick, so if you're looking for a get out of laundry free card, seems like this would be a good time for it."

She slumped into a chair at the dining table and dug through the bagel bag. He grabbed a couple of plates and a toddler-friendly knife. Hannah dashed over, abandoning the puzzle she'd been absorbed with until she saw the food. While Rachel got her set up spreading cream cheese, he found a clean dishtowel and tackled the kitchen.

"I think I'm looking for problems."

Her quiet confession, spoken more to the back of his shoulder than to his face, eased through him. He turned and smiled. "Am I passing the test? Or failing? Whichever you hoped for?"

For the briefest of moments, she rested her forehead against his chest. Then she reached for a sippy cup and filled it with juice. "You keep passing. I keep testing, and you keep passing."

"You seem thrilled by my success."

She shook her head, but indulgent and sweet. What a goner he was. Let her throw all the tests and trials she had at him. Let him work to live up to her staunchest demands.

Clarity. A relief to have it about one aspect of his life, however uncertain her side of things. His sister Helen would ask if he was clinging to his feelings for Rachel because they gave him a roadmap, an anchor while he recalibrated everything else around him. His cousin would reassure him that he knew his own heart best and was old enough to watch out for himself. So what did Helen know, anyway?

In case showing up with breakfast and pitching in with chores wasn't enough to signal his intentions, he waited until Hannah was settled in to her meal and led Rachel far enough down the hall for a modicum of privacy. "We haven't had much chance to talk."

She wrapped her arms around herself. "Not really, no."

Conscious of the child just out of his line of sight, he got straight to the point. "I'm all in. You, us, the baby. Everything."

She hugged herself tighter, eyes wide. He couldn't figure out the hidden message in her body language, either. Not overwhelming glee, anyway. So that told him a great deal.

Pursed lips. Peering in Hannah's direction. Shifting jaw. White knuckles. Yeah. Not overwhelming glee at all.

"I—"

He rushed on, to avoid hearing what he wasn't ready to hear. Later he'd decide if it was cowardice or conviction. "Okay. I can go. I *should* go, I have to be at the lawyer's office in half an hour. I thought I should let you know. Wanted to let you know. That I'm committed. To the baby. Also, and you knew beforehand I think, to us."

"Lawyer?"

Of all the words to snag her attention. Not *committed*, not *us*. *Lawyer*. "Elixir's lawyer. Because of Ron. It's—complex."

The thinnest of laughs, but she unclenched her hands. "I'm sorry. Shit, I should have asked. Hannah, and the bagels, and I am so sorry. What's happening with Ron?"

He shook his head. "Complex." Understatement, but what was he going to say? My business might be folding. I have no idea how I'll support myself and my son and our future child, and side bonus: Hannah's child support will also stop coming in cause I'm looking at letting go all my employees. Not something he could convey in the eighteen—no, fourteen—minutes he had before walking out her door.

Her hand was warm on his cheek. Almost too warm; he scanned her face for signs of fever, but found only exhaustion and concern. "I should have asked. This," she waved her other hand towards the kitchen, "we'll get through this, it's manageable. An everyday kind of thing. Messy, but everyday. Ron and Elixir, that's not. I want you to know you can talk to me about it."

Now he had chills up his nape. "Thanks. It's kind of terrible news all round. And I'm not trying to, I don't know, protect you or withhold information. Talking it through with you would actually be helpful, but you've got Hannah and I've got an appointment and so for now I've got to go it alone."

If anything, she looked queasier. "It's that bad?"

"I don't know. Maybe not. That's what the meeting's for. But listen: no matter what happens, I'll figure it out. Opening a restaurant was always a gamble, and I didn't go into that without evaluating the risks and setting up parameters to protect myself."

"Spreadsheets?" One wry word from her, and he could stop pacing the too-short hallway and cloak himself in calm.

He pressed his back against the wall and tried to sound reassuring. "Yeah, spreadsheets. A few graphs, too. And a business plan and partnership agreement and several quarters' worth of reports. So. Ron wants out. That's the short answer to where we are now. I was ready to work on some kind of trust-rebuilding scheme but he wants out. And that scares me, and I don't know if it's possible to go on without him, or if I even want to, and I love you, but I have to go meet with my lawyer."

Tugging him away from the wall, she circled his waist and held him in a long hug. Her head on his shoulder. Her hands stroking up his ribs. As if she wasn't already carrying enough, and had plenty of strength left to carry him.

"Okay, go. Don't be late. Thanks for the bagels. Call me when you can."

They walked, still touching, to the door. After a brief detour so he could brush back Hannah's curls and feel for himself that she wasn't so feverish anymore, he squeezed Rachel's hand and closed his eyes to savor her brief kiss.

It was only as he pulled into his lawyer's parking lot that he realized he'd let slip that he loved her. And she hadn't said anything in return.

CHAPTER THIRTY-FIVE

THE CAREFUL PLAN involved getting up at four a.m. and driving several hours before Hannah even began to stir, much less got stirred up from too long in the car.

The careful plan did not take into account first trimester queasiness and exhaustion.

They left, instead, a half hour before Thursday rush hour traffic, and made it to Mary Lynn's new home in time for dinner. Goldberg fed everyone his signature cassoulet after Hannah ran through the house, insisting Mary Lynn explain every shelf and corner of every room. Some combination of chamomile tea, stress, tiredness, and relief that she could leave her daughter in loving, capable hands worked to put her to sleep hours earlier than usual.

Mary Lynn woke her at dawn with breakfast and all of her to-go containers full of kid-friendly snacks. "I had her on the potty before I packed all this up so she's back in a deep enough sleep now. Are you sure you're okay to go all that way? Because you can spend the vacation days here, you know. We'll go see miniature horses and play at the lake and Goldberg will make every meal."

She groaned. "Too tempting. I'm not sure my parents would forgive me, though. And thanks to you tiring her out last night, we'll be almost to Abilene before she even stirs, I bet. Plainview's barely a hop from there."

All true in theory, for anyone willing to call three hours of driving a hop. But a thermos of ginger tea and a box of crackers weren't enough to keep her stomach happy. She had to pull over twice, and the second stop roused Hannah. It was past lunchtime before they got to Abilene, and they both had frayed nerves as she navigated to a mall with an indoor play place.

Legs stretched, bladders emptied, stomachs full, she checked Hannah in to a world of kid-sized jungle animals and fake rock tunnels. While her girl clambered up a zebra, Rachel settled herself on a bench to just be still for a little while. She sent an updated ETA to Aunt Johnston and a reassuring message to her friends before texting Theo.

He phoned immediately.

"Hey."

"How are you? How's the road?"

She smiled at the affection she could hear in his voice despite the mild chaos of the mall kids. "It's slower going than I hoped, but we're getting through it. Had some close calls on meltdowns earlier, but she's tiring herself out now, so the rest of today should be fine."

"If you need to take an extra day, I can help with a hotel fee."

She didn't even bristle at the offer. Another day of driving with a toddler might force her to contemplate why Theo getting solicitous didn't raise her hackles anymore. "Thanks, but we'll be fine. It shouldn't be much over seven hours tomorrow, but if I'm feeling rotten we'll stay an extra night with Aunt before we tackle it."

"And the car's okay?" He had a paranoia about her car, born solely from knowing she'd planned on replacing it before she found out about the baby. He'd even tried to convince her to take his for this road trip, as if he wasn't going to be driving his own child all over the state before she and Hannah made it to Colorado Springs and back.

"It's fine. I promise. Anyway, tell me if you've made any decisions yet."

The echoing space she sat in was so ill suited to understanding the nuances of his pause. After he and the lawyer met, he had plans that covered everything from running Elixir on his own to bringing in a new partner to closing entirely. None of them was ideal. None of them guaranteed him success. None of them guaranteed Sergei a job, for that matter, but she reminded him of the man's habit of job-hopping in order to avoid the Attorney General. Keeping her ex employed shouldn't be any kind of factor in his plans.

Even if he discounted her, she made a point of stressing that fact.

"Sorry, I had to shut the door. After lunch I'm going to talk with Marti. Her brother interviewed with Ron a few months ago, but he was too qualified for what we needed. I don't know if he's still available, or if what I need now is too big a stretch for him, or —hell." He sighed. "There are a lot of variables. But at least I came up with one plan that might salvage Elixir. So. That's the goal."

Hannah sent herself tumbling down the back of an alligator. She popped up and checked to see if Rachel had been watching. Seeing her mama smile, she set about repeating her actions. "That's a good goal."

"You think so?" He sounded anxious, and her free hand rubbed at her clavicle. Impossible to give him the assurance he craved, because way too much of the situation was out of either of their control.

One thing, though, she could say. "I do, if it's a goal that fulfills you. Elixir is a great place; you've made something special with it. I don't know if I ever told you that. I know it's a ton of work, but you've created community and a great atmosphere."

He was silent again, or maybe drowned out by the arrival of a crowd of elementary age kids. She stood to keep Hannah in her line of sight.

"Thanks, that's really good to hear."

"I may be biased by the great desserts, especially now I can't drink beer for months."

"Buttering me up again?"

"Ha. You've been pretty clear I don't have to go out of my way to cater to your moods." As she bantered right back at him, her casual words went straight to her bedrock. They were true. Theo wasn't going to hold his goodness hostage if she failed to meet his expectations. He didn't insist she only deserved his best if she lived up to whatever shifting standard he felt like imposing. And he'd never blame her for his own problems. Even now that a significant part of his burden was directly related to her.

He could so easily have said, "I've got too much going on to deal with a baby. It's not reasonable to do anything but terminate the pregnancy. And if you insist on having it, you're on your own."

Instead, even as his business was in crisis and even though they were still so new to each other, he'd said he was all in. He'd pledged to stick by her and the baby.

He'd said he loved her.

She interrupted his jokes about catering. "It's not just you."

"I—what's not just me?"

"All in. It's not just you who's all in, Theo."

His smiling voice warmed her. "Yeah?"

"Yeah. I mean, we have to talk a lot through, and you're busy, and I'm almost a whole state away from you, but ... yeah. It's not just you."

"Okay. Because you know I don't only mean it, that I'm all in, as the baby's father, right? I'm talking about us. Our relationship."

Her heartbeat raced the baby's. She managed to ask, "Are you sure? It's okay if you need more time. It's a lot."

"You were always a package deal, Rachel. You and Hannah. It doesn't scare me off now that the package is bigger than I'd bargained for."

She laughed. "You're joking about my size already?"

"No. Don't turn my beautiful analogy into a bad joke." He was laughing, too.

"Sorry. I knew what you meant. Tension. I didn't come into this mall expecting to end up bowled over by emotion. You tend to steal my breath, Theo."

"Serious?"

She hoped he could hear her own happy sincerity. "Serious."

———

HANNAH LOVED Aunt Johnston's porch swing. Over and over that evening, Rachel had to push them off and add a little side-to-side wiggle so it jostled them in unpredictable paths.

Rachel's laughter died as soon as the man stepped from his truck at the curb. Hannah climbed down to try to push the swing herself, but all Rachel could do was watch Brent Berg mount the porch steps.

"Hey there, Rach. Your aunt told me you'd be by tonight. This your baby girl?"

She stood and picked up her daughter.

"Mrs. Johnston told me all about what a cutie she is. So like her mom, huh? Going to be a real heartbreaker someday." He smirked. She remembered that smirk. She once thought that smirk meant inside jokes. Private confidences that proved she was special. "So, you know I'm still looking for someone for that job. Mr. Steichen says you'll be perfect. Why don't you go ahead and apply?"

"No." She'd refused once via email; she could do it again in person.

"Come on, Rach, you'd be doing me a real solid."

She flinched. And caught herself on the recoil as his 'I'm so confident I deserve your compliance' voice opened a backlash of memory. Doing Brent a solid, back when she was fifteen, meant staying up late baking, so he could strut through game day showing off how her cupcakes were tastier than the other team girlfriends'.

She'd been doing him a solid the first time he'd guided her to jerk him off, two minutes, he promised, faster if he could see her tits, and he would fail his bio test if he was obsessing over how horny she made him.

Doing Brent a solid meant going to his buddy's pool party, playing along when they snickered that they couldn't find a towel for her wet body, letting him perch her on his lap and murmur in her ear that he needed her ass to hide his hard-on from the other guys.

She'd been doing Brent a solid that afternoon she sucked him off in the school parking lot, with his fist in her hair keeping her in place for his thrusts and also keeping her from looking around to see the observers he later claimed he didn't hear approaching.

"No."

"At least let me tell you more about it. You in town for a bit? Come out for a tour. Or leave the baby here and come get a drink with me now."

She settled the solid weight of Hannah against her chest. "No."

She wouldn't elaborate. She didn't owe it to him. He'd taken all her favors, and then some, and Rachel was learning she wasn't that person anymore. The one pleased when someone needed her. The one ignoring her inner voice to yield to the voices around her. The one unsure she was worth it.

She cut off whatever Brent was saying. "No."

He leaned back on his heels, at last silent. "Message received, Rachel. Damn. No need to be a bitch about it."

Her hand belatedly covered Hannah's ear, and Brent had the iota of decency it took to look ashamed. Not that he offered so much as a quiet "sorry" as he turned and left. Not that she needed his apology to feel better.

She felt great. She'd stuck up for herself, and she wasn't even shaking from the adrenaline rush.

"Cricket? Was that Brent Berg just leaving?" Aunt Johnston pushed open the screen door so they could head inside. She set out a plate of crackers and cheese for Hannah.

"Yes, and good riddance. I can't have you talking to him about me, Aunt. There's too much wrong to get into, but he isn't someone I can work for, okay?"

"Well I knew that already. You told me once. I didn't ask him to pester you about it."

"Hmm."

"I did not, so don't take that tone, love bug. I know well you don't want to be moving back here."

"Oh, Aunt. It's not because I wouldn't want to live with you again. Listen, he was aggressive with me in high school, and he thinks he can get me to do what he wants again now. I'm not the insecure girl who has to prove she's worth loving now, you know?"

Aunt Johnston gave the best hugs.

Rachel wanted to confide in her, but it was a lot of story and she needed to turn in early for their next long day of driving. And she'd got it in her head that telling her parents and sister about the baby first would bridge some of the space that stretched between them.

As she settled in for the night, leaving Aunt Johnston to take care of all of Hannah's bedtime tasks, she sent heart and bed and sleep emojis to Theo. He was a man who wouldn't demand anything from her as proof that she cared. His solidity didn't depend on Rachel propping him up in any way. It was a part of him, like his kindness and his intuitive nature and his sexy playfulness and his love.

She hadn't expected his love. And now, the clash with Brent fucking Berg fresh in her mind, she wondered if that was because for so long in her life, love with men was transactional. She had to earn it, or thought she did. With sex, sure, but also by going along with their plans and setting aside her needs and accepting the blame for anything they decided was wrong. With the likes of Brent and Sergei, she always knew the score and how close she was to losing what they thought—what she thought—was love.

Theo, though. His love just was. He gave it to her, and didn't demand a word in return. Or a deed, or a thought, or an action, or a promise. It was hers, unconditionally.

And if she had the right to it without working to earn it.... If that's how real love worked, she needed a serious think about what her own heart was up to.

His cousin texted him: So you and Rachel are a serious thing?

Theo: Where's that question come from?

Tomás: Your son.

Oh, Demeter's ruffled horsefeathers. He phoned. "What did he say?"

"You can't wait ten minutes until you get here and ask me in person?"

"Do I sound a ton like you should be messing with me?" Which wasn't the most graceful way to say thanks for taking Andres for a few hours while he dealt with the company, but Tomás was good at reading between the lines.

"You will be here in ten?"

"Yeah, I'm on my way. Is Andres okay?"

"This little monster? He's got venomous claws that can freeze his victims in their tracks, did you know that?"

"Of course. He inherited them from me."

"Huh, that explains it. Hey, kiddo, go ask Tío Enrique to chop up some mango. Warn him your dad's on the way so he'd better go light on the Tajín."

"Hey."

"Calling it like I know it, primo." Tomás must have held the phone towards the kitchen, because Andres's giggling echoed down the line.

"Seriously, what did he say?"

"That Daddy is dating Hannah's mommy."

"He didn't mention anything else?"

His cousin was also good at picking up on potential gossip. "Anything like what?"

Theo did not want to have this conversation while stuck

behind a tow truck. He'd told Andres about his relationship before Rachel joined them for dinner, but didn't intend to mention the baby until he knew much more about where he and Rachel were headed. Which didn't mean his son hadn't overheard something. "Anything like anything. Like he might be trying to process some big news and isn't sure what it is. For example."

"What big news?"

"Listen, I'm trying to find out what he knows, okay, so I can sit him down if I need to."

"Theo, what big news do you have that might warrant a sit-down?"

"It's—I'm not talking about anything specific."

"Bullshit."

"Hey." He clutched the steering wheel.

"It's fine, he's in with my dad. I'll go outside. Will that make you happy?"

He'd be pulling onto his uncle's street in a couple of minutes, but giving the news without being face to face appealed to him. "You can't tell anyone."

"Híjole! Y'all elope or something?"

"Jesus. No. She's ... we're going to have a baby."

Tomás went quiet. Theo signaled his turn and waited for the cross traffic to clear, listening intently for any kind of response. Nothing. Not a peep.

He cut the call and coasted to a stop at Enrique's curb. When he got out of the car, his cousin was standing in the carport, arms wide. Theo jogged straight at him and let himself be caught up in a massive hug. Tomás gripped his head and planted a kiss on each cheek. "Wow. Are you happy? You're happy. Look at you. Wow. And Rachel? I can see it, man. I really can. She's great. Congratulations, baby."

Theo's heart thudded. He hadn't celebrated at all. He and Rachel, they hadn't celebrated. Maybe she had with her friends or family, but the two of them had gone straight into negotiation and coordination and management of various crises. Even her veiled declaration of the day before was wrapped in layers of logistics.

Tomás's effusive reaction unleashed a reservoir of emotion within him. Because awkward timing and uncertain future aside, the reality was, he got to have another baby. A new tiny person, to hold and marvel at and adore in all the stages and all the days of its life.

His to love and treasure every day.

Theo dropped his head to his cousin's shoulder. Tomás hugged him tighter while he let himself whoop out a laughing cry.

CHAPTER THIRTY-SIX

"WELCOME TO OUR HOME!" Dad said, opening the condo door wide and kneeling to engulf Hannah.

"Say hi to Grandpa." She leaned down to kiss her dad's pate. When they were growing up, it was a game she and Blythe played, planting loud smacks on the top of his head whenever they caught him unawares—slouching at the table, napping on the sofa—to reinforce how much balder he was getting year by year. Now he sported grandfatherly fluffs of hair above his ears, and an otherwise hairless head. It was funny how familiar it was, kissing that baldness, how much more connected to him it made her feel, compared to chatting on video calls.

Hannah kept her arms locked around his shoulders as he stood and backed so they could enter. Mom hugged everyone at once, already asking about luggage and road conditions and bathroom needs and meal times.

"Let's show Grangran all your potty skills, okay?"

They took a group trip to the half-bath under the stairs, which made for a crowd, especially when Rachel had to lean over to help with wiping and pulling up the padded panties. But Hannah enjoyed the fuss and applause, and Rachel in her turn enjoyed the rare chance to shut the door and pee in private.

While her mother and daughter played, Rachel hauled their bags up to Blythe's old bedroom, then joined the others in the den. Dad passed everyone servings of his latest smoothie blend. Cucumbers and beets and apples. He even had a cup with a lid and straw for Hannah, so at some point since their last visit he or Mom had paused by the kid aisle in the supermarket. That was nice.

"Guess what?" Mom was pulling out her iPad.

"Potato," said Hannah.

"Well, no, not that."

"She's got a farming game she plays on my friend's tablet," Rachel explained.

Mom's face cleared. "Oh, right. Well, I can download it, if you want."

"It's fine, she was just making associations. What's your news?"

"I listed you as a co-host for Blythe's baby shower tomorrow. It's going to be beautiful."

She held her hand steady as Hannah took sips of her smoothie. Dad had served the adults in matching glass mugs, nice heavy ones with swirls of color around the rim. Hannah wanted to taste from the green side and the yellow side and the purple side, and was ignoring her grandfather's comments about it being the same as what was in her cup. Experiment over, Rachel wiped Hannah's beet-colored upper lip and set aside her mug. "Blythe's having a baby shower tomorrow?"

"I know, I know." Mom handed over the iPad, which displayed the invite: 'Blythe's Baby Boy Brunch!'

"Blythe's having a son?"

"She didn't tell you?"

She shook her head. Hannah's smoothie was making condensation rings on the coffee table. It was the same table they'd had in their house growing up, the one they played games at and where Blythe did her homework—Rachel had to sit at the kitchen table, where Mom could monitor her progress as she went about her afternoon mom tasks. They'd sold that kitchen table, along with Rachel's bedroom furniture and the plush purple rocking chair and several other items that wouldn't fit into the condo. Rachel kept asking if the rocking chair could go with her to Aunt Johnston's. Mom and Dad kept explaining why she could only take what fit in two suitcases and her backpack.

It was fine. Aunt Johnston's house had the porch swing.

But they'd kept the coffee table all these years, and it, like Dad's bald spot, was a reminder of the safety and comfort of her childhood. And of less comfortable childhood moments, but she grabbed hold of the good and jettisoned the rest.

Mom enlarged the invite so she could see her name there, alongside those of her sister's best friends from med school. "You don't have to tell me it's tacky for the grandmother to host the shower," she said. "That's why it's so perfect that you got here in time. I knew you would stress over dealing with the back and forth emails and researching party favors and such. So I got to do it all, and put your name on it, which worked out great."

When she was little, they had a set of sandstone coasters with pictures of bears on them. A grizzly and a Kodiak and a black bear and a sun bear. A rack on the sofa table held the four of them when not in use, and for a while she cried if she couldn't have the black bear. It had the friendliest pose. Then she learned to alternate her favorite every month, so even if Blythe carried her drink to the living room first, there was a good chance her favorite would still be available. The important thing was to always have a coaster under their drinks. And to their credit, her parents had kept the coffee table ring-free for decades now.

She didn't see the bear coasters. Likely they'd faded or cracked or lost the cork backings long ago. She didn't see any coasters. She guessed it didn't matter if Hannah's smoothie left a sticky stain or two behind. Maybe Mom and Dad were ready to replace the coffee table. It had sharp corners. Her nephew would be safer if it was gone.

The party decorations were green and orange, to match

Blythe's nursery. The menu featured omelets and three kinds of blintzes.

"But I like planning parties."

Her mother paused her litany of event negotiations. "Well, sweetie. I'm sorry. I didn't know that. You used to hate looking things up."

Since she was in a room with two other responsible—if not always thoughtful—adults, she could close her eyes and sink back against the sofa for a minute. It hadn't been replaced, but they'd reupholstered it since the days when she and Blythe woke Dad from his naps with a kiss to his bald spot. Given it some extra foam. Added coordinating throw pillows. It didn't feel like the same spot where she'd curled up and watched countless episodes of *Friends* and *ER*.

Hannah used Rachel's thigh as a handhold as she pulled herself up to lie beside her. "Mama nap?"

She kissed her curls. "I think it's time for us to go meet Aunt Blythe and Uncle Jason for dinner."

"Rachel, we didn't mean..."

"It's fine, Mom. I'm excited about the party."

"Well, of course you are. I knew you'd want a chance to celebrate our grandson."

She refused hear Mom stumbling over her last word. It did her no good to compare Hannah to her forthcoming nephew, like it had done her no good to compare herself to Blythe. Aunt Johnston had drummed that, at least, into her head. "Different people, different relationships. No matter how tempting, does you no good to keep score." An image from that morning of Aunt Johnston waving them off, her face so like Dad's except with profuse hair, was a quick mental snapshot guaranteed to calm her down.

Still, petty and useless as it was, she said, "I am sad you didn't tell me about it before we left. I've been knitting her a blanket, and I'd have tried to finish it in time." It even had a lot of green in it, though she'd picked that because it was cute and gender-neutral, not because she'd heard from her sister about her favorite baby colors.

Dad stacked the empty cups on a tray, wiping the condensation off the coffee table with his sleeve. "Want to get the door for Grandpa?" he asked Hannah, who rolled off Rachel and led the way to the kitchen. He never had been good at sitting in a tense room.

"Well, Rachel, goodness. Your gift is the party."

"So do I write a check to Liz or to Angie?" She knew she was making it worse. Two full days of driving, a two-year-old's favorite playlists on repeat, worry over Theo's business, a sofa that wasn't as welcoming as that of her childhood.

"Don't be ridiculous."

"I should make it out to you, then? If it's more than three hundred I'll have to pay you in installments." She needed a healthy meal and a solid night's sleep and a morning hike, and then she could be a daughter they wanted around.

"Rachel." Mom twisted her fingers together. She'd done it so often, sitting at that old kitchen table while Rachel wrote out spelling words or flash cards full of history facts. Mom suffered a lecture by one of Rachel's specialists, who said no matter how abysmal Rachel's handwriting, she had to write down her own lessons or she'd never learn. So instead of grabbing the pencil to do the work herself, Mom twisted her fingers. By the time she was thirteen, the finger twisting applied to any reason Mom was frustrated with her.

"Fine, then. On the way to dinner we can stop by the mall and you can pick something off Blythe's registry. Will that let you drop this nonsense talk of checks?"

She nodded. Because Aunt Johnston was right, in the end. Scorekeeping was knotting her stomach into tighter twists than the braided cable of her mom's fingers, and it would unravel both of them if she stopped.

Nonetheless, she decided that's night dinner was not, after all, the perfect moment to tell her family she was pregnant.

"So are you going to take her kayaking or something?"

"She's two, Theo. She doesn't like sitting still. Or getting her head wet."

"Okay, Ms. Colorado, I was joking." He closed out his report and leaned back in his desk chair. "What are you up to today?"

She's told him neither of her parents had taken time off work to spend with them. Not even a half-day.

"We'll go up to Santa's Workshop in a bit. Dad got me a coupon."

"What's Santa's Workshop?"

"It's an amusement park. She can go on most of the rides, and there's, you know, entertainment, pictures with Santa, all that. Do you want a souvenir ornament? Do you guys even celebrate Christmas?"

"Of course. But last time I had him at Christmas, we spent the whole week up with my family, so I didn't decorate. Can't do that this year."

She didn't ask why not. He'd offered Marti's brother the job as head brewer and was working with his accountant and lawyer to take on full ownership of Elixir. Ron agreed to stick around for a month to transition, in exchange for no criminal charges. Theo felt like he was pushing his luck, but that morning he'd submitted a proposal to pay Ron out in stages, instead of adding to his loan. And while he hadn't undervalued Ron's shares, his appraisal used forced liquidation values for all their equipment. As he'd explained while talking it through with Rachel, if he couldn't buy Ron out, they were going to have to sell out. He gave Ron a chance to meet with his own advisers and come up with a different valuation. Now he just had to wait for the man's response.

"Okay," she said, and he appreciated her brisk cheer. "I'll look for the most hideous ornament for your tree, and what's more, I'll help you decorate. That way I can be sure you're displaying it prominently."

"Damn but I love you."

"I love you, too."

He closed his eyes to savor her words. No ambiguity, no hesitation. Just a statement, from her to him, and it eased everything in the world.

"I quit."

He sat up and found Sergei in their office doorway. "Sorry, Rachel, hang on."

"That's what I thought. First you accuse me of stealing, next you force Ron out, now you're running off with my wife. I don't need to put up with it."

"Serg, hold up."

"Oh, he's got his 'world is working against me' tone happening," Rachel said. "I'm going to go pack up to head to the North Pole. Call me later, love."

He looked at his mobile, but she was gone. Sergei, not so much. "Sit down."

"No thanks, *re*." Clear as the Aegean he was reverting to the rudest meaning of the interjection.

"You're going to walk out on me? I explained about Ron and the money."

"How do you explain stealing my wife and daughter?" The man had a world-class sneer. He took note of it, as a warning to himself. If he was ever tempted to replicate it, he'd know he was way off track from who he wanted to be.

"Ex-wife. And I'm not stealing either one of them. Loving them isn't theft."

"My mother warned me about your intentions."

"Does your storming out mean you're not having Depy's name day dinner here tomorrow?"

Sergei crossed his arms across his chest. "I'm giving my two weeks' notice."

He rubbed his temple. "Fine. I appreciate that. Give me your company card. And send Marti in on your way back up front."

She could be ready to move up to manager, if he had her

shadow Sergei for a few weeks. And he could still take Andres up to his parents' for their scheduled visit without stressing every single day about how the place was functioning.

In the ensuing quiet moment, he googled Santa's Workshop. Looked a little old-fashioned, but tailor-made—elf made—for Hannah to have a blast. Maybe they'd all go back sometime, him and Rachel and Andres and Hannah and the baby. They could take Rachel's nephew, too. All the other in-laws could decide for themselves if they wanted to tag along, but they wouldn't mind either way. With him on board, Rachel wasn't anyone's afterthought. And neither was he. Because they loved each other, and love meant choosing each other, every day.

CHAPTER THIRTY-SEVEN

MOM SPENT ten minutes justifying the early dinnertime, as if Rachel hadn't started eating dinner at five thirty from the time Hannah started solid foods. She grinned, wondering if her nephew or her sister's schedule would triumph. "It's fine, Mom. We're as happy to eat now. I'd have to give Hannah Banana a snack otherwise."

She kept grinning. She'd felt bubbly all day, planning to make her announcement over dinner. She'd told them already about Theo, leaving out Ron's stealing and Sergei's quitting. After Mom looked up Elixir's website and followed the links to some of the good reviews, she'd smoothed her hand down Rachel's hair, fluffing it a bit and telling her he seemed like a nice companion.

So: that was good groundwork. And after Blythe let Hannah explore her abdomen during the baby shower, she knew her girl was ready to adapt to the idea of a sibling. Back in spring, her daycare friend Rishi's brother was born, which put Hannah on a campaign for a baby of her own. She'd settled down about it after a while, but Rachel was ready to answer her girl's many thousands of questions once she shared the news. She'd even picked up a couple of picture books that afternoon, while filling the time until her parents returned from their jobs.

All this groundwork, and Blythe and Jason wanting to eat so conveniently early. She was glad she hadn't shared the news that first night, when she was tired from the road and everyone was focused on the shower. Now no one could accuse her of creating drama and stealing focus from Blythe.

She showed them all the photos from Santa's Workshop, and everyone admired the ornament Hannah, for whatever inexplicable reason, picked out to be her treasure. It was a cow wearing a quilt, but who was she to question her daughter's passions?

"We'll have to take the baby up for his first picture with Santa," Mom said. "Grandparents get free admission, isn't that so nice?"

Rachel closed out the photo app on her phone.

"He'd freeze his little nose off waiting in line."

Mom got misty. "Oh, Blythe, but imagine it, him wearing that cute snowsuit from Jason's brother?"

Dad laughed. "Does your brother think he'll be skiing before he can walk?"

Jason shrugged. "We almost were, ourselves. But we could at least stand up first. I think lessons won't start until next winter."

"Baby's first ski lesson. You have to send me video of that, when it happens," Rachel said.

"That reminds me, I need to get a new phone with more memory."

Before Mom and Dad started one of their technology debates, Rachel cleared her throat. The bubbles still elevated her, no matter how off the track of her own life things got. The four of them were used to dinners together. Of course they had patterns to sink into, even when Rachel and Hannah visited. "I was thinking. Maybe you all could come down to Houston for Easter."

Blythe and Jason exchanged a baffled look, and Dad said, "Easter?"

"Well." She grinned again. "It could be really special. Because, the thing is, Blythe, by Easter? Your son will have a new baby cousin. How sweet would that be? If they can share their first Easter together?"

Everyone but Hannah stared at her. The saccharine cheer of her announcement soured on her tongue. Looking to be handed praise again. As always. Because Mom was right all those years; it was almost impossible for her to learn.

Blythe's hands rested on her pregnant belly. "Oh. Well. I'm supposed to be back full time by then. I'll need to check if we can take the time to go all that way. But maybe." She tugged at her left ear, and Rachel couldn't guess if she was fidgeting or passing along their long-ago warning to be quiet until Mom had her say.

"A cousin. I mean, another cousin. Nice." Jason nodded at Hannah, like Rachel might have forgotten the existence of her own child.

She smiled at him, because she was at the point of collecting any scrap of approval from anyone in the room.

Mom said, "You've gone and gotten pregnant again?"

"Jason, I've been meaning to ask you about this mole on my back. You mind coming back to take a look at it?" Dad left the table without waiting for an answer. Maybe the way Jason kissed Blythe's temple and followed was another part of the shorthand these four had from all their meals together.

She licked her lips. Took a sip of water. "I—Theo and I both— we're excited about it."

"You barely know the man."

"I know, Mom. But he's such a good soul. You'll like him, I'm sure. And we know we love each other."

"Like you loved Sergei?"

Blythe spoke up. "Mom, she was so young then. I'm sure she's smarter about relationships now."

"I am. I am so much smarter." She didn't trip once over the words. All those times Theo praised her cleverness must have worn a smoother pathway through her brain, allowing her to own her worth. Well enough to proclaim it to her mom and sister, anyway.

"Well, Rachel." Mom's fingers knotted together. "It's good you feel that way. But it's still a big step for people who just met."

She helped Hannah to the floor. "Go find Grandpa and Uncle Jason."

"It's almost like you planned it as soon as I told you about my baby." Blythe said.

She would not add rolling eyes to the list of everything else her mom was tallying up about her wrongness. "I didn't even know Theo back then. And this was very much unplanned."

"Well, Rachel. You don't have to just let this happen to you, you know. We could even schedule something for while you're here, so Dad and I can help out with Hannah while you recover."

Blythe's hands rubbed at her abdomen, and Rachel found herself mimicking the action. "Mom. We talked about it. That's not our choice."

"Well, did you, though? Because this is a big deal, Rachel. You're barely getting by with one child. And I'm sure your Theo is all you claim, just lovely as can be, but you can't expect him to stick by you forever when you haven't even known him half a year. There's no shame in terminating. If he's as nice as you claim, he might stay with you afterwards long enough for you to make a baby on purpose."

Red and bright and sharp color shards plunged around behind her eyelids. Rachel kept the tears at bay, but her jaw was stiff when she spoke. "I know there's no shame in termination. I'm pro-choice. We both are."

"I didn't know that. All those years living in Texas."

"Dad lived there longer than I have."

"But he got out. You were there all those impressionable young adult years. Living in that state changed you, Rachel."

"Mom, maybe—"

"No, you know what?" She interrupted Blythe, but also tugged on her right earlobe, in apology, in case her sister still had any attachment to their old code. "You're right that Texas changed me. Or that I changed after I moved there. After you and Dad sent me there, two suitcases and a backpack, and suddenly I had to make friends with people whose parents grew up with each other. I had to figure out the rhythms of Aunt Johnston's house, and learn to trust her when she told me my problems with school weren't the whole measure of me. I left here thinking I wasn't worth a penny to anyone, and in Texas I found out that's not true. I have value. Not just because I got myself through school and college and have those degrees you never thought I could manage. I matter, Mom. I'm good at my job, and I'm a kind, supportive friend, and most of all? The thing I'm most proud of, what I know I'm doing so well, or trying to do so well, every single day? And you never say it. I don't know if you can't see it or if you don't mention it because you forgot years ago how to compliment me. But I am a great mama to your granddaughter. That girl and I aren't 'barely getting by.' We are *thriving*."

THEY WERE in the middle of singing about the wheels on the bus when her own tires stopped going round and round. Rachel coasted onto the shoulder and set the parking brake before, one slow peel at a time, lifting her fingers from their grip on the steering wheel.

Hannah continued with the song, unperturbed by calculations of how much further to Plainview, and why hadn't she let Aunt Johnston know they'd fled Colorado early, and what blight hit this stretch of the freeway and killed all the shade trees?

The engine wasn't cranking at all, and the car's interior grew toastier by the second. She called Aunt J's house but got the machine. Her cell went to voice mail, and not once in her dozen years of deigning to own a cell phone had Aunt Johnston figured out to check her voice mail.

And Hannah said, "Mama, it's peepee time."

Because of course it was.

The tow truck arrived while she was teaching her daughter to squat in the great outdoors. Rachel wanted a shower. And a nap. She tried not to act helpless and relieved as the driver, Kari, latched the car seat into her cab. But Kari picked up on some level of her distress. She offered to drop them at Aunt Johnston's house on the way to the mechanic. Turned out she knew one of Aunt's neighbors, so she caught her up on the local drama: the man spray-painted all the gnomes in the garden across the yard. Not some teen prank. The vandal was fifty-eight years old and he'd coated each gnome with a different color. "Used drop cloths and every-thing, said he didn't want to ruin Thelma's grass."

"Courtship ritual?"

Kari's laugh was sarcastic. "Boneheaded one."

"You got that right."

"When I was in, I don't know, second grade? Kid in my class kept poking my back with the eraser end of his pencil. Swear to god, though it sounds like a euphemism now. Mom told me to take it as a compliment cause it meant he had a crush on me. Imagine the message there. Acting like a prick is supposed to flatter a girl."

"I think I met that guy in high school."

"Hon, we all met in that guy in high school."

She laughed, but. Yeah. The amazing thing was, her newfound ability to laugh about it.

"Thanks for the lift. It was good to meet you."

"No worries. All in a day's work. You got Ray's number for the car?"

She nodded and sent Hannah up to tackle her beloved porch swing while they unloaded all her gear. Still no answer from Aunt. After settling Hannah down, she called Theo. They'd talked during the morning's drive, so she could decompress and update him about her change in plans. It settled her, hearing his voice and knowing the worst of her trip was behind her.

"Hey, you make it to Plainview?"

"Almost."

"What happened? Are you okay? Hannah?"

"No worries; we're both fine. The little one, too." She cradled a hand over the tiny bump of their baby. "We're at my aunt's house waiting on her to come home. She's in for a surprise. My car died just outside town—tow truck driver gave me a lift. I think it's the timing belt."

"Rachel, hell. You're terrifying me."

"We're fine, I swear. It's just car trouble. And I left so darn early this morning I even made it here before nap time. I'll lay down with her in a bit. I wanted to let you know what's happening. Anyway, Evan, that's Natalie's fiancé, remember? He's getting a new car next weekend and is going to give me a good deal on his old one, so I only have to get us back home. If the mechanic can't fix this cheap we'll take the bus."

"If the timing belt's gone it'll cost more to repair than it's worth."

"I know, Mr. Mechanical-All-the-Sudden."

"I looked it up."

"Just now?" She laughed. "Of course you did."

"Hey. I like looking things up."

"I know. It's cute. Anyhow I'll have the real expert give me an opinion soon and let you know what we're doing."

"I'll come get you."

"Theo. You're with your family."

"Rachel. You're my family, too."

She dropped. Just landed on the sofa like she'd meant it. How did he always find casual phrases to shatter her to her core like that?

"We can fuss about it later. It might be something simple. Okay, listen, Aunt is here, talk to you soon."

"Bye, love."

"Bye."

She kept staring at her phone until Aunt Johnston walked in. "Doodlebug, what's happened? I didn't expect you till Sunday. Are y'all okay? Where's your car?"

She lifted a finger to hush her aunt, tilting her head to the back room where Hannah napped. "I'm pregnant."

And then she curled up in Aunt Johnston's lap and sobbed.

"Rachel. Oh baby girl, it's okay. We can sort it out. It's fine now, you hush. Don't let those hormones get the best of you, come on. Good strong breaths. That's my girl. Well, now. I'm going to make you some tea, and you just sit here a minute for me."

Oh, hell. She wiped at her face, realized her hands weren't absorbent enough, and shut herself in the bathroom to clean up. When she emerged, Aunt J had tea and an afghan waiting for her. So many comforting memories started out that way. It all helped settle her into a peaceful state.

She explained about the car and then told her about Theo, the baby, everything.

"Well, you've always been my busy bee. Okay, now. I can't say I'm not a tad worried about if you're forcing your own hand here, going forward with this, but the man sounds a thousand times better than that ex of yours."

"So much more than a thousand. I'm not the numbers person you are ... I don't know if I can explain it. The way he's always standing beside me, and thinking about what's most important for me. Not all high-handed, I mean, but thoughtful. And I can disagree with him. He doesn't shut me down, or make me feel small."

"Doodlebug."

She ran a mental eye over what she'd said. Blew her nose. "Maybe I never told you everything about my marriage."

Aunt smacked a kiss on her cheek. "You think not?"

"Well, we can talk about it if you want. But listen, I've had lots of counseling and space since then. It's mostly in the past. Not just because of Theo. Except one thing I really think is him."

"What's that, then?"

She found herself gripping her aunt's hand. "This hit me on the drive today. I was so upset, leaving Colorado, but before Theo, that always came with this voice in my head, you know? This horrid, mean voice that was all Sergei. The way he got into my head to tear me down. The minute I had a problem I couldn't handle, or worried I was messing up, or ... anything, really. Sometimes just if I stubbed my toe or let out a curse in front of Hannah. Big things, little things, always there was Sergei sneering away in my brain. But not anymore. Or not nearly so much. I didn't even realize it was going away until I was crossing back into Texas this morning, and there was the sun rising higher above the wind farm and everything looked wide open and bright and I thought, 'hey, everything going on and not once has that toxic weasel crawled out of his hole to tell me what a pathetic loser I was and it was no wonder my family didn't have time for me.' And it could be that's me getting distance from him. But I think Theo's influence has a bunch to do with it."

"Oh, June bug."

"No, but it's so much better now, that's what I'm saying."

Aunt Johnston planted both hands on Rachel's shoulders, so she knew it was a question she had to answer without evasion. "My girl, you know I'm pleased as spicy pickles to have you, but why are you here three days earlier than you planned? What did your mom and dad do this time?"

And there was the one thing she'd avoided confiding to her aunt. She half-pulled away towards the bedroom, but before she could make an excuse about checking on Hannah, Aunt said, "If I need to call my brother and interrogate him, you know I have no qualms about it."

"It wasn't like they kicked me to the curb. I just couldn't stay. I thought if they were the first to hear the news about the baby— well, I don't know what I thought. They're so excited about Blythe's son. Did you know it's a boy? I didn't. And I get there, and they have this whole baby shower planned, and that's fine, they live near her and it's not like I even had a shower for Hannah, what with the divorce and living with Depy and everything. So that's fine, I guess, even if it wasn't the most kid-friendly brunch place I've ever been. Lots of fancy glassware and quaint rickety chairs."

Her aunt snorted.

"But all their plans for him, Aunt." She told her about the ski lessons and her foolish attempt to surprise everyone with her news and Dad leaving the table.

Aunt snorted again.

"Well, when has your brother ever been good at confrontation? I swear I learned to never stand up for myself from him."

"You taught it to yourself just fine, cricket."

She nodded. Because it was true. And Rachel deserved to accept all the true things about herself. And then she told Aunt Johnston about the rest of it. "And Mom said, 'If you think your aunt is the only person in this family who loves you maybe you should go back now to see her instead of suffering through a visit with us the rest of the week.' So I said I would. And here I am."

They ran out of tissues and her tea had long since gone cold. She was a certified mess, but for the first time in all her long days of driving, she felt blanketed in peace.

CHAPTER THIRTY-EIGHT

His parents, his sisters, his sister-in-law and brother-in-law—everyone thought he was being ridiculous. Fine. He didn't have to share their opinions, or heed them, or explain why he and his son were leaving Austin early to get to Rachel and Hannah. Andres downloaded a couple of movies to watch on the way up. They picked the most interesting hole-in-the-wall burger place in Sweet-water for lunch. They counted cows for a while. When they got closer to the feedlots, they counted types of cows instead, and he had to explain the beef industry. Andres said he wasn't ever eating cow again and they talked about vegetarianism for a few dozen miles.

He wouldn't say the trip flew by, but he wasn't making life miserable for his son, no matter what his family said. And when they got to Plainview, there was Rachel. And Hannah, who latched on to Andres and unloaded every toy from every bag in the place.

When his son handed over the books they'd bought her, her adoration of him was set in cement.

Speaking of adoration. "Hi."

"It's so good to see you, ridiculous man. I can't believe you drove all this way." She glowed. Not some kind of pregnancy thing, or probably not. Hell, she'd been pregnant for all but like the first three weeks they knew each other. But no, the glow predated the sex. It was those eyes, all those blue hues playing catch and release with the light.

Theo deepened the kiss and she was right there with him. The kids giggled but she didn't tug her fingers out of his hair, so he continued to stroke the beautiful strong arch of her spine.

"Well, howdy. You must be Andres."

Rachel pulled back and dissolved into laughter, hiding her head in his chest. He looked past her to find his son fist bumping the woman who'd shepherded Rachel through her teens.

"Aunt, this is Theo and Andres. Guys, Karin Johnston."

It was all very friendly. Iced tea and chatter about the broken car and preparing a beef-free dinner. After the kids were in bed, his new favorite person Aunt Johnston said, "I'll listen out for them. Cricket, you go and show Theo what passes for a town around here."

Yes. He was half-flustered, making sure she had his number in case Andres needed him, trying to figure where Hannah had stashed his shoes, remembering not to grope Rachel in front of her aunt. Then they were in his car, and he said, "Nearest place with a modicum of privacy?"

And she gripped his thigh—not helping—and laughed—extra not helping—and very helpfully directed him to past strip malls and drive-ins and down a dark and empty country road. "Here."

He took it in. "Serious?"

"Serious. Now are you going to sit there or are you going to hop a graveyard fence with me?"

Grabbing a blanket from the back of the car, he followed her into the darkness. And into an actual cemetery, trusting her to keep them from getting caught. Or haunted. Or both. They fetched up beside a maintenance shed, which was a relief. A little more shelter than the headstones; a lot less creepy. "You are working me into a state, love."

"Don't even pretend like you weren't planning on getting very naked with me tonight. I know you didn't drive all the way up here just to be sure our kids got a chance to bond like you've been scheming for all summer."

"Hey. They're going to share a sibling soon. They should be pals."

"Agreed. But maybe let's talk strategy later and get naked now?"

He couldn't. Not until he got another taste of her. Not when touching her, any part of her, holding her and feeling her press against him was more vital even than hearing her say 'I love you' in person. Contact with Rachel. Lips, hands, bodies and lips and smiles and eyes shining in the darkness. It was everything he needed.

"I love you, Theo."

Okay, he'd lied to himself. Those words, her hands playing in his beard as she said them, the utter conviction in her voice. That was everything he needed.

"I love you, too. An entire world of love."

"Good. Strip."

He kicked off his shorts and shrugged off his shirt, managing to drop them in a pile on the corner of the blanket. Her sandals and t-shirt landed in the same general area, and that was as far as she got before he rolled her under him and kissed his way along her jaw, her neck. That spot on her shoulder that made her giggle; he knew that spot so well. He would always know that spot, and if he was the luckiest person around, it would always make her giggle.

"I MISSED YOU." Truest words, but she paired them with shoving down his boxers so it might not be obvious that being with him again set her on the verge of tears.

"Hey." He stripped her body and her heart bare.

Was this this price of love? A man with constant access to her emotional core?

She hoped her kiss had the same effect on him. Probably it did. Probably that's why he'd spent all day driving to rescue her, and was happy to be exposed to all the summer heat and mosquitos in the middle of a cemetery where she and her friends once set off a nonsense amount of fireworks and got away before anyone caught them.

"You need to be inside me right now."

"Why, are we worried about cops?" He shackled her wrists above her head and slow motion explored her torso with his tongue.

"No. Just bugs. That's not the point." She undulated to be sure he knew what the point was.

"You are so impatient."

"Fuck yes. It's been like a century."

"I know," he said and covered her breast with his free hand. "I've been counting the seconds."

"And guess what?" She wrenched back her hands and propped herself on her elbows. "I didn't even tell you the best part."

His mouth seemed to think her navel was the best part. Or lower. He bit at her hip. "There's a best part?"

"Theo, pay attention." She tugged at his hair. His back arched and his cock jerked against her, so she did it again. He smelled so much better than she ever had after driving six hours. Mint and oranges and Theo. "When I went to the doctor, she did an STD panel. We're clean."

He tilted his head at her. "I think we knew that already?"

"Well sure. But since we're clean, and we're already pregnant...."

She didn't have to finish her leading statement before he thrust into her. Smart man. "Oh fuck. Rachel. You. This. Amazing."

Totally amazing. Not the sex with no barriers. Or not just the sex with no barriers. Not just the hand he cradled under her head to keep it from the bumpy hard ground. Not just the other hand he slipped between them to drive her to a fever pitch. Not just the slick of her palms over his body, the moan as his tempo increased, the way he pressed his thumb hard to her clit when her breathing went ragged and he caught her mouth in a kiss that stole everything from her. Her orgasm, her screams, her heart.

No barriers, that was the amazing part. He was fully in her. Even after his thrusts deepened and she wrapped her legs around his back and demanded his release and he bucked and moaned and nipped at her lip and neck and shoulder and it sent a jolt straight to where they were joined. After they came and crashed back to the blanket and used their shirts as inadequate blankets over their sweaty, cooling skin. Humming and holding her hand and leaning over every few seconds for another gentle kiss. Even then, he was fully in her.

He'd gone and foraged around her soul, leaving alone the walls she still needed. Found space for himself. And it was so comfortable, having him in residence. She didn't think she'd ever be able to let him leave.

EPILOGUE

THE KIDS JOSTLED each other hopping down the hallway-turned-raceway. Giggling. So much giggling.

For a few fall weekends, she and Hannah joined Theo on his treks up to Fort Worth so Andres could get to know them. Not every time, because Andres deserved his dad's undivided attention no matter what else was happening in Theo's life. In September, the kids thought dashing through the connecting doors of their hotel rooms to leap onto each other's beds was a glorious game. In October, they'd insisted on a sleepover. Neither of them could settle down that night, and in the end Rachel curled up with Hannah and Theo with Andres. In November, they didn't spend money on a second room.

Over Thanksgiving, when both kids were with their other parents, Rachel moved into Theo's townhouse. He'd given Andres's big bed to his aunt and uncle after their house flooded, leaving room for twin beds and an influx of Hannah's possessions in the kids' bedroom.

It wasn't yet a squeeze. But they'd only just now stacked a messy, towering pile of gifts from Colorado under the Christmas tree. There was plenty of time for Andres and Hannah to get sick of being together all the time. She watched them go back to their starting line. Hannah wanted to race crab-style like Andres. Every time he came up with a new way to slow himself, she copied him and the playing field was uneven again.

"You're borrowing trouble," Theo said, bumping his hip to hers.

"Open the oven for me?"

He did, and she slid in a tray of cookies. They'd already mailed tins full of baked goods to Aunt Johnston and her parents and Blythe's family. And Annalisa and Theo's sisters and his parents. So much more holiday baking now. Good thing her beloved was an excellent dessert maker. They'd turned down the invites to visit Austin and Plainview; their first Christmas as a family was for the four of them.

"I'm not borrowing trouble. I'm monitoring in case trouble arrives, so I can jump in first thing."

"Pretty sure that's the same thing." He stopped rubbing her back long enough to pass her a towel so she could wipe the flour from her shirt. The baby bump was nothing but an expanse waiting to be covered in spills.

Little One kicked at her to protest the characterization. "She wants more of your pecan pie."

"Does she now?" Theo reached around and splayed a hand over their child, who seemed to be copying her siblings, crab walking around inside of Rachel. "Nope. That's not what she wants."

"Oh, really?" Her in-house expert. All his organizational drive, now he'd gotten Elixir back up and profitable, seemed focused on the stages of the baby's development. Every day another tidbit about how she was growing. "What does she want? A green smoothie? A walk?"

"A wedding."

She spun to face him. He wrapped a hand round her nape and pulled her in for a deep kiss. Well, as deep as he could manage with her trying to talk through it. And with his grin. And with the kids suctioning themselves to their legs. And with the oven timer going off.

"Theodoros Andreas Melis, did you just propose to me?"

"Everyone back up so we can get the cookies before they burn." He winked at her while scooping up Hannah. Winked!

She gave Andres the potholders and set a steadying hand on his crown while he leaned in to slide out the baking sheet. If her hand trembled a little, no one mentioned it. If she stared at the golden edges of the pfeffernüsse longer than necessary, everyone let it slide. Tears under control, wobbly smile in place, she faced her family. "Is that a yes?"

"I think that's my line," he said, pulling her in to his side. Hannah pushed away and he let her wriggle to the ground. "Out of the kitchen, you two. Go wash up for dinner."

"Is dinner even ready?"

He moved so she could see the timer on the Instant Pot.

"Is that a yes?" She laughed a little while repeating herself.

"Yes, dinner is ready. Yes, I'm proposing. Yes, I want you to say yes. Yes, I want to spend forever with you and our children. Yes, my heart belongs to you. Yes, I'm thinking about a summer wedding, if you and Little One are up for it by then. Yes, there's more pecan pie. Does that cover everything?"

She was nodding, because words were tricky things. Hard for her shallow lungs to push through her tight throat. The easiest decision she'd ever made, but hard to say.

"So. Rachel. My goddess, my companion, my love. Is that a yes?"

She swallowed. Whispered, "Yes."

"Yes? Serious?" He voice was rough around the edges, too.

"So serious."

The dinner timer went off, Hannah got obstinate about sitting in Andres's favorite seat, Little One opted to sit on her bladder. She could not stop grinning.

"I was going to ask you, you know."

Theo lowered his fork. "What?"

"Already put a ring in your stocking and everything."

"You did?"

"Andres, go get your dad's stocking, can you?"

Hannah trailed after him. While they waited, Rachel twined her fingers with Theo's. "Don't get too excited about the ring. I found it in the dress-up section of the toy store. But I wanted you to know—want you to know, in case you ever wondered, how much I want to spend my life with you. Not because of Little One, or because Hannah loves you or because I love Andres. It's you, Theo. You're everything to me, and I'm choosing you."

She didn't know which of them was trembling, and which of them was holding the other up. Maybe a lot of both on both sides. But together they made a solid unit, and together, they'd keep supporting their family through whatever adventures lay ahead.

Rachel and Theo took off from my heart, and I hope they found a home in yours.

Ratings and reviews help me grow as an author, and I appreciate all of your feedback. Please take a moment to review me! Goodreads ~ Bookstore

Not done with me yet? Read on!

My 'also by' page has links to the rest of the **Roll of the Dice** series, as well as my other books. My 'about the author' page has links to my newsletter, website, and social buttons. I'd love to connect with you!

Happy Reading,

Melanie

ACKNOWLEDGMENTS

This novel was in draft stages for … well, let's redact the exact number of months. It's a strange delight to let it out of my mind and into the world. Over those months, family, friends, and readers have cheered me on. Every word of support was a bolster.

I'm grateful to many for providing helpful info as this book unfolded onto the page, especially the following: Rachel and Jasmine for the cute facts about their two-year-olds, Brooke for the pie tutorials, Casey for her lessons about restaurant work, and Jessica for sharing her emergency contraception soapbox with me.

My beta readers—Claire, Kira, Robert, and Violet—are insightful, kind, sharp people. Their skills exposed my weaknesses, which gave me the opportunity to reshape this manuscript into a stronger novel. Thanks, y'all!

My family always gets a shout-out in the acknowledgements page, and you'd think after seven books I'd run out of things to thank them for. You'd be wrong. Robert, your everyday support is extraordinary, and your special occasion support is a gift I can count on every day. Thanks for spending half your life with me.

ABOUT THE AUTHOR

Melanie Greene lives in a little cottage in a giant city, with her husband and kids and cat and dog and all the people inhabiting her imagination.

For more info, visit her at www.melaniegreene.com, where you can sign up for her newsletter to access new releases and bonus content. Also visit her at Facebook.com/MelGreeneBooks and Twitter.com/Daki_MelGreene.

www.ingramcontent.com/pod-product-compliance
Lightning Source LLC
Chambersburg PA
CBHW051649180726
48284CB00006B/1921